TULA ROSE

A TRUE STORY THAT YOU WILL NEVER BELIEVE

SUZANNE MONDOUX

BALBOA.PRESS
A DIVISION OF HAY HOUSE

Balboa Press books may be ordered through booksellers or by contacting:

Balboa Press
A Division of Hay House
1663 Liberty Drive
Bloomington, IN 47403
www.balboapress.com
844-682-1282

Because of the dynamic nature of the Internet, any web addresses or links contained in this book may have changed since publication and may no longer be valid. The views expressed in this work are solely those of the author and do not necessarily reflect the views of the publisher, and the publisher hereby disclaims any responsibility for them.

The author of this book does not dispense medical advice or prescribe the use of any technique as a form of treatment for physical, emotional, or medical problems without the advice of a physician, either directly or indirectly. The intent of the author is only to offer information of a general nature to help you in your quest for emotional and spiritual well-being. In the event you use any of the information in this book for yourself, which is your constitutional right, the author and the publisher assume no responsibility for your actions.

Any people depicted in stock imagery provided by Getty Images are models, and such images are being used for illustrative purposes only.
Certain stock imagery © Getty Images.

Print information available on the last page.

ISBN: 979-8-7652-5660-2 (sc)
ISBN: 979-8-7652-5661-9 (e)

Balboa Press rev. date: 10/26/2024

1

It was a typical quiet Saturday morning on the Nort riverbank. The river flowed low and slow. It meandered eastbound throughout the quaint and artistic Nort village and into the Nort estuary.

The riverbank's smooth grassy surface was just right to walk comfortably, and bear a foot down into the river. The willow trees along the bank dangled their branches over the water. The birds flew from tree to tree, collecting the trees' soft fluff to line their nests amid the slender twigs.

Just a few yards away from her backyard, Amy, being an early riser, sang with the birds on the riverbank. That morning was a particularly special morning for Amy. She skipped along the riverbank and sang to the melody of the birdsongs *I am eight years old today. I'm having a party with my friends and we'll eat chocolate cake. Chocolate cake is my favour...*

She stopped dead in her tracks. Her mouth dropped wide open, but no sound came out. Even the birds stopped singing. She took a deep breath and released the loudest screeching scream. The entire village woke to a shriek crackling through the air.

The Lins jumped out of their bed. Their daughter's voice could not be mistaken for any other little girl in Nort. At the speed of light, Tom ran to the river. He searched frantically, calling out for his daughter. After she checked on the twin boys playing video games in their room, Joyce was right behind her husband.

On the riverbank, Tom found Amy under the largest weeping willow, screaming. "Daddy's here sweetheart." He took Amy into his arms and rushed away from the corpse.

He turned his head and looked back at the body. The body lay face up and was stretched out along the edge of the water. The decomposed hands held a birthday gift on what remained of the chest. It was wrapped in pretty yellow paper, with pretty little birds on it, and was finished with a pretty purple ribbon and bow.

From the decomposing face, Tom could barely make out who it was, but he did recognize the silvery-white ring made of spiralling bone. It was worn on the right hand's middle finger, and it belonged to only one person in the village.

He held Amy tight in his arms and walked faster back to the house. Halfway home, they ran into Joyce and he said in a firm voice. "Call the sheriff."

Joyce hugged them both. "Sweetheart. Mommy is here, Amy." Amy was crying uncontrollably. "Tom, you look like you've seen a ghost. What's going on honey?"

"Keep the boys in the house." When they reached the house's porch, he placed Amy into her mother's arms and led them into the house.

"Tom, please you're scaring me. What's going on?"

Tom ran into the bedroom and grabbed his cellphone from the night table, next to the bed. He looked out of the bedroom window overlooking the river, and autodialed the sheriff.

✤

A cloud of dust followed two cars. Sheriff Emily Berg and her deputy Aten Omar were at the Lin's house by 7 a.m. Emily was nursing a hangover from last night's wine party with two orange pekoe tea bags steeped in her large travel mug. She wasn't much of a drinker, but she loved wine. Aten, on the other hand, was feeling rested and refreshed. He nibbled on his granola bar and sipped his mint tea.

When the two patrol cars rolled up in front of the house, Tom had been waiting for them in the driveway. He ran to Emily's car and opened the door for her before she could even reach for the door handle. "Emily, come this way." He offered his hand to help her out of the car. "Thank you Tom, always a gentleman."

"Aten, this way." Tom pointed with his finger.

"Tom, where's Joyce and the kids?" Aten asked. He followed Tom and Emily.

"Inside." Tom hurried Emily along by stepping in front her. "Follow me."

On their way to the corpse, Tom described in detail what had happened from the moment he heard Amy scream, as well as what he saw, until the moment when he called the sheriff.

Emily had been sheriff for 25 years, and Aten her deputy for 15 and, in their time together or before, they had never heard or seen anything like what Tom was describing to them. Nothing ever really happened in Nort. The word crime was a word mainly heard on the daily news, and it was always something that happened somewhere else.

Emily and Aten also knew that the ring Tom described on the corpse could only belong to one person in the village. No one else in the village owned anything like it. It was a very unique ring that held a great deal of mystery for everyone in the village, because every time anyone asked about it, they were never given a clear answer. Even though the ring owner had been a resident of Nort for as long as anyone could remember, she was a woman of great curiosity to the villagers, as well as a well-respected member of her community. Charlotte Bourbon was known for her kindness, generosity, and beautiful and delicious cakes and all manner of baked goods.

"She immigrated from France when she was in her 20s or so." Aten said.

Tom stopped them a few feet away from the body. They looked down at Charlotte's corpse, with a gift in her hands.

"She always seemed ageless." Emily said. She kneeled down on the ground to take a closer look at the area and the body. "We need to get a team here ASAP, Aten."

"Making the call now." Aten searched his contact list on his cell and clicked on it to make the call.

"What team and who is he calling?" Tom asked. He knelt down next to Emily.

"Look at her body. I saw her just last night. She was with Aten and I.

"And?"

"She was with Aten and I until 2 a.m. We drank wine and talked about my Norwegian family, Aten's Egyptian family and Charlotte's family. Tom, Charlotte knew the history of her ancestors all the way back to the 10th century, when Scotland as we know it today came to be known as Scotland."

"Really. I didn't know her family hailed from Scotland."

"I thought I knew a lot about my Viking ancestors. What we know from the history books and all that. Charlotte knew the history of her Scottish ancestors, as I said, from the 10ᵗʰ century into the Middle Ages during the departure of the Romans, up to the adoption of major aspects of the Renaissance in the early 16ᵗʰ century extremely well. She said her people from Scotland were a melting pot of different groups. The Britons, the Picts, the Angles, the Gaels, and the Norse. Then, in the year 1295, I think that's the year, an alliance, what did she call it? Oh yeah, the Auld alliance."

"Never heard of it."

"Neither did I until she told us. It was an alliance between the Kingdom of Scotland and France against England. This alliance was established because Scotland's and France's shared needs to curtail English expansion. Somehow, this arrangement of military and diplomatic alliance brought tangible benefits for the population, such as the pick of the finest French wines, and that's how, over time, her ancestors emigrated to France, I think around the time of the signing of the Treaty of Edinburgh in 1560, which played a significant role in the relations between Scotland, France, and England."

Tom was staring at Emily and said. "Wow. You remembered all that. That's actually quite fascinating."

"Yeah. I know. It seems Charlotte's people were quite important members in their communities, and that's all I know. Anyway, Amy found Charlotte around 7 a.m.. It means that she died between 2 a.m. and 7 a.m. this morning. That's only 5 hours. I'm not a forensic expert, but I know that a body cannot decompose as rapidly as what we see here."

"Me too. I'm a sculptor and, when I realized it was Charlotte, I also didn't understand how her body could have decomposed so fast. As for Joyce, she's a paediatrician and couldn't understand it either when I told her what I saw. We saw Charlotte yesterday around 4 p.m. when we grabbed a coffee at her shop." Tom leaned in closer to get a better look at Charlotte.

"Chocolate oatmeal cookies." Emily said.

"What?" Tom said.

"That's what's in the box. She baked chocolate oatmeal cookies for Amy this morning. She knew that Amy was an early riser and would be at her favourite tree this morning for her birthday, and to watch the birds build their nests. Charlotte wanted to surprise her with freshly-baked cookies. She told Aten and I this last night."

By 8 a.m. the news of Charlotte's ring which had been found on a corpse had reached everyone in Nort. The entire village was is disbelief. By 9 a.m. the Halifax police and forensic team were on the scene. By 10 a.m., Chief Investigator Anika Patel was in the Lins' home.

On her way to the kitchen, Anika admired the Taiwanese painting on the wall. It was taken from the Lins' home in Taiwan, with a lush forest and mountains. Next to it, Tom pointed to the portraits of their parents and grandparents.

At the kitchen table, she drank coffee with Tom and Joyce, and took notes on everything they could tell her about Charlotte. By her second cup of coffee, she learned that Tula Rose, the local bookstore owner, was Charlotte's closest friend. Tula was described as a classic beauty. She was a woman in her mid-50s, an author of adult and children's fiction books from her adventures around the world, and the go-to person for any spiritual advice and guidance. They say Tula was born with a special gift. The dead loved her. She could see and hear them when they came to visit her, and spirits communicated with her all the time.

Anika held no such beliefs in what the villagers described as Tula's special gifts. With a PhD in criminology and psychology, Anika opted to keep her boots on the ground, be a voice for those who could no longer speak for themselves, solve their crimes, and bring those responsible to justice. However, she did believe in God, and that was as far as it went for her. Her relationship with God was a private one, and with a 98 % conviction rate, she was determined to get to the bottom of Charlotte's mysterious death.

After her visit with the Lin family, Anika returned to the scene of the crime. The forensic team studied the riverbank and the surrounding area. The imprint of the body on the riverbank was all that remained of Charlotte at the scene. The yellow tape wrapped around the periphery of the crime scene flickered in the breeze.

She sat in the grass several yards from the cordoned-off area and looked out at the village, wondering: "What's going on here?"

Anika was known by her family, friends, and colleagues to be quiet and introspective. They said it was her process. It was why she was so good at her job and, on this day, she was officially 25 years on the job. She celebrated with a salmon sandwich and a coffee.

After taking in all that she needed to consider from the vantage point of the riverbank overlooking the village, she closed her notebook and walked into the village.

2

When Anika arrived at *Le Gâteau*, Charlotte's café and bakery, the sign on the front door read *Closed Until Further Notice*. Next to *Le Gâteau*, she looked up at the sign *Tula* over a large window. It was beautifully decorated with roses. Next to it was a brilliant orange wooden door with a forest etched from top to bottom.

The sign in the window read "Closed", but she saw someone walking into the store. She looked down at the strange and unique doorknob. With her hand on the elephant head with its trunk curled up, she twisted the trunk to the left, opened the door and stepped through the entrance.

"If Tula and Charlotte were best friends, why is Tula at work today? Why is she not home mourning the loss of her friend?" Anika thought.

When she took another step into the dimly lit store, Anika heard a voice. "I'm sorry. We are closed."

Anika followed the voice and said. "I'm sorry to bother you. I'm Chief Investigator Anika Patel. I'm here about…"

"I know why you are here." Tula stepped into the sunlight. "Please. Take a seat here." She directed Tula to the green velvet antique sofa in the corner. It was the perfect spot in the shop to read by natural light. Tula put out her hand and introduced herself. They shook hands, and Anika introduced herself again.

Anika was struck by Tula's beauty. They were right about how they described her. Tula's silver hair flowed chin-length and glittered in the sunlight. Her perfectly-shaped dark brown eyebrows and dark brown eyes smiled against her beautiful and flawless olive skin.

On the wall behind where Tula stood, Anika looked at the black and white photo of a woman holding a baby in her arms, and said. "I see a resemblance."

Tula turned her head around to look at the photo and back at Anika, and added: "Yes. She is my great-great, let's say I am the fifth generation. She is grandmother Laetiti

a Pannan, an Algonquin woman. There is me, my father, my grandmother, her mother, that's the baby in her arms, and her mother, Laetitia."

Anika was still holding Tula's hand. She released Tula's hand and sat on the sofa. Tula sat next to her and said: "How can I help you Chief Investigator Patel?"

Anika looked around the store. Old books lined the shelves from floor to ceiling. She noticed how well organized and neat everything was. It wasn't messy or dusty. It was clean and fresh. The store resonated a sense of calm and peacefulness. It's what she felt when her hand touched Tula's hand. She felt as though she had been put under a spell because her mind slowed down, and she was admiring everything she saw in the store, even the things of a spiritual nature, from the spirit world, and what could be conceived as calling the dead to her right here in this store.

"Chief Investigator Patel." Tula said.

"Yes." Anika said.

"Can I offer you a cup of tea?"

"Yes. Thank you."

Tula reached over to the teapot on the table next to her. She placed two small cups in front of her, and poured the tea. She took a cup in her hand and presented it to Anika, and said: "For you."

"Thank you." Anika took a sip and looked up at Tula. "This is my favourite tea. Chamomile tea. Usually taken before I go to bed."

"Yes." Tula said and smiled. "Sometimes it's nice during the day just to calm our mind and soothe our body.

Anika looked at Tula and wondered. "She knew someone like me would be coming here today after she heard about Charlotte. The villagers would let me know that they were best friends, surely."

Tula sat quietly and sipped her tea, waiting patiently for Anika to ask her questions about Charlotte.

Anika placed her teacup on the table and said. "Ms. Rose."

"Tula."

"Yes. Thank you." Anika said and shifted her body to face Tula. "I understand that you and Ms. Charlotte Bourbon were close friends, Ms. Rose. Tula, I'm sorry for your loss.

"Thank you, and yes, we were."

"Do you feel you can answer some questions about Ms. Bourbon?"

"Yes. What questions would you like to ask me?"

Anika reached for her notepad and pen in her jacket pocket. "I'll be taking notes. Are you comfortable with this?"

"Yes. Go ahead. Charlotte was a very interesting and brilliant woman, and she always preferred being called by her name Charlotte instead of Ms. Bourbon."

"Noted." Anika opened the notepad to a blank page. "When did you first meet Charlotte?"

"I met Charlotte..."

Anika's cellphone rang. She looked down at the caller. It was from the coroner. "I'm sorry. I must take this."

Anika left Tula sitting on the sofa and walked outside to take the call. "Yup? What can you tell me?"

"I'm not sure."

"Sami. What do you mean you're not sure?"

"I mean. I read the report, time of death, you know everything I need to do."

"Sam. What are you trying to say?

"I mean, at first glance, because I haven't completed the full autopsy yet. But..."

"But what?"

"A body doesn't usually look like this when dead for only five hours or so."

"Yeah. I thought that was a bit weird as well, and so did the guy who found it, as well as the sheriff and her deputy. We all thought the same thing. So, what are we looking at here?"

"I'm not sure yet but I would say longer than five hours."

"How long? The whole town saw her the day before, and she was with the sheriff and deputy until 2 a.m. Can we make sense of this?"

"Anika. Remember my first job after graduation?"

"Of course, Sami. We visited your parents in Sudan before going to Egypt. Your parents were so proud to have a doctor in the family, not the kind of doctor they thought, but a doctor for the dead. Sorry. I don't mean to laugh, but I'll never forget the look on their faces when you explained it to them. I loved your office amongst the mummies. Great first job. A forensic anthropologist in the Grand Egyptian Museum of Giza. Wonderful memories. However, what does this have to do with a dead 55 year old French woman in Nort?"

"Well. That's just it. This case takes me back to when I worked at the museum."

"What do you mean?"

"A mummy is a dead human or an animal. Well, here we have a human whose soft tissue and organs have been preserved by either intentional or accidental exposure to chemicals, extreme cold, very low humidity, or lack of air, so that the recovered body does not decay further if kept in cool and dry conditions."

"Are you telling me the French woman is a mummy?"

3

Tula opened the shop's door and stepped outside. She smiled at Anika who was still on the phone. Anika was pacing back and forth, just off the curb on the sidewalk. The sidewalk in front of *Le Gâteau* was covered with flowers and candles. The villagers loved Charlotte.

Tula told Anika that the sheriff's phone was ringing off the hook from villagers who wanted to know what had happened to such a vibrant and kind member of their community. If she didn't answer her phone, they would show up at the sheriff's office. It was clear to Anika that Charlotte was well-loved by her community.

Tula placed the key in the keyhole and locked the door.

Anika raised her hand to signal to Tula to wait for her. Tula nodded her head with acknowledgement and waited for Anika.

"Tula. Thank you. I'll be just one moment."

"Sam. Send me photos of everything."

"Already done. I'll send more as I progress with the autopsy."

Anika's phone dinged several times before she hung up with Sam.

"Tula. Thank you for waiting. Can we continue from where we left off?"

Tula zipped up her jean jacket and said. "Let's continue on the way to my house. It's a short walk across the river."

Anika admired Tula's elegance. She dressed very well, but comfortably, and the only jewellery she wore were small heart-shaped gold stud earrings, as well as a gold ring band with the design of the tree of life. She was also a natural beauty. No make-up. She also loved the scent of her perfume.

Upon seeing her reflection in the shop window, Anika thought. "After giving birth to four kids, the last one is barely still at home; two at university and one married. I look pretty damn good. I still have it going on. Also, I'm stylish."

Tula smiled at Anika and signalled with her hand. "This way."

By the time they walked across the village to the small bridge arched over the river, and the only footpath to Tula's house, Tula had answered all of Anika's initial questions. However, Anika's curiosity peaked when Tula recalled that Charlotte was never sick, nor did she feel ill or ever complained about any physical ailments or discomfort, for someone who had died so suddenly. They had been avid hikers, they enjoyed white water rafting, and had gone trekking in the African and South American jungles just to see wildlife and meet the locals. Tula was an explorer at heart. She loved nature, all the creatures that came with it, and she enjoyed meeting people from different places and cultures.

Before going to the bookstore, Anika did a search for Tula Rose and her books on her cellphone. From what she had read, and from what Tula had shared with her during the question period of their walk, it was clear to Anika that Tula's real-life adventures merged into the fantasy worlds that Tula had created in her stories. Tula was a self-published author who wasn't yet well-known, but she was a well-known figure in Nort and the surrounding area. Tula was a writer at heart and an explorer; a life she had chosen that not many women would have chosen for themselves. She was single, had had lovers, no children, but she'd had one miscarriage. She had friends from all over the world and, long before Charlotte's death, she had shed many tears and grieved the loss of many friends, animal friends, a lover, family, and African children she had cared for throughout her life. With that knowledge of Tula's life, Tula warned her not to mistake her serene and composed disposition as being untouched by Charlotte's death. "Every painful feeling will surface in its own good time." Tula said.

Charlotte and Tula had met on the ferry to Nort the day Charlotte moved to Nort. Charlotte was booked into a bed and breakfast for her first night before getting the keys to *Le Gâteau*, which she named when she purchased the café/bakery while still living in France. Tula loved that Charlotte had bought a place sight unseen. Charlotte said that she had done her research, trusted her instincts, and followed her heart. She knew that Nort and *Le Gâteau* were where she needed to be.

Le Gâteau's property extended far back into the forest and along the river. Plus, the land was home to a small beautiful and historic house. It was an old house that needed a lot of work, and until the work was completed, there was nowhere for Charlotte to sleep but on the floor.

By the time Charlotte and Tula walked off the ferry, Charlotte had shown her numerous photos of *Le Gâteau* and the house. Tula was very familiar with both places, and invited Charlotte to stay with her until all renovations were completed, and she could move into her new house and sleep in her own bed instead of sleeping on the floor.

Charlotte built a beautiful patio that stretched out to the back of *Le Gâteau*, with a walkway that linked to Tula's bookshop. Ever since then, both shops received guests from all over the area and the world, where they enjoyed reading their books with a side order of delicious cake.

When Anika asked Tula about what she could tell her about Charlotte's life before she left France, Tula said that she had gotten to know Charlotte over the years. Tula knew nothing of Charlotte's life until Charlotte talked about her life before Nort, and Tula had never asked. She figured that Charlotte, like everyone else, would share what she wanted to share with others in her own time. Otherwise, Tula never asked her, and never felt a need to know about Charlotte's first 20 or so years of her life in France. However, when Charlotte talked about her ancestors, Tula noted that she spoke of them as though they were the ones with whom she had lived with in France before moving to Nort. Sometimes she spoke of them with love in her heart, sometimes with pain, and other times, she spoke of those she wished she had never known.

Anika was absorbing and processing loads of mental notes as well. "Here is a woman who died suddenly, without any history of illness or cause of death, on a riverbank in a crimeless village, and where most of the villagers knew her for some 30 years, but really knew nothing about her. She spoke of her ancestors with greater detail than anyone living today could really know about their own parents, let alone the generations before them, and who is now lying on the coroner's table, looking like a mummy."

"Anika, we're here." Tula said. "This way."

They stepped out of the forest and into Tula's backyard. A sea of wild spring flowers welcomed them, even when they walked on the stone path between the forest path and the house.

"It's beautiful." Anika said. She scanned the area and looked at wild flowers as far as the eye could see. "Is that the river I hear over there?"

"Yes, we will see it from the other side of the house." Tula stepped onto the stone path. She led the way to the back porch. It wrapped around a single level beautiful green house that was shaped like the crescent of the moon. It wasn't quite a glasshouse, but windows dominated the design.

When Tula whistled, two cats and two dogs came running out from the side of the house.

"Hello my darlings."

Lune, the grey tabby male, jumped into Tula's arms, and Étoile, the calico female, rubbed her body against her legs, and then she rubbed her entire body up against Anika's legs.

Anika was fond of animals. The dogs sensed that she was a dog lover, and they walked calmly right beside her, one on each side of her. When they reached the porch, the cats ran to the cat door. Mopo, the Basenji, and his brother Ndoki, ran up the three steps in one leap onto the porch.

"Your cats and dogs look different from other domestic cats and dogs I've seen." Anika said as she followed Tula up the steps.

"They are African. The cats come from Guinea, and the dogs come from the Congo. Brazzaville, Congo, not the Democratic Republic of Congo. They are rescues."

"They are beautiful. I have a rescue mutt lab-husky mix or something like that, and two rescued cats as well. My Marmalade and Lemonade are sisters. One is more orange than the other." Her phone dinged several times in her back pant pocket. "Excuse me Tula." She stayed on the porch. Tula went in the house.

Anika looked at her phone. Sam sent her 10 photos with a text message: *"Look at these now and get over here ASAP"*.

4

Anika scanned the photos of Charlotte's face and other body parts. Anika could not believe her eyes. She speed dialed Sam.

"Yup. I know you have lots of questions, Anika, and I'm working on it."

"The photos you just sent. I don't understand. It's like she's disintegrating right before your eyes." Anika put Sam on speakerphone and tapped on the photos that Sam had just sent her less than 30 minutes ago.

"I know. The video camera is recording the entire autopsy as well. She's literally decaying right before my eyes. It's pretty much what happens to a mummy when it is exposed to the outside world. It usually decays within matter of hours, but nothing like this. This is much faster."

Anika sat in the chair on the porch. "So, we don't have much time."

"Not much."

"How much time would you say we have, then?"

"At this rate, less than three hours before there's nothing left of her. Maybe less. It's a tricky one Anika."

"Can you tell me anything about the cause of death?"

"Nothing yet. From what I can gather from what's left of the organs when she arrived on my table, there wasn't much left to sample from. When I checked, everything appeared to be normal. You know what I mean. There was no sign of…"

"Let me guess, no sign of illness or abnormalities?"

"That's what I observed and recorded in the report, for now, but I did find something on the skin over her right hip. I sent you the photo. It's the last photo I just sent."

Anika tapped open the last photo. She enlarged it to get a better look at the bright orange birthmark. "A triquetra."

"Yeah. The ancient Celtic symbol of rebirth."

"The unbreakable cycle of time and life, the unity of land and sea. Why does a dead woman in Nort have a birthmark symbolizing immortality?" Anika looked closer at the photo.

"I don't know, but the three overlapping and interconnected arcs are clearly seen on the decaying skin. It's as though it was made from an insertion of the pigmentation under the skin, and that it was done fairly recently. The three-cornered knot looks as though there is no beginning nor end, as it should for a triquetra. I've seen many birthmarks, but I've never seen one of this colour or formed in such a very specific shape or symbol before. Nothing like I've seen before."

"Ok. Thanks. I'll be there in an hour, tops, but call me if there's anything else."

Anika took a screenshot of the birthmark and went into the house. She walked through the house looking for Tula. The house was clean and tidy. It was beautifully and tastefully decorated, with a mixture of modern and antique furniture, paintings, masks, statues, and other ornaments from around the world. From every room she could look out at the river. When she reached the kitchen, she found Tula feeding the animals.

"Tula. I must return to Halifax immediately, but I want to show you something before I go." She tapped on the screenshot of the bright orange triquetra birthmark photo and handed the phone over to Tula, without telling her what it was or where it had come from. "Can you tell me if you know what this is or if you recognize it?"

Tula looked at the photo and handed the phone back to Anika. "Yes. It's the triquetra. Charlotte had this exact birthmark over her right hip." She curled her hair behind her ear with her finger. "Like this." She pointed at the heart-shaped stud earring with the triquetra at its centre. "Charlotte gave me these earrings as a thank you gift when she moved into her new house. She said they had been handed down to her from generation to generation, and it was how she wanted to show her appreciation for our friendship."

Anika stepped forward to have a closer look. "Very nice. So, you have seen this birthmark on her body?"

"Yes. Is that photo taken from Charlotte's body?"

"Yes. It looks like a fresh tattoo. It's so clear and bright for a birthmark at this stage on decomposition. Did Charlotte do anything to it, if that's possible?"

"No. I don't think so, but Charlotte's birthmark looked just like that, clear and bright when I first saw it."

"What do you mean?"

"Charlotte and I went swimming all the time over there in the river." She pointed with her finger. "She loved wearing her bikini. The first day she stayed here, we went for a swim, and that's when I saw her birthmark. That was 30 some years ago."

Confusion washed over Anika's face. "Thank you Tula. You've been a great help today. Again, I'm sorry for your loss."

"You're welcome."

"I'm expected back in an hour tops. Sorry to dash off."

"It's faster if you take the ferry. The road you drove in on is the longer way to Nort from Halifax. It's a beautiful drive. They kept the ferry from Halifax to Nort many years ago when Nort became a tourist destination. The ferry continues on from here to other remote communities along the coast that have minimal to no road access. However, the ferry is quicker. It leaves in 10 minutes. I'll drive you to your car and call the captain to let him know that you're on your way. He will wait for us."

5

After dropping Anika off at the ferry, Tula returned to the shop. She kept the *"Closed"* sign on, and locked the door behind her. She went to her reading chair beneath the skylight at the far end and private area of the shop. The light shined down on the chair. It illuminated the pink velour with a beautifully crafted wooden frame. It was an original antique from 17th century France. She loved the silky feeling when she rested her arms on the armrest. She had the other chair from the set in her bedroom by the window, where she loved to read. The chairs once belonged to a Duke during the Baroque period, and somehow, they found their way to an estate several miles from Nort. During an estate sale, she found the chairs alone in the library, with no other furniture but the books and chairs. She placed her bid and, by mid-afternoon, she was the owner of the most spectacular chairs she had ever set her eyes on. She later learned from the estate manager that she was the only one who had placed a bid on these chairs.

The estate sale was where she had also purchased the majority of her oldest and most precious first print books. Some of them, for which she had paid a pretty penny, dated as far back as the 12th century, but the estate manager also assured her that the collections she had purchased were not what his usual clientele desired. He assured her that she still purchased them way below their market value. He also informed Tula that the owner had clearly stipulated certain parameters in the will for the buyer of the books she bid on, as well as the chairs, and she fit the bill. It was almost as though the owner knew exactly who he had in mind as to whom would procure themselves of these specific items. No one else in Nort or the area, or much further afield, fit the bill that suited Tula to a tee.

Tula dropped her body in the chair and cried until the sunset. She stayed there with her head resting back, and watched the moon. The moonlight shined down onto the walkway between the shop patio and *Le Gâteau*. She reached for the bottle of red wine on the floor next to the chair. It was just two nights ago that she was sitting here with Charlotte, drinking wine and eating pastries. The box of pastries was left on the bookshelf next to the chair, and next to it was a glass of wine. She pulled the cork out from the already opened bottle of Saint-Émilion and poured the remaining wine into her glass. She hoped there would still be a chocolate éclair in the box of pastries. When she opened the box, she grinned with delight. Two éclairs remained. She griped one with her thumb and finger, opened her mouth wide and stuffed half of it in her mouth, and washed it back with a gulp of wine. That was how she ate both éclairs. She licked her fingers clean and reached for a new bottle of Saint-Émilion behind the chair.

The pop of the cork from the bottle echoed throughout the shop. She looked at the front door, expecting Charlotte to walk through it. Then she looked out at the walkway, waiting for Charlotte to walk along it to the shop's back door. Both times she was surprisingly disappointed that she could not manifest her best friend back in the shop with her. Nonetheless, she poured two glasses of wine. She placed a glass of wine on the table next to Charlotte's favourite chair, the blue velour rocking chair she brought with her from France.

Tula raised her glass and said. "Chin chin, Charlotte." She leaned forward and clinked her glass up against Charlotte's.

Tula gulped her entire glass, and then reached for Charlotte's glass and gulped it down as well.

∽

It was 3 a.m., and Sam and Anika were still in the morgue and standing over Charlotte's corpse. It was disintegrating right before their eyes.

Anika tapped on a photo of Charlotte that Tula sent her earlier that day, and the text read: "This is what she looked like."

"That beautiful black pixie haircut is no longer, neither are her bright green eyes." Sam said. She looked closer at the photo.

"Caucasian. Five-feet and four inches, and 130 lbs. Her skeleton is all that's left of her. Anika returned the phone to her back pant pocket.

"The entire autopsy is recorded on video. The lab work will be back by morning. I put a rush on it. We should have more answers by then."

"What do I tell the villagers? The sheriff wants answers, and so do the villagers. How do I explain this? The only thing working in our favour right now is that Tula, her best friend, told me that she was Charlotte's benefactor. She had the will, as well as other documents. Charlotte was explicit that her ashes be sprinkled in water. She also didn't want a viewing of her body at the funeral. Of course, this won't happen. It can't happen now."

"You have a tough one this time my friend." Sam covered the skeleton with a white sheet. "Let's get home. Your husband will think that you found someone else to spend your nights with."

Anika rolled her eyes and smiled, and said: "I love him like no other."

Sam pulled a white sheet over Charlotte's skeleton and rolled the table into the cold room. "She should be ok here for the night. I can't think of anything else changing after this transformation." She stepped out of the cold room and shut the door. "Let's go."

⚮

Tula woke up from a bad dream. She felt cold and was shivering. She fell asleep in the chair. Her neck and back were stiff, and the empty glass of wine dangled upside down between her first and second finger. She tapped her phone that was set on the window ledge to see what time it was. It was three a.m. She looked out the window, jumped up from the chair and dropped the glass on the floor, and called out: "Charlotte." Charlotte was standing on the far side of the walkway behind *Le Gâteau*.

Tula ran to the back door, opened it and ran outside. There was no one there. "The shadows from the trees are playing tricks on me." she thought. Tula was used to visits from those beyond the grave. Growing up, she knew of no one else who could see and hear dead people, and it remained so until her 20s, when she started to randomly meet other people with this very same ability.

Tula had been sought out by many as a conduit to communicate with their loved ones, but Tula never advertised her ability or promoted it in any way. Everyone who came to her was by chance, and word of mouth through unique and unexpected circumstances. Eventually, the whole of Nort knew this about Tula.

The villagers knew she never gave psychic readings or held séances, but if you needed her help, she was there to give it. She even helped find missing people. One time, an elderly man wondered away from a seniors' home, and they could not find him. A friend of a friend asked if Tula could see where he was. Tula's only experience with missing people was from the TV. When she saw or heard on the news that someone was missing, she would close her eyes and could see where the person, often dead, was to be found. When she was asked to help find her friend's friend grandfather, Tula said yes. Within minutes of the call, Tula told them where the man was to be found. Later that day, they found him exactly where she had said he would be. This news spread like wildfire and eventually reached Nort, but the villagers of Nort respected Tula's gift and her privacy, and never bombarded her with requests. They knew her help would always be available whenever it was needed.

The villagers also knew that they could speak with Tula about anything, and often without revealing too many details, and that Tula would somehow speak with them about the very matter that troubled their heart. Everyone left their visits with Tula feeling as though they had communicated with their guiding angels through her, and that was enough for them.

Tula was also the recipient of visions that guided her life. She didn't always abide by the guidance that was given to her, and she quite often lived the consequences of her choices. She often wondered if those choices were meant to be a part of her life's journey as well. She had a strong bond between her human form and her spirit, her soul, and because the dead loved her, Charlotte gave her the nickname of *The Soul Collector*. The whole village agreed that it was an appropriate epithet for Tula. They loved it and she loved it. She smiled every time someone addressed her as such.

Her visions also served to inform her about what was to be for others. She kept those visions to herself until the recipient of the message crossed her path or came to her for guidance. Otherwise, the message from her vision always remained with her.

Sometimes she had visions that made absolutely no sense to her. She didn't understand the scene, the characters or the message. This always left her feeling anxious and confused. She always wanted to understand these mysterious visions that left her feeling blind to a world she knew so well.

That night, she woke to one of those visions, and with the sight of Charlotte appearing and disappearing, she felt even more lost in the spirit world she loved living in and with. She described her ability as breathing air. Without it she would die. In spite of all the troubling and frightening visions she received, she wouldn't have it any other way. This ability, her gift, was a part of her soul. It was who she was.

6

Tula remembered a book that Charlotte had given her. When she moved into her new house and unpacked her books, Charlotte felt that Tula would enjoy reading about the ancient soul collectors. It was the most beautiful pocket-sized book she had ever seen. The book cover was made of layers of purple silk to give it a rich and thick texture, with an embroidered gold triquetra at its centre. The pages were adorned with beautifully-painted and brilliantly colourful illustrations. Each one told a story of eternal spiritual life.

Tula looked up at the waning moon. She locked the shop backdoor and headed home on the same path that she walked earlier that day with Anika. She loved walking in the village in the middle of the night. It was quiet and ghostly. She walked with the shadows and talked with the whispers in the dark.

When she arrived home, the cats and dogs were sleeping on the porch and were waiting for her.

"Good morning my babies." She patted each one on the head. Tula let out a big yawn. She was usually an early riser, but today, she was exhausted and all she wanted to see was the inside of her eyelids for as long as possible, and to sleep in her comfortable bed.

Sami was in a deep sleep when her phone rang. She rolled over reluctantly and reached for her phone on the night stand. With her eyes squinting, she searched the answer button, pressed it and dropped the phone on the floor.

In her tired voice, she said. "Hello. I'm here. Just a minute! I dropped the phone." With her arm dangling over the bed and her hand on the floor, she swept the area in search of her phone. Her fingers rubbed up against the phone, and she gripped it and brought it to her ear.

"Hi. I'm here. Why are you calling me at this hour Norm?"

"Sorry to wake you, but you said the lab work on Charlotte Bourbon was a rush and a rush like no other."

"Yes, and thank you for making it a priority. What can you tell me about the lab work Norm?"

"Well, it's a good thing that you flagged it as a priority, Sam."

"Oh, yeah? Why's that?"

"Well, every sample you've sent us, the skin, the hair, the blood, the bone, from the organs, everything you sent…"

"What's with all the suspense Norm? You're talking slower than you normally do."

"They're gone Sam."

"What do you mean, "gone"?"

"I mean, as we were working on each sample, we noticed that they were disintegrating right before our eyes."

Sam sat up in bed so fast that she practically woke up her husband who was snoring next to her. She got out of bed and went to the other room. "Tell me exactly what you mean and please tell me we at least have something, some information before they completely disintegrated."

"It's as I said. Moment by moment, we watched each sample gradually disintegrate. Ashes to ashes, dust to dust."

"Fascinating. And?"

"Yes, we did manage to do the analyses, including the radiocarbon dating to see why a 55 year old woman dies and, within hours, she looks like you got her from a mummy shop in Egypt."

"And what can we interpret from the lab results?

"Well. Charlotte Bourbon is much older than 55 years old."

"How old is she, approximately?

Norm cleared his throat and said. "Approximately 5,000 years old or so."

"That's older than the Great Pyramids of Giza. Send me everything you have, including the photos and video recordings of the disintegrating lab samples. You did a video recording of all this, like I instructed, I presume?"

"Of course. I'm sending it all to you right now."

"Thank you Norm. Excellent work, and I appreciate you staying there all night for this. Please go home and I'll talk to you later."

Sam jumped into her jeans and t-shirt, and skipped into her boots while speed dialing Anika.

Anika answered her phone before the first full ring.

"Holy shit Anika, did you get any sleep?"

"Some. What did we find out?"

Sam filled her in on all the details. "It's 5 a.m. I'll be at the morgue in 15 minutes. Meet me there."

"I'm already in the car."

By the time Sam drove into her parking stall, Anika was waiting for her at the front door.

"How fast were you driving Anika? It usually takes you at least 25 minutes to get here." She unlocked the front door, and they ran to the cold room.

When Sam opened the door, she noticed something odd about the sheet that she had used to cover Charlotte's skeleton. It was flat against the table.

She turned to Anika and said. "Well, she couldn't have walked out of here!"

"It's been a weird 24 hours. I'm expecting just about anything at this point."

They stepped forward towards the table where Charlotte used to lay. Sam gripped the top end of the sheet with both hands and pulled it back.

"Ashes to ashes, dust to dust." Anika removed her phone from her back pant pocket and took photos.

"That's what Norm said."

"Do we know the cause of death?" Anika asked as she kept taking photos.

"Inconclusive. Norm found no cause of death. He could not provide any evidence as to why Charlotte Bourbon died."

Anika stopped taking photos and looked up at Sam. "Nothing?"

"Inconclusive." Sam pulled the sheet back over the ashes. "I'll store them in a temporary urn until her friend, Tula, you said that was her name..."

"Yes. Tula Rose."

"…until she gets an urn for Charlotte's ashes."

"Yes. Thank you. I will go see her. I can catch the ferry if I leave now."

"Go ahead. I'll look after things here until I hear from you."

"Thanks Sam."

7

Anika rang Tula while she was driving to the ferry. She could tell from Tula's voice that she had been sleeping, and she could tell, from the tone of one's voice, when someone was exhausted. However, Tula remained gracious and invited Anika to have breakfast with her.

When Anika arrived, the cats and dogs greeted her at the front door. The screen door was unlocked and she walked into the house and announced her arrival, as Tula had instructed her to do. Anika followed the smell of brewing coffee and other delights cooking in the kitchen, at the far end of the moon-crest shaped house.

"Good morning Tula. It smells wonderful in here."

"Good morning Anika, and welcome! I hope you were able to get some sleep last night."

Anika knew she looked like someone who had not gotten much sleep, if any at all. Tula, on the other hand, looked great in her spring dress. She just moved a bit slower from the fatigue, and with a few yawns, she made no effort to hide it.

"Please. Take a seat."

Anika sat at the table where a place had been set for her. "Thank you Tula for inviting me to have breakfast with you. This must be a very difficult time for you."

"It's my pleasure to cook for someone and share breakfast with you." She reached for the coffee pot. "Coffee?"

"Yes. Please. Just black."

She poured coffee into Anika's cup and said. "Charlotte's people are Scottish, from way back, all the way back to the tenth century."

"Thank you. The coffee smells great. Oh really, when did her family emigrate to France?"

While Tula cooked breakfast, she told Anika the same Charlotte ancestral story that Emily had shared with Tom, and of how, over the course of a few hundred years, Charlotte's family came to France in the 1500s.

"I hope you like crêpes. It's Charlotte's recipe. Everything we'll eat this morning is from her recipes."

Anika glanced at the jams, eggs, and fruit salad, all nicely displayed in beautiful porcelain dishes on the table. "It all looks delicious."

Tula let a crêpe slide off the spatula and onto Anika's plate and said: "Voilà!"

"Wow. This smells amazing. Thank you." Anika said as she sipped her coffee.

Tula served herself and sat across from Anika. "Bon appétit."

While they ate, they talked about this and that regarding Nort. They talked of the spring music and artist festivals, the summer theatrical festival, and other seasonal events that drew people together from all over the world, and Tula shared a bit more about Charlotte's life with Anika.

Anika listened as Tula weaved a beautiful and heartbreaking story of a woman whose father was a chef, and of a mother who was a tailor and an embroiderer. She had three older brothers who all became successful in their own rights. She grew up in the medieval village of Provins, located one hour from Paris, and preserved as a UNESCO World Heritage Site. A few years after Charlotte arrived in Nort, she met Scottish actor Duncan, who flew his own plane to Nort for the summer theatrical festival. They fell in love and married that fall. Two years later, during a flight to Scotland, his plane crashed in the sea. His body and plane were never recovered. A few years later, Charlotte fell in love with another Scottish man, Logan, who sailed from Scotland to Nort alone on his sailboat. They were together just over five years. They sailed around the world and brought Tula along as well. She flew to a destination and joined them on the sailboat for a few weeks at a time. The last time she joined them, Charlotte flew back with Tula. A few weeks later, a rogue wave capsized the sailboat. Logan and the sailboat were lost at sea.

Anika wanted to remain sensitive to Tula's pain. She could clearly see that she was grieving the loss of a dear friend every time Tula spoke

Charlotte's name, and that she relived the memories they had had together, took a bite of food, and touched anything that she said Charlotte had given her.

She wanted to wait for the right time to share the autopsy results with Tula since she was Charlotte's benefactor, and she was also listed as her next-of-kin.

Tula poured herself a second cup of tea and said: "What did we learn from the autopsy?"

Anika swallowed half-chewed food and washed it down with a sip of coffee and said: "What we've learned is very interesting."

Over the course of the morning, Anika reviewed every photo, as well as the findings from the laboratory results, including the radiocarbon dating with Tula. It took a while to cover everything since Anika respectfully paused from photo to photo, as well as for each discussion points. These graceful moments of intermittence allowed Tula to process the information, and for her to share anything that came to mind to Anika. However, it was Anika who did most of the talking, while Tula listened quietly.

8

With a fresh pot of ginger and lemon tea, Tula joined Anika on the porch. Anika sat in the rocking chair and watched the river flow. The cats and dogs were playing in the tall grass, chasing one another. Anika could see from Tula's red puffy eyes that she had been crying. Tula smiled and poured them each a cup of tea and said: "I love this tea. Fresh from my garden. It was also Charlotte's favourite tea."

"You have a lemon tree?"

"Yes, over there in the greenhouse."

Anika leaned forward and arched her head to look where Tula pointed. "You've made this place into your own little oasis Tula. It's beautiful and peaceful."

"Yes. I love it here." She removed the book from her dress pocket and placed it on the table. "I've seen many places. However, I love making a home for myself and sharing it with friends. You're welcome here anytime, Anika."

Anika was touched by the genuine invitation. She sipped her tea and let Tula settle into the rocking chair next to her before talking about the real reason for her visit, and asked her about the book with the beautiful purple silk cover and embroidered gold triquetra at its centre.

Tula placed her teacup on the table and said. "I would like to show you something Charlotte gave me a long time ago." She took the book from the table and placed it in the palm of her hand. She told Anika about the nickname Charlotte had given her, and explained why she thought she would enjoy reading the ancient story of soul collectors.

"Soul collector." Anika said. "That's a unique and interesting nickname. Thank you."

Tula handed her the book. "It's like a flipbook animation in the earliest and simplest form of a frame-by-frame animation. Each illustration, or each frame, is painted on a separate page of the book. You can gently flip through rapidly in order to create the illusion of a continuous motion sequence. You see? Like this.

As Anika flipped the pages of the book, Tula recited the story frame-by-frame. Anika listened intently to the story of a once ancient people who lived a very long time ago in a remote village, on an island. The circular-shaped village was flanked with cliffs, and a vast sea that was home to many seabirds and other wildlife.

One early morning, a little girl was walking along the beach, collecting stones for her stone garden, when she came upon a gigantic water bird resembling a cormorant. The little girl had never seen such a big bird on the beach before. She dropped her basket of stones and ran the other way. The bird chased her and picked her up in his bill.

The little girl kicked, screamed, and waved about trying to free herself from this bill. The bird landed gently and released the little girl. When she was about to run off again, the bird told her not to be frightened of him. The little girl didn't know that birds could talk. She approached the bird and asked it questions so that she could hear him speak again. The bird answered all her questions until she had nothing left to ask, except for one last question. She wanted to know why the bird wanted to speak with her. The bird told her that the only way he could answer her questions was for her to climb onto his back and fly with him.

The little girl agreed and she jumped onto the bird, and up and up they went. The little girl looked all around, and when she looked down at the cliffs, the other islands and the sea, she noticed a shape she had never seen before. The islands' arms overlapped into a triangular figure and were interlaced with the circle of her village at the centre. Bird told her to always remember what she saw.

When she returned to her village, she carved the triangular figure with her village at its centre into a piece of flat stone. The next day, she returned to the beach to find her bird friend. She waited all day but he never came. When she returned home, she found the entire village gathered outside her home with her parents and brothers all gathered around the piece of flat stone with the carving of the triangular figure, and their village at its centre.

Everyone wanted to know why she had carved this figure and where she had seen it. The little girl told her story of the bird flying over the village, and she drew what she had seen. Silence fell over the crowd and all eyes were on the little girl. Her parents put their arms around her and smiled.

Anika rubbed her finger gently over the lines of the triquetra that was beautifully painted on the page. Her phone rang. The ring tone and vibration in her back pant pocket snapped her back onto the porch with Tula. She felt Tula had transported her to the little girl's world. She grabbed her phone and said. "Excuse me Tula." She walked over to the end of the porch. "Yup, Sami."

"You'll never believe it."

"What? The ashes are no longer…"

"No. The ashes are safely put away until…"

"I didn't get to that part with Tula yet. What's going on?"

"I just received a call from Arthur Moore."

"Is that a name that's supposed to mean something to me?"

"Yup. Arthur. The cute British forensic anthropologist I worked with in Egypt."

"Oh yeah. Dr. Arthur Moore. AKA. Dr. Sexy."

"The one and only. We've stayed in touch over the years. You know, work stuff."

"Didn't he return to England?

"That's right. More than 15 years ago now. Anika, look at what we've accomplished in this time as women in our careers, on our own steam."

"He's transferred to the Royal Anthropological Institute for some years now. He's the head."

"And. Why is he calling you now Sami?"

"He's still married to the same woman we met in Egypt. Happily married. I called you to tell you something far more interesting."

"What's that?"

"I hope you're sitting down. If you're not, hang onto to something so you don't fall over."

"This is quite the build-up for you Sami."

"Arthur called to tell me about a few mysterious deaths. MI6 requested he help with their investigation."

"Wow. MI6. Are we talking mummy mystery here?"

"You got it. Six bodies. Just as mysterious as Charlotte Bourbon's."

Anika turned to look over at Tula. Tula was sipping her tea and rocking back and forth. "Sami. Six other bodies, and they all appeared to be mummy-like? Were they all healthy before their deaths? And no cause of death was ever determined?"

"Yes, and they all died around the same time. In their time respective zones of course. One Scottish man. One Scottish woman. One French man. One French woman. One British woman. One British man."

Anika repeated and wrote what Sami just said in her notepad, and then added: "And we have one French Charlotte. That makes seven, Sam." What were their ages before they died?"

"They were all around the same age as Charlotte."

"Including the radiocarbon dating?"

"Yes. Everything was the same, Anika."

"Sam, why did Arthur reach out to you? How could he have known about Charlotte?"

"He didn't know about Charlotte. He called me because he wanted to pick my brain. He didn't tell me exactly why he was calling me at first. He just told me that he was working on something and wanted my professional input. I know him too well to know that he doesn't reach out to anyone for input or insight on anything, unless he really feels something can be offered. It's how he shows that he values someone's opinion. He's a pretty smart cookie, and when he asks for your input about anything, it's only because he's really stumped and that almost never happens. So, I must admit that I was pretty flattered when he called me. Then he said something that caught my attention."

"What's that?"

"He mentioned that each of the bodies had a bright orange birthmark of the triquetra over their right hip. Then I dug into him even more, and he told me everything. Now I'm on the phone with you about this. Your case has just gotten bigger, more complicated and international."

"Can he send you everything he has?"

"Already done. I told him about Charlotte Bourbon. He will see what he can find out about her."

"Can you send…"

"Already done."

Anika's phone dinged several times from the photos and emails that were coming in. "Thanks Sam. You're a star, as always."

"Of course. This is very exciting."

"I'll call you later." Anika quickly scanned the new photos. When she turned around to rejoin Tula, Tula wasn't there.

Anika noticed her teacup had been topped up. She walked around to the other side of the porch and called out to Tula. By the time she came back to the table and rockers, Tula was back in her rocker, eating chocolate mousse.

Tula smiled at Anika and said. "Try it. It's Charlotte's recipe of course. I love eating anything chocolate, anytime of the day."

"It's 10:30 a.m. and it's chocolate mousse time already!" Anika smiled. She sat in the rocker next to Tula and ate the chocolate mousse served in a beautiful glass cup with roses etched around it. She loved the mousse. It wasn't like any other chocolate mousse she had ever eaten before.

9

Between the spoonfuls of chocolate mousse, Tula questioned Anika about Charlotte's mysterious death. She dissected what Anika had told her up until the moment when she told her that Charlotte's remains radiocarbon dating suggested that she was 5,000 years or so.

Tula repeated and rephrased every question Anika had asked her about Charlotte and her mysterious death, and she went through every photo again that Anika had shown her of Charlotte's body on the riverbanks, to the ashes on the table in the morgue, as well as the bright orange triquetra birthmark. Her questions searched to understand why there appeared to be no conclusive cause of death, and why the radiocarbon dating suggested that Charlotte was approximately 5,000 years old.

At first, Anika was taken aback at the innocence of Tula's questions. They were like those of a child asking a parent how babies are made. Why is the sky blue? And then, the questions evolved. They revealed to Anika that Tula was very inquisitive. She observed the way Tula framed her questions. They were so well-framed that she wondered if Tula was really a seasoned detective. Anika knew she couldn't get away with answering her questions with a simple yes or no, or any which way.

The deeper Tula searched for answers, the greater her philosophical mind was revealed. Anika could see that Tula was trying to resolve something in her mind that she had yet to tell her, and that's what she desperately wanted to know. However, she knew that she couldn't just blurt out *"Tula, what is it that you're not telling me?"*, because Tula was much too clever and too strong to crumble under that sort of interrogation.

Tula returned the book of soul collectors to her dress pocket, and tidied-up the table. She placed the dishes on the tray and stood up.

Anika was disappointed that story time was over. She really wanted to know more about the little girl and the triquetra, and why Tula had chosen to show her the book and tell her this story. She also wanted to know how the little girl's story ended, as well as Charlotte's story, and about the other bodies.

"Anika. When can I collect Charlotte's ashes? Charlotte wants her ashes sprinkled in the river near the estuary, and the village wants to celebrate her life as well before I do that."

Anika stood up from the rocker. "Anytime Tula. I will accompany you. Just let me know when you want to come to the morgue to get them."

Tula placed the tray of dishes back on the table and sat down. "They will have questions. They will want to know how she died, why she died, and I won't have any answers for them. Also, I can't possibly tell them about the radiocarbon dating. We don't even understand this, so how will they?"

Anika sat back down in the rocker. "I don't know Tula. However, let's do this one day at a time. We will figure this out together."

Tula put her hand over the dress pocket with the book. She looked at Anika as though she wanted to say something, but she stopped herself short of saying anything.

Anika leaned in closer to Tula and put her hand on her shoulder. "You can talk to me about anything. Is there anything you wish to tell me?"

Tula smiled and picked up the tray. "Thank you. That's very kind." She stood up from the rocker and walked into the house.

❧

Back at the office Anika went through Charlotte's entire file in great detail. It was the first time that she could not connect the dots. On average, 96 hours was Anika's record for submitting all the evidence to the prosecutor that was needed for a solid conviction. She was on day 2, and she wasn't any closer to solving the case.

By the 96th hour, she was no closer to knowing anything about Charlotte's mysterious death, and Anika could not find anything on Charlotte to help her solve the case. There were also no other findings for the six other bodies in Scotland, England and France.

On day 5, Anika wasn't ready to give up, even if it was now past her record-breaking time for solving a case. She was determined to get to the bottom of this mystery. Her office walls were covered with photos of all the bodies, and at different stages of disintegration, with Post-It-notes. She watched the videos over and over again. She researched the towns where each person had lived, where they grew up, where they went to school, and she found nothing out of the ordinary that could help her get any closer or wiser about the mysterious mummies.

∞

That same week, Tula was busy organizing a celebration of life for Charlotte. The entire village set aside an entire day to rejoice and recognize Charlotte's contribution to her community. People from all over the world whose lives she had touched were arriving in Nort for this very special day.

On the 5th day that Anika wasn't even close to giving up on Charlotte's case, Tula had gone into town to meet Anika in order to collect Charlotte's ashes. This was an opportunity for Anika to spend more time with Tula, and to get to know her and ask her more questions. She suspected that Tula knew more about Charlotte's mysterious death than she let on, and she wondered if Tula knew anything about the other six bodies. "But how could she know about the bodies?" she wondered.

Anika picked up Tula at the Ferry, and they drove to the morgue. Sami was waiting for them at the entrance when they arrived. After the formal introductions were over with, Sami escorted them to the family room. There, Sami called someone to bring in the Charlotte's ashes. Within seconds, the assistant was in the room with the urn.

Tula sat quietly in the chair across a beautiful table made of white marble. She watched Sami remove a metal urn from a box. She read in her head the name written on the box. Charlotte Bourbon. Tears came to her eyes. She lowered her head and took a deep breath.

"Are you ok Tula? Do you need a moment?" Anika said.

"Thank you. No. I'm ok." Tula removed from her bag an urn made of bright purple stones. She handed it over to Anika. "We can transfer Charlotte's ashes into this urn please. It's what she wanted."

"Of course." Anika looked at the gold triquetra that had been carved into the urn, and placed it on the table.

Sami and the assistant transferred the ashes from the metal urn into Charlotte's urn. Tula watched until every grain of ash was transferred into the urn. She didn't like that, no matter how well they transferred the ashes, some of Charlotte ashes would no doubt be left inside it, a film of her would be washed away down a drain.

"Can I take the metal urn?" Tula asked.

Sami thought it was an unusual request at this point, but replied: "Of course."

"Thank you."

Sami returned the metal urn into the box and handed it to Tula. "And there's something else." Sami removed a small pouch from her white coat pocket. "This is Charlotte's ring." She placed the pouch with the ring in Tula's hand.

"Thank you." Tula removed the silvery-white ring made of spiralling bone from the pouch. She looked at the ring for a moment and cried. After whipping her eyes, she placed the ring on her middle right hand finger. Tula sat in the chair. Her left hand covered her hand with the ring, and she stared at both the metal urn and the purple urn.

"Would you like a moment alone?" Anika said.

"Yes. Thank you."

Anika, Sami and the assistant left the room.

Tula sat quiet and hugged the metal urn and the purple urn.

The others were waiting for her in the hallway. "Anika. I have something else to tell you."

"What's that Sami?"

"It's the ring. It's quite unusual. We did a test on the ring. I wanted to see what it's made of because we couldn't identify from sight what it's made of."

"And what did you discover?"

"No known material on Earth? We don't know." Anika heard a noise from inside the room.

Tula put the urns in her bag and walked towards the door.

"I think she's coming out."

"Anika. Why did you give it back to her?"

"Because you told me that she asked for it, and that she wanted the ring when she collected the ashes. Also, we only just got the results a few minutes before you arrived with Tula."

Tula opened the door and joined the others in the hallway. "Thank you."

Anika put her hand on Tula's shoulder. "Is there anything you need before you go?"

"Charlotte's celebration of life is tomorrow. The community is grateful for your help, and we hope to see there."

"Thank you Tula. We will be there." Anika said.

The drive back to the ferry was a quiet one. Anika could tell Tula wasn't up to talking. She looked out the window and said nothing. Halfway to the ferry, Tula burst into tears. Anika pulled over at the lookout point overlooking the ocean. Tula was inconsolable. Anika placed a box of tissue on the front dash. She stepped out of the car and left Tula alone to grieve in private.

10

The next day, Nort was humming. People from everywhere walked the streets. The ferry held extra special trips just for Charlotte's celebration of life. Anika, Sami and the assistant showed up. Anika gave them a tour of Nort before taking them to *Le Gâteau*, the epicentre of the celebration. From there, the celebration fanned outwards, along the river, the estuary, and by the sea. Every seasonal festival was on display that day.

Titi, Charlotte's sous-chef, had prepared a feast for the day. Tula met Titi in Mauritania. Titi's mother was the housekeeper in the house where Tula lived in Nouakchott, during one of Tula's African expeditions. Titi was only 8 years old at the time. Titi was curious about everything. She wanted to know everything about Tula and why she was travelling and writing books. The greatest discovery Titi made one day when talking about the animals that lived on the planet, was that she discovered dinosaurs were actually real and once lived on Earth, and that they were not only made up in the movies and cartoons that she saw on television when she walked by a shop that had a television. She could not believe that such big creatures had actually walked the Earth. From that day forward, she never left Tula alone. She wanted to learn more about everything and anything.

Six months later, when Tula left Mauritania, Tula, Titi and her mother were very close. They were like family for Tula. Tula gave them a cellphone and enough money to live comfortably, and call her as often as they needed. Tula also continued to support Titi's education in Nouakchott, and when Titi completed high school, Tula helped Titi and her mother emigrate from Mauritania to Nort.

Over the years, Titi also came to know Charlotte through many video calls with Tula, before she came to Nort. During these calls, Titi discovered the culinary arts and wanted to become a chef, just like Charlotte. She had no idea that there was so much food in the world, especially the cakes and other goodies that Charlotte prepared while on the calls with Titi.

Titi was now married with her own children. She could not believe her ears when Tula told her that she had inherited *Le Gâteau* and Charlotte's house. Titi was always paying it forward with every opportunity that presented itself. For this very special occasion, her entire family helped her prepare a feast that reflected everything beautiful about Charlotte.

As the sunset and the moon rose, everyone gathered by the estuary where Tula canoed from the river into the estuary. She paddled across the estuary until she was several feet, bobbing in the sea. The moment of silence had arrived. The sound of the waves on the shore was all that could be heard. In the light of the moon, Tula took the metal urn from the bottom of the canoe. She removed the lid and gently dropped the urn into the water. She watched it bob up and down for a few seconds, until it filled with water and sank to the bottom. She removed the purple urn from the bottom of the canoe and removed its lid. She leaned forward over the water and slowly poured Charlotte's ashes into the water. When there was nothing left in the urn, Tula pressed the urn into the water and watched it fill with water, and she let it go. She watched the urn sink to the bottom. It seemed that the moonlight latched onto the gold triquetra. It glowed until she could see it no more.

11

The next day, Anika called Tula to see how she was doing. She still wanted to talk with her and see what else she could tell her about Charlotte, but there was no answer. She left her a voice message. Three days later, after leaving her a few messages, Tula had not returned her call. She was curious as to why Tula was not returning her calls. She took the next ferry to Nort to catch up with Tula in person. She figured that Tula could not ignore her if she showed up at her shop or at her house.

When she arrived in Nort, she had returned to the quiet Nort she first encountered. Everyone was going about their business. She was greeted by smiling faces as she walked along the sidewalk to Tula's shop. The sign *Open* was facing the street. "Good, she's here." Anika thought. She opened the door.

Someone at the front counter said. "Good morning. Welcome."

Anika didn't recognize the person's voice with a thick ascent. "Good morning. I'm here to see Tula."

"Oh. I'm sorry. She's not in. Can I help you with anything?"

"No. I'm Chief Investigator Anika Patel."

"Yes. You're the one investigating Charlotte's death."

"That's right. Can you tell me when Tula will be coming in today?"

"I'm sorry no. She's not coming in today."

"Is she at home?"

"I'm not sure."

"Sorry. It's rude of me. What is your name?"

"Antonio."

"Nice to meet you Antonio. What's your last name?"

"Rossi."

"Italian?"

"Yes."

"Have you worked here long?"

"For some time now. I started working here when I met my wife Titi. We arrived in Nort at the same time. She works next door, at *Le Gâteau*. Tula asked my wife and I to look after things for a while. She said she needed a rest."

"Thank you for your time Antonio."

Anika left Tula's bookshop and went over to *Le Gâteau* to speak with Titi. By the end of the conservation, she wasn't any more informed about Tula's whereabouts, and if she was at home or not. All she knew was that Tula had asked them to look after things for her.

When she left *Le Gâteau*, she walked the same path to Tula's house that she had walked with Tula. At the junction of the forested path to her backyard, she was greeted with only quiet and a field of wild flowers. She figured the cats and dogs must be in the house. When she stepped up onto the porch, she knocked on the back door. There was no answer. She walked around the porch and looked into the windows. The house appeared to be empty. The cats or the dogs were nowhere to be seen or heard. When she reached the front of the house, she looked left and right of the river to see if she could see Tula taking a walk with the animals. Tula told her she did this every day. However, she didn't see or hear anyone. After several more knocks at the front door, she gave up and walked over to the river.

On the riverbank, she found footprints of one person and four animals. She followed the path in the hopes of reaching up to Tula. After 20 minutes or so, she recognized the dogs and cats in the distance with someone else but Tula. As she approached them, the dogs recognized her and ran towards her. Now she was greeted with the expected joy of doggy love. She returned the same love. Eventually, the cats greeted her as well. The man fishing in the river turned to see whom the animals were so happy to see.

"Good morning. My name is Chief Investigator Anika Patel."

"Good morning. My name is Frank Walsh. How can I help you?"

"I'm looking for Tula Rose."

"Oh yes. She told me that you might come here."

"Why's that?"

"She told me who you are and what you're doing to help solve Charlotte's case. She's really happy you're on the case."

"I went to her house but she wasn't there."

"I'm sorry but you won't find her there."

"Where can I find her?"

"I'm not sure where you can find her. She just asked me to look after the house, the gardens, and the cats and dogs until she returns."

"She returns from where?"

"I don't know?"

"Did she say how long she would be gone for?"

"No."

"I left her a few messages at the number I have for her." Anika showed Frank the number she had in her phone for Tula.

"Yes. That's the right one."

"Do you know if there's any other way I can reach her?"

"I'm sorry. I don't."

Anika looked around the river and the willow trees and wondered. "Where is she, and why didn't she tell me that she was leaving Nort?"

"Thank you, Mr. Walsh. If you hear from her, can you please let her know that I need to speak with her? Here's my card in case she asks for my number."

"Thank you. I'll let her know if she calls me." He put the card in his shirt top pocket.

12

Tula sipped her Guinness after a day of touring Scotland's Highland village of John O'Groats unspoiled scenery, fascinating wildlife, and the breathtaking array of birdlife on the local cliffs, as well as seals in the surrounding waters. This most northerly spot in Scotland was home to about 300 people throughout the dispersed village, with a linear centre with council housing, a sports park and a shop on the main road from the nearest town of Wick.

John O'Groats also received many tourists to view the Northern Lights, and Tula was one of them, even though she had seen them many times before. She went back to her room for a small rest, and when she saw the lights from her bedroom window, she went back outside and walked to the cliffs, and stretched out on the grass from where she watched the lights.

The next morning after breakfast, she enjoyed a day tour from John O'Groats to the Orkney Island, by ferry. The ferry crossing was rich in marine wildlife, puffins, and orcas along the way.

When they arrived at the World Heritage Island of Orkney, Colin Ridel, her 72 year old private tour guide was waiting for her, next to a small pick-up truck. He was holding a sign that read *Tula Rose*. Her first thought was, *he looks just like his photo on the website.*

When they shook hands, Tula admired the lines on his face. They moved with each smile, and he smiled all the time. Tula wanted to know the story behind those lines. "Who is this mysterious man I'll be spending the day with?" she wondered.

Colin had the hands of someone who had worked with his hands all his life. They were big, strong and scared.

Once in the truck, Colin said. "Our first stop is Churchill Barriers. It was built during the First World War."

Colin knew the answer to every one of Tula's questions. He knew everything about the islands' history.

"Our next stop is Kirkwall. Orkney's capital city."

While Colin waited by his truck, talking with other tour guides, Tula visited the St-Magnus Cathedral, the shops, and the museum. When it was time to visit the scenic harbour, she invited Colin to have a snack with her.

"After this, we continue along the northern coast of Scapa Flow to admire the beautiful views of the Hoy hills." He pointed with his finger the direction in which they were going.

During snack time, Tula learned that Colin was a retired veterinarian and a hobby historian. He advised veterinarians from time to time when they had difficulty with a patient, but he spent most of his time giving private tours because he loved the Orkney Islands so much.

"From here, we will drive slowly to Stromness, a picturesque town."

Tula really enjoyed her time with Colin, and she knew that he had seen everything there at least a million times, but she invited him to come along anyway, and he gladly accepted. Together, they strolled through the winding streets, visited the museum, and had another snack.

"Tula, our next stop is the Neolithic village of Skara Brae. It was established in around 2500 BC. It's older than me and older than the Pyramids." They laughed. "The village was hidden under sand dunes, perfectly preserved for thousands of years."

"I really want to see this place." Tula said. She looked at the time on her phone. "Can we make this our last stop? I would like to spend more time here before we have to return to the ferry.

"Of course. We can continue on the road and follow the route onward along a narrow stretch of land between the lochs of Harray and Stennes. There, we can stop at the mystical Ring of Brodgar and the Standing Stones of Stennes."

Tula loved Colin's narration of everything they saw while driving between each stop.

When they left Standing Stones of Stennes, they drove the same route back to get to Skara Brae.

Tula waited for Colin to get seated comfortably before he entertained and educated her on their next and final stop, Skara Brae Neolithic village.

He stepped on the gas and said. "Tula. Skara Brae Neolithic village is located on the Bay of Skaill, on the west coast of the Mainland, the largest island in the Orkney archipelago of Scotland." He pointed on the opened map and tapped to the dash of the truck. Tula leaned forward to have a closer look.

Colin motioned with his hand when he spoke. "The Stone Age village was covered for hundreds of years by a sand dune. In 1850, a great storm exposed it. It was later excavated in the 1860s. Then after 1926, further excavations were undertaken, and so on and so forth."

Tula couldn't wait to see Skara Brae. She loved history and old places.

When they arrived, Tula felt like she had stepped back 5,000 years in time. She invited Colin to join her. She wanted to know as much as possible about what she was about to see.

Colin looked around and said. "Skara Brae was a thriving village long before Stonehenge and the Egyptian pyramids were built."

Tula remembered Anika saying *Charlotte's radiocarbon dating suggested Charlotte was approximately 5,000 years old. That's older than the Egyptian pyramids.*

Colin continued. "My entire family was born and raised in Northern Scotland, and we hail from these original settlers."

Tula was even more curious to see where Colin hailed from. She was in awe of the site's preservation.

Colin walked next to her, describing what she was looking at. "The dwellings were built on slabs of stones from the beach, and because there were no trees on the island, it was suggested that the furniture had to be made of stone."

Colin stayed close to Tula to answer her many questions.

"Tula. The village is made up of several on-room dwellings, as you see here. Each being a rectangle with rounded corners." They entered through a low, narrow doorway. "And entrance can be closed by a stone slab."

Tula looked closely at the furniture that the people used so long ago.

On the outside of the dwellings, tools and other artefacts the people used every day were on display where they would have been used.

"Tula, the inhabitants of the village lived mainly on the flesh and milk of their herds of tame cattle and sheep, and on limpets and other shellfish, and they probably dressed in skins as well. Life in Skara Brae was probably quite comfortable. They probably had contact with other communities for trading of various commodities. The villagers were settled farmers and probably self-sufficient." Colin pointed to the different tools.

Tula examined everything as though she was an archaeologist searching for something. She was so engrossed with her careful examination of everything and at the wealth of knowledge Colin furnished with the answers to her questions, that Colin had to remind her of the time.

"We must return now so you don't miss the ferry."

Tula was sad to leave. She wanted to spend more time with Colin. He answered all her questions and talked about things she didn't even think to ask all the way to the ferry. They arrived just in time. They were the last ones to board the ferry.

13

The night of Charlotte's celebration of life, Charlotte visited Tula in a dream. She told Tula that she was to travel to the Scottish Orkney Islands, and Tula thought that was very specific for a vision.

Then, flashes of many other visions she could not decipher flooded her dreams, and all the faces from previous visions that made absolutely no sense to her flooded back. She still didn't understand the scene, the characters or the message.

She woke up feeling more anxious and confused than when she had had these visions in a waken state. She felt blind to the spirit world she thought she knew so well. However, this time, the faces she did not recognize were calling out to her. The next day, she was on the first plane to Scotland.

The evening of her day trip with Colin, Tula was back at the same table, sipping a Guinness beer and looking through the book of the soul collectors. After what she had seen on the islands, she knew that Charlotte had brought her to this place to show her that the Orkney Islands were the home where the little girl had once lived. "But why?" she wondered.

She looked at each illustration again and again. The underground houses, circles, standing stones, earth house, the cliffs and the wildlife that she saw with Colin had been perfectly preserved in the book as well. Today, Tula had a glimpse of what this little girl's world had looked like. The little girl was even painted with a light brown skin dress, with a belt wrapped around her waist, and skinny boots with braided strings up just below her knees.

That night, Tula booked a private helicopter ride to travel over the area and the islands. She hoped to get a bird's eye view of what the little girl had seen when she flew with the big bird.

"Anything else, Tula, before we close?" the bartender called out to her with his cheerful voice.

She was the only one left at the pub. "Thank you Bruce, no." She paid her bill and went up to her room.

When she checked her phone for messages, she noticed that she had 12 missed calls, 5 text, and 3 voice messages from Anika. Tula felt guilty for not responding to any of her messages. She wasn't ready to tell her about her visions and why she was in Scotland.

Tula was also determined to understand what had happened to Charlotte. She also wanted to understand why her visions were now calling her name. She wanted to know why she was sent on this mysterious journey.

⁂

The next morning after breakfast, Tula was in the helicopter getting ready for take-off. Tula put on the headpiece with a microphone to hear and speak with the pilot. She was seated right next to him.

"Brodie. I have a question."

"Yes. Go ahead, Tula."

"Do you have a set flight path for this morning's tour?"

"Yes." He removed a map from the pouch on the side of his seat. He unfolded the map and followed the flight path with his finger."

She remembered the flight path the big bird had taken with the little girl. She pointed on the map and said. "Can we also take *this* path?" She outlined the path with her finger on the map.

"Yes. It's within the boundaries of this tour. No problem."

"Thank you."

Before she knew it, Tula was in the air looking down at the pub's roof. They followed the cliffs and then headed in the direction of the Orkney Islands. From there, Brodie flew the flight path Tula outlined on the map.

Tula was speechless. The view of the mainland and of the islands from the sky was more beautiful than she had ever imagined. She could see everything from the marine life in the water, to the curvature of the land, and what she was really searching for, the formation of the triquetra.

One of the many climatic changes that had transpired over the many centuries was that the sea had risen over the islands' arms that once overlapped into a triangular figure and interlaced with the circle of the little girl's village at the centre. However, when she looked down, she could see the interlaced arms submerged below the water, and since she had seen a perfect replication of the area in the book, she recognized Skara Brae as the village at the centre of the islands, woven into the triquetra.

14

By noon, Tula was eating lunch in the pub and saying goodbye to her tour guide Colin Ridel over the phone. He agreed to see her that afternoon to tell her more about the area and the islands. Members of his family were descendants of the original settlers of Skara Brae of Orkney Island, and Tula grabbed her first opportunity to tap into that knowledge. After lunch, she drove her rental car to the town of Wick where Colin lived.

The day she spent with Colin at Orkney Islands, she learned as much about him as she did about the Islands. When she enquired about his family, she learned that Ridel was one of the earliest surnames found in Scotland. It occurred during the reign of David I, King of Scots from 1024 to 1053, long after the original settlers of Skara Brae had arrived. Colin highlighted as well that Ridel was an Anglo-Norman name, which had become hereditary in England before arriving in Scotland.

The drive from John O'Groats to Wick took about 25 minutes. Tula drove a little bit slower than the speed limit, south along the southwest coast, and enjoyed the scenery. As there were no other cars behind her during the entire way, she was even able to slow down almost to a full stop from time to time, just to take in the view.

Thirty minutes later, she was approaching Wick. Her mind went back to when Colin told her that Wick's origins were probably in the later 14th century, and when they talked on the phone, he suggested that she stop in first to visit the Old Man of Wick, a castle dominated by its four-storey tower, a grand sight near the town of Wick. This is exactly what she did.

After her visit to the castle, there was plenty of time to spare before meeting Colin and continue on to Wick. She drove slowly through the town. It straddled the River Wick and extended along both sides of Wick Bay.

Her head turned from left to right, and she looked everywhere at the twin gullies and cliffs, and at the colossal sea stacks.

Once she was in the village, she continued to follow every one of Colin's instructions until she arrived. When she reached the end of the village, she drove ¼ of a mile and took the first left on the dirt road to Colin's farm. She looked for the sheep in the field on the right-hand side of the road, and stayed on the road until she reached the small stone bridge over a creek, and followed the winding road to the cottage made of stone. Colin's truck was parked in the driveway at the side of the house.

The day before, during her chats with Colin, she learned that he lived alone. His wife had died during childbirth, and he raised their newborn baby girl Iona, 2 year old son William, and 4 year old daughter Ava on his own. However, his youngest daughter, Iona died at the age of 5. Ava and William were grown up and living elsewhere.

His oldest daughter, Ava, was a veterinarian and living in Uganda, working with a wildlife conservation group. His son William was a famous playwright and actor, living in London.

His brothers, sisters and the entire village helped him with his family, and in return, he provided a great deal of veterinary services for free. Even though he was a top-notch veterinarian, his friends always told him that he may have missed his true calling in life, and that he should have been a historian. Colin always replied that he was.

If he wasn't doing veterinary work, and caring for his children, he was always reading history books, and everything and anything that had to do with anthropology and archaeology. It was all history to him. His vast historical knowledge of the area reached far and wide. From numerous universities around the world, historians, archaeologists, and anthropologists with a keen interest in Northern Scotland and surrounding areas always called on Colin as their principal advisor and to help with field studies.

When she parked the car, Colin stepped out from the other side of the house, with four chickens in tow. He scattered the last bit of grain from his hand onto the ground and waved at Tula.

"Good afternoon, Tula." Colin greeted her with a warm and strong hug.

"Good afternoon Colin." She hugged him right back.

"Let me show you around the place. Then we can go in."

Colin gave Tula the grand tour of the barns. One was a modern and well-organized veterinary clinic. The next barn over served to store farm vehicles and mechanical tools and equipment. He had free ranging chickens in one area, and pigs in another, and sheep in the field.

"Let's go to the cottage." Colin led them away from the third barn with the doors closed. It was larger than the two barns and painted white, with bright orange shutters and doors.

"What's in that beautiful white and orange barn, Colin?"

"The horses. They are far out in the field. They'll come back later."

"I love horses. I hope we can see them before I go."

He opened the back door to the cottage. "Please, come in."

Tula stepped into a mud room where coats and boots where kept. He removed his dirty boots and slipped his feet into indoor shoes.

"You may wear these." He handed Tula a lovely pair of indoor slip-on shoes that fit just right. "Thank you."

He opened another door. "Tula. Please come in."

Tula stepped through a low entrance into a magnificent kitchen. She could see that Colin kept a tidy and very clean house. The kitchen was not too big and not too small. A wooden rectangular table with four chairs was the kitchen's centrepiece to gawk at, with its beautiful and intricate carvings.

"I've prepared tea and sandwiches for a snack. Then I will gladly answer any question you may have. After that, we can go into town for a beer at the pub, if you wish."

"Sounds like a perfect day to me! Thank you Colin for preparing all of this, and for making time to see me in spite of your busy schedule."

"It's no trouble at all."

While they ate, Tula learned that Colin was the 28th descendent to inherit the land since the reign of David 1, King of Scots. His relatives, including first and distant cousins, still lived mainly in Northern Scotland, with a few who had left for England and France, during the same time and for the same reasons as Charlotte's ancestors had emigrated from Scotland.

Tula wasn't surprised by that news since many had left Scotland during specific periods throughout the course of Scotland's history. However, she was none the wiser as to why his family believed to be the descendants of the little girl in the book on soul collectors.

When they finished eating, Colin cleared the table and set the dishes in the sink. "Come. Let me show you the rest of the cottage."

Tula followed him out the kitchen and into the hallway. Beautiful wallpaper decorated with soft coloured roses covered the walls. "My wife decorated the entire cottage. I haven't changed a thing."

"Your wife had great taste."

"Mora. That was her name."

"Beautiful name."

"Here she is." He pointed at a portrait of her hanging on the wall. It was the first thing you saw when you walked through the front door of the cottage.

"She's beautiful."

"She was 25 in this portrait. We had just found out that she was pregnant with our 3rd child."

Tula looked up at the portrait. "You always have her with you."

Colin smiled and said. "And through here." He stepped into the main room.

Tula followed and her eyes fell upon two sofas made of wood and silk. They faced one another, and in the centre, a stone table was carved in a slight oval shape. A green velvet chair was set in the corner, by the window, and there was also a bookshelf filled with books on the other side of it. She could see that the chair had been well used. She walked past the bookshelf and glanced at Colin's diverse and eclectic book collection. He read everything and owned copies of very rare and expensive books.

The furthest round corner of the room housed a baby grand piano. Colin described everything she was looking at with great passion. Everything was Mora's idea.

"My wife was the one who played. I play a little, but she was the maestro."

Tula touched the keys with her fingers, and she looked at the music sheet that read on the top, *Stillness* by Rose Ridel. "Rose was also a composer?"

"Yes. She could do anything she wanted."

Tula looked at the sea of photos covering the piano. "And these?"

"These photos are of family and friends, my ancestors, people I grew up with. Ava has the four children. William, 55, never married and has no children."

Tula walked around the piano and looked at the photos. Near the back, she noticed a photo of a group of young men and women gathered in front of a stone building. She went to pick up the photo in order to look closer at the faces, but she didn't dare touch anything. She could tell every photo was well organized.

"Where is this photo taken Colin?"

"That's the London Academy of Music and Dramatic Arts. He pointed at his son. It's when William graduated."

Tula leaned in and looked at the young man standing next William. "Do you know who that is?"

"Sorry. No. Everyone you see is from William's graduating class of '92, 31 years ago or so. These kids came from everywhere to study at this school."

Tula focused intently on the face and in her head she said, *this is Duncan.* She knew it was Duncan. She remembered the first time she met him as though it were yesterday. It was after a play at the Nort Theatre, and in the pamphlet, Tula had read that Duncan had studied at the London Academy of Music and Dramatic Arts, and he later mentioned this a few nights later while having dinner with her and Charlotte at Charlotte's house.

"Is everything OK, Tula?"

"Yes." Tula stepped away from the photo.

"Do you recognize anyone in the photo?"

"No. We have a great theatre in Nort."

"Yes, you mentioned that the other day. Are you an actor as well?"

"Yes, sometimes. Only theatre. When I'm cast for a part."

"Now, let's get comfortable and talk about the real reason you came by to see me today."

15

Tula sat on the sofa across from Colin.

"Tula, would you like anything? Tea, before we get started, maybe?"

"Thank you, but no."

Tula wiggled a little in her seat trying to gather her thoughts. Seeing Duncan's face shocked her. She gathered her thoughts and sat back with her back resting against the cushion. When she relaxed, she realized the sofa was very comfortable for a piece of furniture that was as old, if not more so, than Colin. Everything in the room was beautiful, old, well used, but well maintained as well.

Tula thought she knew where she would start the conversation, what questions she would ask Colin before she got here. However, right now, she wasn't so sure what she wanted to ask. She had prepared so many questions about why his family believed they were descendants of Skara Brae.

Instead, she told Colin about Charlotte, when they met and how they had met, of their adventures together around the world, and of their life in Nort, with the exception of mentioning Duncan and Logan, and only that she had been married and was a widow, with no children.

Then it took every bit of strength that she had to say that she had died recently. She didn't tell Colin the reason she came to Scotland. Instead, she said she wanted to see where Charlotte's family had come from in Scotland, before immigrating to France.

When she talked about a book Charlotte had given her, she removed the book of the soul collectors from her bag. Without providing a narration to each illustration in the book, she gave a summary of what she understood to be the little girl's story, up to when she carved the triquetra in the flat stone. After that, she didn't really know what she was looking at. She could only say what she was seeing in the illustrations, but she could not decipher the entire story.

She noticed how similar the illustrations had captured everything they saw at Skara Brae, and what Colin had told her about how they had lived and what they thought they wore for clothing.

Up to that point, Colin remained quiet and attentive to Tula's story. When he saw the book in Tula's hands, he leaned over and put out his hand. "May I look at the book?"

"Yes." Tula placed the book in the palm of his hand. She noticed how minuscule the book looked in the palm of his big and strong hand.

Colin gently examined the front and back cover of the book. He opened the book to the first page with the tip of his big fingers. He didn't look up the entire time he flipped from one page to the next. Then, he closed the book and returned it to Tula.

Without saying a word, he stood up and walked over to the bookshelf that was located behind Tula. Tula turned around to see what he was doing. She watched him scan the top shelf of his old and expensive collection, which she figured were first editions. After a few seconds, he pressed his first finger against the top of a book and tipped it towards him, and removed it from the shelf. He returned to the sofa and sat next to Tula with the book.

16

Colin stroked the front cover of the book with his hand.

"Embroidered here is what you would call a coat of arms. It's not the Ridel coat of arms. What you see here is the underground houses, circles, standing stones, earth house, the cliffs and the wildlife of Skara Brae." He followed the lines of thread with his finger.

Tula followed his fingers with her eyes.

"May I?" She put out her hands.

Colin placed the book in her hands.

"It's lovely." She stroked the front cover of the book with her hand.

"Next to the Celtic Psalter, this book is one of the oldest books from this area. What I mean is that it wasn't a book as we see here. I should say that this story is one of the oldest stories transcribed from oral storytelling to a written and illustrated story."

"The Celtic Psalter?"

"May I."

Tula returned the book to Colin.

"The Celtic Psalter is described as Scotland's Book of Kells. It's a book of Psalms. A prayer book. That too was a pocket-sized book, and that book, science suggests that it was created in the 11th century AD, making it Scotland's oldest surviving book. It's now housed at the University of Edinburgh where it went on public display in 2009 for the first time. I'm only referring to the Celtic Psalter because of how old it is. This story that we have here in this book you see here." He followed the letters embroidered on the front cover with his finger. "Skara Brae Anaman. This means Skara Brae Souls. In Scottish Gaelic Anaman means souls, and Anam is soul."

Tula looked closely at the words on the cover of the book. "The people of Skara Brae did not have the material to create such a book."

"That's correct, but they still had the means to tell stories and to draw with the tools they had. Just as you see in your little book."

"And what material was used to inscribe the prayer book?"

"The same that is used in your little book, Tula?"

Tula took the book from the table and opened it. She stroked the thin page and examined it closely. "What is it?"

"Vellum." Colin opened the book to the first page of his book. "This material is Vellum as well."

Tula touched the pages of her book again. She couldn't believe what she was feeling. "Animal skin."

"Yes. Vellum is prepared animal skin or membrane. May I?"

Tula placed her little book in his hand.

Colin opened the book to the illustration of the carved triquetra on the flat stone and said. "The stone was the easiest material she could find in her immediate need to draw what she saw."

"My little book is somehow well preserved. Its extraordinary illuminations in vivid green, red, purple, gold and other colours survived these many centuries. Is my little book from Skara Brae when the little girl was alive? How can that be? It must be an excellent copy of sort. Taking animal skin and turning it into a book like this one, with a purple silk front and back cover. No?"

Tula's head was spinning from so much information and questions. The mystery surrounding Charlotte's death and life, woven tighter into a more unknown place, than giving way to answers to her questions she had hoped to clear up while in Scotland.

"As these books passed from hand to hand, they were no doubt damaged. The book covers were modernized, reflecting a time when their repair was required, just like the silk cover of your little book. The inside pages remain the same. You see? It's difficult to tell with the naked eye, but these marks in the skin tell me that they are the original pages. The radiocarbon dating from the sample of a page in this book confirms what my family suspected all along. A friend from the university did this for me without revealing it to anyone, as I requested. This book is one of a kind."

Tula looked closely at the pages in her book. She found their marks in the skin now that she knew what to look for. She also wondered why Colin didn't want the scientific world to know about his book.

"My book read as a first edition on the inside cover before it was printed. It's only the front and back covers of the book that do not date back to Skara Brae's original inhabitants, when the little girl in your book lived there." He showed her the difference in material from the front and back covers, to the vellum inside the book.

"Now, you came here today to know why we believe to be the descendants of this little girl's people."

17

Colin sat back comfortably against the sofa. Tula did the same thing. She waited with anticipation to hear the story that Colin was about to share with her. He opened the book to the first page and said: "What I'm about to tell you will seem impossible. This story is considered by many to be a local legend or a myth."

Tula was open to hearing anything that could possibly help her learn more about Charlotte's life and death, and of the six other mysterious deaths she overheard Anika talking about on her phone, and who was found in the same condition as Charlotte and with the birthmark of the triquetra. When she overheard Anika on the phone, she rushed into the kitchen to look over Anika's shoulder as she scrolled through the photos of the six bodies' faces. With the shape of the kitchen's window in the shape of a moon crest tip, Tula had a good vantage point to see clearly what Anika was looking at.

When Tula saw the photos, she could not believe what she was seeing. They were the same faces that came to her in her visions, calling her name. She stepped away from the window and searched her mind for answers. Then she stopped and said to herself, and to these faces and any spirit who was listening, *What are you trying to tell me?*

She could hear that Anika was about to end her call. As an excuse for going in the house, she came back out with the chocolate mousse that she had prepared for supper that night. Lucky for her, the mousse was ready to eat, and she was telling the truth when she said that she liked eating anything chocolate at any time of the day.

"Let's have tea before I begin." Colin stood up from the sofa and went to the kitchen.

Tula recognized that it wasn't a question. Tea or no tea? She turned the pages of Colin's book and looked at the illustrations. The only words in this book were on the front cover. There were no inscriptions other than the illustration throughout the book that she could see.

A few minutes later, Colin walked in with a tray carrying a teapot, two cups, milk, and sugar, as well as a plate of biscuits. He set the tray on the table and served Tula a tea and offered her biscuits. She graciously accepted the tea even though she already felt full of tea, and took a biscuit, which she placed on her saucer.

Colin filled his teacup and took a biscuit as well. He dipped the biscuit in the tea and ate it slowly.

Tula had no other choice than to do the same. She could see that she could not rush him or show how eager she was to hear his story. By the time she had dipped her last bite of biscuit, Colin placed his empty teacup on the table and filled it up again. This time, when he offered Tula a top up, she showed him that she still had half a cup. He took a sip and sat back comfortably against the sofa and placed the book on his lap.

He opened the book to a page near the beginning of the book with an illustration, and said: "Let's begin with the big bird that the little girl saw on the beach that day."

"Colin, you have my undivided attention. Again, thank you for sharing your story with me. Trust me, nothing seems too far-fetched at the moment."

Colin looked at her. "Why is that?"

Tula realized that she probably shouldn't have said that. She sipped her tea and smiled. "Oh. Sorry. Nothing really. Please. Continue."

"As I was saying, the big bird. The Boobrie."

"The Boobrie."

"Yes. It is said to be a mythological shape-shifting entity which inhabits the lochs on the coast of Scotland."

"I see, and is it a mythological entity?"

"You're catching on. No. It is not."

"And how do you know this?"

"I know this because I have seen the Boobrie myself, and I have spoken to it."

She opened her little book to the illustration and pointed. "Was it the same bird that the little girl spoke with, here in this illustration?"

"Something like that. It commonly adopts the appearance of a gigantic water bird resembling a cormorant or a great northern diver, but it can also materialize in the form of various other mythological creatures, such as a water bull."

18

Tula had no reason to think that this old man was shy of a few screws. He was strong and healthy in every way, educated and worldly. She had no reason to be suspicious of him since she, herself, was born with the gift of vision, a seer, a medium, and a psychic as many have been labeled. More often than not, she had encountered people from all over the world who did not believe or condone such things, and often, she had to keep it a secret from others. She did meet many by chance who believed in such things, and did not condemn her in any way when they discovered her gifts. From her visions of the six faces calling her name, she had no reason to doubt anything that Colin had told her.

"And when was the last time you saw it?"

"The day before we met." Colin smiled. "I can summon it when I desire, or it comes to me unexpectedly."

"Did you summon it or did it come to you?"

"It came to me."

"And what shape did it take?"

"Cormorant."

"And why did it come to you?"

"To tell me that you have come here to learn about the Anam and the collection of their souls."

"And what do I need to learn?"

"That is your journey of discovery Tula, not mine."

Tula sipped the last of her tea and reached for a biscuit. "I think I need a top-up." She reached for the teapot and filled her cup. "Colin?"

"Yes, thank you." He extended his arm with the teacup in the palm of his hand.

Colin sat back against the sofa. The phone rang in the kitchen. He got up and went to the kitchen to answer it. When he returned to Tula waiting for him on the sofa, he said: "Sorry. I must help my neighbour. There's an emergency with his sheep in the field you drove past."

"Of course. Can I tag along Colin?" She stood up from the sofa.

"Yes, absolutely."

Tula followed Colin to the mudroom where she had come in, at the back of the house.

"Here, put these on. They're my daughter's boots. They should fit you."

"Thank you." She slipped her feet into the green gumboots. They were a perfect fit.

She followed him outside to the veterinary clinic, and watched him in action. He grabbed an already-prepared medical bag, and a few other bits of sterilized medical equipment. Within minutes of the call, they were in the truck and on their way down the same road that she had driven up on, parallel to the field where she had passed the sheep.

When they arrived, his neighbour was standing at the already-opened gate for Colin to drive through.

"That's Angus Scott." Colin said.

Once Colin was through the gate and Angus had closed the gate, Angus jumped in the back of the truck, and Colin drove in the direction Angus had called out.

Thirty seconds later, they had arrived at a sheep that was stretched on its side on the ground. Angus' wife was with the sheep, waiting for them.

As they stepped out of the truck, Colin quickly made the introductions. Bonnie looked up and smiled at Tula. Tula stayed by the truck and watched Colin help the sheep. From the quick and anxious conversation Angus and Bonnie were having with Colin, Tula learned that the sheep was having difficulty giving birth and she was premature.

Colin instructed Bonnie and Angus to do this and that in order to help him better position the doe and keep her steady. He called to Tula and ordered her to come by his side. His medical bag was open on the ground, and he instructed her to assist him when he asked her for something from his bag.

Tula was there in a flash and on her knees in the wet grass, helping to

66

give birth to a newborn lamb. She could never have predicted this for her day or any other day for that matter.

Colin wasn't dressed as a usual farm veterinary ready to help birth a lamb. He was dressed smart and casual for his visit with Tula. However, he rolled up his sleeves and did what a veterinarian needs to do to get a lamb out of its mother, and did so safely for both mother and baby. Before Tula could look away, Colin was holding a newborn lamb in his hands, and the mother was safe and well.

Bonnie and Angus sighed with relief. They could not thank Colin enough for saving them both.

Colin finished up and gave instructions about the care of the mother and lamb to the Scott's. "Let's load them up at the back of your truck and then you can be off to the barn." Colin added.

Bonnie carried the lamb, wrapped in a blanket, to the truck.

Colin and Angus carried the doe in their arms. Tula followed behind, carrying the medical bag.

The tailgate of Scott's pick-up truck was already opened and lowered when they got to it. They were prepared and had everything ready for the doe. When Colin and Angus raised the doe in their arms to slide it into the truck, Colin's pant belt loop snagged the corner of the gait and dragged down his pants. With his shirt no longer properly tucked into his pants, the bottom of his shirt rose when he lifted the lamb. Tula was standing by the truck at the ready, in case Colin called out another instruction. She bent down to help free Colin's snagged pants from the truck, and when she bent over, she saw an orange triquetra birthmark next to another birthmark of the Tree of Life. Its far-reaching roots and high-stretching branches were arranged in a circle and slightly overlapped the triquetra which was located just above Colin's right hip, where the skin was exposed. The triquetra was the same birthmark that she had seen on Charlotte's right hip, as well as the same birthmark found on the six other bodies, when she overheard Anika talking with Sami on the phone. However, she had never seen the Tree of Life's birthmark.

19

Tula and Colin watched Scott drive off. Colin gathered his things and returned them to the truck.

"Is this your first time Tula?"

"Yes. Sort of." Tula walked over to the passenger side of the truck and opened the door.

"What do you mean, sort of?" Colin was in the truck and closed the door.

Tula knocked her foot on the edge of the truck to remove the mud from her boots. She looked up at Colin. She really wanted to talk about his triquetra and the Tree of Life birthmarks but she said: "When I traveled in Africa, I volunteered at various wildlife rehabilitation centres. I was fortunate to see and assist animals give birth."

"Those are beautiful memories."

Tula jumped in the truck and closed the door.

When they drove back towards the gate, it was Tula who had to get out of the truck to open it and shut it after Colin drove through. Before Tula got back in the truck, she looked around for a moment. She wanted to see what the people of today and Colin's ancestors would have seen. Her intuition was guiding her to look at the land, to pay attention to the landscape and to see what was beyond what she could see in front of her. It was only there and then that some of the images she saw in her visions started making some sense to her. She felt that she had been here before and seen this very same place. It's now that she was feeling that she was having memories of Skara Brae. She had seen this village before as well. Everything she had seen since the moment she first arrived in Scotland was beginning to feel familiar.

Colin stepped out of the truck and went to Tula.

"Are you having troubles closing and locking the gate?"

Tula turned to Colin. "No. It's ok. It's closed and locked." She jiggled the gate to show him it was secure. "The sheep can't get out." She smiled.

"Great. Thank you for your help today. You did a great job."

"My pleasure. This was my first baby lamb." Tula smiled from ear to ear. She was genuinely pleased to have been a part of this. She had a great love for animals, and this was a gift for her.

Tula stepped away from the gate and turned back to see Colin leaning against it. He was looking around the same way she had just been looking at the beauty of the area. He turned to her and said. "The triquetra is considered one of the oldest Celtic symbols."

Tula walked back to the gate where Colin was standing. Just as she was to ask him about his birthmark, he continued.

"They say it dates back as far as 500 BC, but we know it was much earlier than that."

"Why's that?"

"My ancestors. Over the many centuries, the triquetra was used to symbolize many things, depending on who looked at it and what it meant to them, their society of that time. It was symbolized as the triple goddess, meaning maiden, mother, and crone."

Tula rubbed her earrings and wondered what her heart-shaped stud earrings with the triquetra at the centre meant to her.

"And amongst Christians in Ireland, it became a symbol of the Holy Trinity."

Tula remembered the day Charlotte suggested for Tula to order specific books on the triquetra for her bookstore, and all the different meanings it had held over time.

Colin looked out at the field. "And the symbol is also often used to represent the three fundamental elements. Air, water, and earth or the infinite cycle of life."

Tula had a flashback of Charlotte talking about the infinite cycle of life.

Colin put his hand over Tula's hand. "It is also known as a rune of protection."

Tula didn't move. She felt as though a bolt of lightning rushed through her body. The energy vibrating through her veins wasn't like anything she had ever felt before in a vision.

She opened her eyes and said. "Yes, and in modern times, the triquetra has become a design element in knot-work, jewellery, emblems, logos and so on." Tula remembered when Charlotte suggested she not cater to these requests when people came to her shop. Everything Tula had in her shop in reference to the spirit world had been made and designed from her visions, and her books were for a clientele who sought literature from ancient and original scripts that had been discovered at archaeological sites, and authenticated to be from such sources, instead of new age and contemporary charlatans.

Colin walked back to the truck. "The three-fold today symbolizes the promise of a husband to his wife, love, honour, and protection, the family, father, mother, and child, and the passage of time, past, present, and future, and many other things. Many have defined it as they desire."

He got back in the truck. When Tula closed the door, he added: "And the circle represents the bond between the three elements: air, water, and earth. The infinite cycle of life. A rune of protection." He put his finger over his right hip where his pant covered the triquetra birthmark. "This is how we know we are the descendants of the Skara Brae people." But he made no mention of the Tree of Life birthmark, and Tula didn't feel like she should ask, not just yet.

20

Back at the house, Colin returned his medical bag to the clinic. Tula helped him clean the equipment, put everything away, and prepared a fresh medical bag for another emergency call.

"Tula, please put this medical bag in the truck, and I'll meet you back at the house."

Tula was eager to get back to talking about why she was there. When she returned to the house, she found Colin sitting in the living room on the sofa with his book on his lap, and a bottle of Scottish Whiskey with two glasses on the table.

"I suppose we should get back to this before we head over to the pub." He handed her a glass of whiskey.

Tula sat next to him. "Agreed. Thank you."

Colin opened the book at the first page. He remained quiet while looking at the beautifully painted oak tree, with far-reaching roots and high-stretching branches arranged in a circle.

"This is our Crann Bethadh." Colin followed the lines of the tree with his finger.

"The Celtic Tree of Life."

"That's correct. How did you know this?"

"My friend Charlotte had one in her house and she told me what it was, and I have this ring." Tula raised her hand to show him the gold ring with the Tree of Life design. She lowered her eyes in memory of her friend. She held back her tears and put her left hand over the orange ring on her right hand.

"Charlotte was Scottish?"

"Her family was."

"This tree symbolises the longevity, strength and wisdom of our ancestors, as illustrated throughout this book. Trees are the actual ancestors of man and provide a gateway to the spirit world."

"Yes. I remember Charlotte telling me that as well."

"Also, did she tell you that the Tree of Life embodies rebirth and new beginnings, safety and the home, the universe and the inevitable cycle of life and death?"

"She did, and I learned that as a child as well."

"How did you learn that as child."

Tula really wanted to tell him about her visions, her gift, but she answered: "Books." However, it really was the visions that led her to specific books. It was how she came to read the most unusual books not found in the general bookstores or bestsellers. Just about everything she read was guided by divine intuition through her visions.

"Have you read, in those books, that it is believed that the Celt Tree of Life symbol is one of many designs to come from an ancient group of tribes known as the Celts, and that the Celts lived across Europe, which many believed were Irish or Scottish. In fact, they also say that the exact origin of these ancient people is unknown."

"No. I didn't read that exactly."

"We know where we come from."

"Do you mean you, as Scottish Colin, or do you mean the people of Skara Brae?"

"We are neither. It is only the name of the region that has been given to us over the many inevitable cycles of life and death. However, for simplicity, we agree to call ourselves the descendants of Skara Brae." Colin turned his body towards Tula. "As I mentioned in the truck a little while ago, the triquetra birthmark you saw today is the mark of this ancestral line."

Tula sipped her whiskey. She wasn't used to whiskey, but she liked the flavour. "It's delicious."

"Top up?"

"Yes please!"

While Colin topped up his glass, he said: "There is more to my ancestral story." He turned the page.

Tula looked at the page Colin pointed at with his finger. Her first thought was: *"If I didn't have my own visions, and my own unexplainable experiences with the spirit world for which many believe me to be crazy or a liar, and if I had not seen Colin's triquetra birthmark, Charlotte's and the other six, as well as their unusual deaths, I would think that Colin is an absolute nut job."* She followed the painted lines of a large, dinosaur-like creature in a narrow arm of the sea and, before she could say it, Colin said it.

"Yes. What many know as the Loch Ness monster is believed to be a myth. However, we have our own gigantic water serpents in the area and around Skara Brae."

"Serpents. Plural you say, Colin?"

"That's correct. We have lived with many of them for centuries."

Tula was fascinated and confused. She could not connect the dots. "What does any of this have to do with Charlotte, the other six, and her visions, as well as her reasons for being in Scotland, and with this mysterious and interesting man, Colin?"

"These serpents protect us."

"From what?"

"From the many threats we've endured over the centuries from anyone who believed they could steal from us."

"Are they still here?"

"Yes. More than ever."

"Is there a chance that I can see one?"

"There's always that possibility."

Tula turned her head towards the window. "I think I saw a horse walk by."

Colin looked up from the book and at Tula. He closed the book and walked to the window. "Yes. The horses are coming in from the field."

Tula walked over to the window to have a better look at the horses. She walked from window to window to get a glimpse of them. "Can I go out and see them? Will they be ok with a stranger?"

Colin looked out the window for a moment and back at Tula. "Follow me."

Tula was filled with excitement. She loved being around horses. She didn't ride horses because she never felt right being on a horse when she was given the opportunity to do so. She always preferred to walk next to them and to just be with them.

She followed Colin to the mudroom. Colin laughed at her excitement to see the horses. She was practically tripping over herself. She couldn't get out there fast enough.

"They've gone to the barn." Colin said. He followed the horses' footprints.

Tula walked right behind him. She was practically on his heels.

"We will go in through the far doors at the other end of the barn. I always keep these doors closed. The horses prefer the one entrance at the other end."

Tula followed Colin to the far end of the barn. When they turned the corner, Tula was greeted with a horsetail swatting her face. She laughed and stepped back. She wiped her face and eyes.

"Hello Ròs, my pretty girl." Colin stroked her long silver mane.

Tula wiped her eyes and listened to Ròs' neighing. When she opened her eyes, Ròs turned her head and greeted Tula. Tula stood frozen with disbelief. She could not believe what she was looking at. She giggled, and then her giggle grew into an uncontrollable laughter. She kept repeating to herself: *There's no way Anika and Sami will ever believe any of this. I can barely believe it myself.* She laughed some more while Colin and Ròs just stood there, watching her.

Then she burst out even more with laugher when two more unicorns came out of the barn to see what was going on outside.

21

By now, Tula was on the ground in stitches. She looked up at three unicorns staring down at her, and Colin smiling and making introductions. "Again, she's Ròs. Over here, he's Gorm, and over here, she's Lilac." Colin pointed to make sure Tula knew who he was referring to, in her fit of laugher.

"Hi. Nice to meet you." She couldn't stop laughing no matter how hard she tried.

Gorm nudged Colin. "Is she going to be OK?" He stepped over to Tula.

"I think so." Colin lowered his hand to help Tula off the ground.

Lilac walked over to the other side of Tula. "She's wearing Charlotte's ring."

"And they talk too." Tula reached for Colin's helping hand. It took a few pulls to get her up because she couldn't stop laughing.

Tula finally managed to stand up on her own. She looked up at the three unicorns. They were very tall. The top of her head, which was at 5 feet and 4 inches barely reached the top of their front legs. She looked up at their faces. They all looked alike. They were all white with bright silver manes, with the exception of their eyes. Ròs, had bright rosette-coloured eyes. Gorm, he had bright blue eyes, and Lilac had bright lilac-coloured eyes.

"How do you know that I'm wearing Charlotte's ring?" She raised her right hand with the silvery-white ring." She realized that she might be focusing on the wrong thing here, in this moment. She was standing in front of talking unicorns. She dropped her hand back to her side.

Lilac looked down at Tula, and said: "We know it's Charlotte's ring because we gave it to her. It's one of a kind, as they say."

Tula brushed the dirt off her clothes and hair.

"You have some more here." Ròs pointed with her nose at the dirt on Tula's right cheek.

Tula cleaned the dirt from her face. She giggled at the thought of a unicorn telling her she had dirt on her face.

Colin walked over to the bench on the side of the barn and sat down. He waved for Tula to come and sit next to him. He figured it probably was the safest position for her to be in should she fall to the ground again. This way, he could catch her before she fell over.

Tula sat next to Colin on the bench. She looked at the unicorns gathered around them and smiled. "This is real. This is all real? Isn't it?"

"Yup." Lilac said.

"I don't understand any of this."

Colin turned towards her. "In the book I showed you, the page that follow the serpents are a painting of these three." He pointed at the unicorns. "It is said that the unicorn is first mentioned in a long-lost book about India, in about 400 BC."

Tula looked up at the unicorns. As much as she loved Colin's historical stories, this was the only moment that she just wanted to be told something not completely idiotic. She looked at Colin and tried not to laugh. She put her hand over her mouth. "I'm sorry. Please continue."

"It is also said that, eventually, the unicorn was adopted in Scotland, as you know it today, as Scotland's national animal in the 15th century. That's why you can see it everywhere. The unicorn has been in these lands, now Scotland, since long before that."

"As long as the giant serpents living in the lochs?" This was Tula's attempt at a serious question.

"Yes." Colin smiled. The unicorns laughed out loud.

"Maybe we've been around longer than that sea dragon." Gorm said. He laughed.

Tula couldn't contain her laughter. "And what else do I need to know?"

Lilac stepped forward. "The myth about unicorns is that we are a symbol of purity, innocence, and power."

Gorm laughed. "Purity and innocence."

"My thoughts exactly." Ròs grimaced.

"But was is true is that our horns can purify poisoned water. This is one of our strengths…one of our healing powers." Lilac said as she lowered her horn.

Colin placed his hand over Tula's hand with the silvery-white ring. "There is a reason you are here, Tula."

Tula noticed that he wasn't smiling. She felt his energy through his hand. A sudden energy of fear rushed through her body. "Why am I here?"

"The unicorn is not the only mythical animal that makes up the fabric of Scottish folklore. There's the Kelpie."

"What's a Kelpie?"

Ròs lowered her head to be eye-to-eye with Tula. "The Kelpie is also a horse-like animal. We are land-based with a single horn on our head, as you can see. The Kelpie is an evil water spirit that haunts the Scotland's lochs. The real problem is that it takes on the shape of a horse, which you can find around any one of these farms throughout Scotland. The other danger is that the Kelpie can also pose as a human, and this human can go anywhere."

Colin gripped Tula's hand a bit tighter to reassure her. "This shape-shifting spirit is often seen as a black horse-like creature. Some accounts of his sightings say that the Kelpie retains its hooves when appearing as a human. However, the Kelpie's shape-shifting abilities have improved over the centuries. It no longer needs to shape-shift from horse to human. It can shape-shift directly, posing as a human without any traces of hooves or any other horse-like features. With its powerful evolution, it shape-shifts into a grey foggy film of energy."

Tula put her other hand over Colin's hand and looked up at the unicorns. "I need to tell you something about Charlotte." Tula's tears rolled down her cheeks.

Colin put his arm around her. "We know about Charlotte's death."

Tula wiped her tears. "How do you know?"

"She would have to be dead for her ring to have been passed on to you." Gorm added.

"I don't understand. Why do you say she would have to be dead? And why to me? I don't want her dead. I preferred when she was here with me. She was my friend, and how do you know her? What does she have to do with all of this?"

"We are sorry for your loss, Tula. We loved her dearly as well. She was our friend." Lilac said. She lowered her horn. "Please touch my horn."

Tula touched Lilac's horn.

"Now touch the ring." Lilac said.

Tula touched the ring. "It feels the same." She looked up at the unicorns.

"That's because the ring is made of our horns." Ròs said.

Tula looked at her silvery-white ring made of spiralling unicorn horn. She wrapped her hand around the ring and began to cry. "I don't understand. Why would Charlotte want me to have this ring? I miss her so much. I don't understand why she died, how she died and what happened to her body. What about the others? I don't understand any of this. I miss my friend."

"It's probably best for us to continue this conversation with a little something." Colin said. "We will tell you everything." Colin hugged Tula and left her with the unicorns.

When he returned from the cottage, he had a book under one arm, two glasses in one hand, and the bottle of whiskey in the other. Tula had stopped crying and was hugging the unicorns.

Tula sat on the bench. Colin sat next to her. He poured them each a glass of whiskey. Tula gulped down every drop.

"Another Tula?"

"No thank you."

Colin opened the book to the unicorn page. "Let's begin."

22

Colin opened the book to the page with the three unicorns and began narrating a tale that Tula had never heard before.

"A very long time ago, even before the world, the little girl lived in Skara Brae, the Boobrie, the unicorns, and the serpents shared a world with human beings. It wasn't a perfect world. There were people who did good things and there were people who did bad things. Some wanted power. Some wanted riches. Some wanted what others wanted, just as you see in today's world. Human beings pretty much remained the same throughout history. Some things got better over time, others we aren't quite sure of yet, but what we do know is that evil continues through every century. The evil the humans suffered back then is the same evil they suffer today. Through the persistent and relentless pursuit of anything that they imagined as theirs for the taking and at any cost, came the creation of the Kelpie."

Colin flipped through the pages of the book. The illustrations told the story of the many wars and battles, the friendships, the discoveries, the arts, and many other wonderful human accomplishments in the ancient world.

Tula placed her hand on a page. "This one."

"Yes, the serpent rising out to the water."

"So, the serpent as you said at the beginning, is not a bad creature?"

"No. The serpents are the protectors of the waters. They keep guard and protect the human beings."

"Protect them from what?"

"At first from themselves as best as the serpents can do. Humans have great minds and imaginations, but they did destroy many things in the world they live, just to get what they want. They pollute their water. The unicorns then heal the water. The serpents are the knowledge keepers of the water: sea, lake, river, any water. They shared and passed on this wisdom to humans. Some humans used this knowledge to do bad things, instead of doing good things. They believed they knew better and wanted to create a world where achieving certain outcomes was for the greater good of all humans. It's an age-old tale that hasn't changed much over time."

Colin turned the pages with the serpents and stopped at the page with a serpent fighting the Kelpie. Tula put her hand over the grey horse rising out of the water, trying to reach land."

"Why would evil choose to shape-shift as a horse? What a beautiful animal! And why would people be scared of a horse?"

"For that exact reason." Ròs said. "The Kelpie appear to their human victims as a beautiful horse, entice them to ride on their back, then carry them down to a watery grave."

"The Kelpie returns the human to the world where they were created." Tula said.

"Yes. Something like that." Gorm replied.

"That is how the evil can continue to live and thrive." Colin said.

Tula turned the page. "And what happened to the Kelpie?"

Colin placed his hand gently over Tula's hand. "The story continues." He turned the page and resumed the narration.

"The Boobrie are messengers. The unicorns are healers. The serpents are guardians of the water. In those ancient times, there also lived a different kind of human being. They were and still are the Anam Duines, Soul Human, you see Tula." Colin turned to the next page. He pointed at the triquetra. "The three interlaced arches, one represents the Boobrie, the other the unicorn, and the third the serpent. The circle that loops through each arch represents the Anam Duines, the Soul Humans."

"How do you know if a human is a Soul Human or a regular human?" Tula asked.

"By the orange triquetra birthmark you saw on my hip earlier today. We all have it."

"And Charlotte?"

"Yes. She was one of us." Colin replied.

Tula touched her earrings with her fingers. "And where did the Soul Humans come from?" She had many questions rushing through her head. As she thought back to the first day where she met Charlotte, bit-by-bit, everything she didn't know about Charlotte, or didn't question at the time, as well as her mysterious death, was slowly coming into focus. She looked up at the setting Sun. She was further north, and the Sun set around 9:30 p.m.. "This day is like no other." she thought.

Colin closed the book. "It's getting late, Tula. We can continue this tomorrow."

"No. Please go on."

"Let me go in a make us some sandwiches. We need to eat something before we continue. Stay with the unicorns."

Tula smiled at the thought of being with the unicorns. "My pleasure."

"I'll be right back." He left the book on the bench. "Go for a walk with them. It will do you good to walk around before we begin again."

Colin disappeared around the corner of the barn. Tula put her hand on the book, but Ròs poked Tula on the shoulder to get her to stand up and follow them for a walk in the field.

23

Tula and the unicorns walked towards the sunset. They listened to her questions and concerns, the story of her friendship with Charlotte, her death, Chief Investigator Anika Patel's investigation and the death of the six others who bore the triquetra birthmark, up to the day where she sprinkled Charlotte's ashes into the sea.

With a string of unanswered questions, the unicorns took turns recounting the story from where Colin had left off, in an attempt to make this as easy as possible for Tula to understand the whole story. The unicorns continued the story and started with the Boobrie.

The humans of Skara Brae wanted a better world for all humans. They also wanted to help those humans who used their powers for evil instead of good. However, they didn't know how this could be done.

One very early morning, the Boobrie shape-shifted into a cormorant and brought a message to the humans of Skara Brae. The Boobrie told the humans about the power of the human imagination, and how their imagination would guide them in their quest to making a better world for all.

That night, the men, women and children gathered around the only tree in their village, the oak tree. The oak tree was also the only tree for miles and miles.

Over the centuries, the Skara Brae people gathered around the oak tree for many rituals, and the ritual for the well-being of human beings was a new ritual.

The oak tree was a sacred tree because of its size, durability, and nourishing acorns. They even believed that the oak tree held magical powers. They made magic wands from its branches that naturally shed from the tree, and gathered acorns at night because they believed this would bring them great fertility.

Nine months after the Boobrie brought the message to the humans, many babies were born in Skara Brae. The parents raised their children and their new babies with the knowledge of their imagination's power, as well as the power of their imagination which proved to be true magic. New tools were created, hunting and fishing became easier, the whole of their life had improved incrementally.

Eight years after the Boobrie's message, a little girl saw the Boobrie on the beach. The unicorns summarized the story Tula already knew about the little girl, up to when her parents found the carving of the triquetra in the stone. From there, the unicorns added that the little girl was Charlotte.

When the Boobrie delivered the message, the villagers were told that, with the power of their imagination, they could create the Anam Duines, the Soul Human, just as the power of their imagination was used to create the Kelpie.

The Anam Duines walked the Earth as human beings with the very special powers of imagination. They were strong influencers that helped the humans to achieve amazing and wonderful things. The Anam Duines guided the human beings' souls with every personal growth and advancement, which was also good for all of humanity, to new ideas, creativity and everything imaginable in the evolution of a whole human.

Nonetheless, the Anam Duines were not immune to the danger of the Kelpie. The Anam Duines were always on their guard. They guided and veered away as many humans as possible from the Kelpie's seductive lure. Since they both walked the Earth in human form, it was impossible for humans to know who was Anam Duine and who was under the influence of the Kelpie.

When Charlotte returned from the beach and drew the triquetra, it was only then that her parents knew that she was Anam Duine. It was also then that the orange triquetra birthmark bloomed over her right hip. This was a seal of an Anam Duine. That night, the villagers celebrated with a feast, dancing and music around the oak tree. Charlotte had completed the circle that looped through the interlacing arches of the triquetra.

Before Charlotte knew she was Anam Duine, she had embraced the power of her imagination and lived her very young life without ever knowing who she truly was. She followed her heart and did what made her feel good. She also noticed that this was always good for her, her family, her friends and everyone else.

24

Tula and the unicorns returned to the barn. Colin was sitting on the bench, eating a sandwich. A tray with sandwiches, pickles and a fresh pot tea were placed on the bench next to him.

"Tula, please sit there. Have something to eat."

Tula sat on the bench. Colin placed the tray of food between them, and the unicorns went inside the barn to eat as well. It was silent while everyone ate a late supper.

"You were hungry!" Colin looked down at the empty plate of sandwiches and pickles.

Tula smiled and wipe her mouth. "I love to eat, and yes, I was hungry. Delicious sandwiches by the way!"

"Thank you. I made them all by myself, even the bread."

"Charlotte made delicious sandwiches as well."

"Yes, she did."

The unicorns rejoined Tula and Colin. Ròs looked up at the night sky. "It's going to be a beautiful night."

Colin sipped his tea and returned his cup to the tray. He opened his book to the page where the unicorns ended up in Charlotte's story. "What you now know is all in here, and in your little book as well, Tula."

"Why did Charlotte die? And why did the six other Anam Duines die as well? I'm assuming they were Soul Humans as well?"

"Yes, they were." Colin pointed to the painting of the six people who died. "This is them."

Lilac looked down at the faces in the painting. "I remember them well. We remember them well."

Colin motioned to Tula's little book, which she held in her hand.

"Charlotte was the first Anam Duine. Then, over the years, for centuries, humans gave birth to other Anam Duines."

Tula raised the teacup to her lips. "And how is it that you can live for so long and all be of different human ages? And what really happened to Duncan and Logan?"

"Yes. Duncan and Logan." Colin turned the page of his book. "This is Duncan and this is Logan. They were born just a few years after Charlotte."

Tula recalled a strange feeling when Charlotte met them. It was as though they were already familiar to her. Looking back at their encounters, and knowing this story, it was clear how well they knew each other. "I suppose I would know someone pretty well if I knew them for 5,000 years." Tula thought. "But you said you didn't recognize Duncan in the photo on the piano next to your son."

"It was too soon to tell you anything."

"Are your children Anam Duines as well?"

"Yes."

"But your baby…"

"Iona died and my wife Mora died because the doctor ignored her concerns during her pregnancy. My wife was human like you. She was not Anam Duine. The Kelpie succeeded in twisting men's views about women and childbirth. Sadly, my wife and child were not the first to die from male doctors making women feel that everything was in their head."

"I'm sorry. Yes. Men have a knack for gaslighting women, and you say Soul Humans can be with humans like me? Did Mora know about all of this?

"Yes, she did."

Tula opened her little book to an illustration where Charlotte was a grown woman with two men at her side. "How is it that Duncan and Logan died in accidents?"

"Forces of nature. No one is immune to those. We can die from such things as you do, but it was also their time, just as it was Charlotte's time as well."

"What do you mean? And the age? Charlotte was in her 20s when we met. She died in her 50s, in my years."

"We are born and grow like you. We live and adapt to the world in which we live, and we die at the average age of death, depending on the place and the period in history in which we live. We blend in as much as possible. Some of us marry, some of us have lovers, some of us live on our own, we have friends, and we have children. When we are alive, our affairs are in order. We ensure that we have a will that stipulates exactly our desires. As you know, when we die, our body quickly disintegrates to ashes, and these ashes must be sprinkled in a lake, a river, or in the sea. It is in the water with the serpent and the unicorn that we complete our cycle."

"How do you mean by "complete the cycle"?"

"When the body we inhabit dies, we rejuvenate. A few days after our ashes are in the water, the magic of the unicorn brings us back to life in human form.

However, our life cycle is not infinite. We do not live forever. If we rejuvenate on the day of the winter solstice, this is how we know that we are in our final life cycle. It means that we have one last life to live as a Soul Human, an Anam Duine in a human body. We all have different life cycles. Some have only one. Some have hundreds, and some have thousands, like Charlotte.

However, if we did not rejuvenate on the winter solstice, it means that we are not living in our final life, and if we are murdered by a human, we cannot be rejuvenated. We must complete our natural life cycle to be rejuvenated. This is the power of the Kelpie. It wants to kill us to weaken us, to weaken and completely annihilate the power of the triquetra."

"So, Charlotte knew this was her final life."

"Yes, and you asked about the age. When we rejuvenate, we return in human form at the age of 22. Our face, our body, everything about us, appears as a 22 year old man or woman would for the place and time in which we live. However, we don't always look quite the same as we did in our previous life cycle. I look a bit different than I did in my last life, and if we've had children, our children recognize us when they see us with a different face. Our physical appearance does not change much, just enough to not create confusion and hysteria in the general public. We retain everything we've learned over the course of our various lives.

"I've died in my 20s, 30s, 40s, and so on. Our life cycle is not cut short if we are a solider fighting in a war or if we die from an accident. The reason we can die in a war is because it is our way of being in this society in which we live. Most of us have managed to escape being a soldier, as we are not permitted to kill any other human. However, if we are killed in a war, it is not the same as being murdered because humans are forced to be soldiers due to the way society has created their world. Our life cycle must end naturally. Our heart just stops beating. However, as I've said, we can be murdered. This would only be done by a human who is under the influence of the Kelpie. This would not be a natural ending to our life cycle. I have been 72 several times throughout the last few centuries.

Tula smiled. "That's why you know so much about history."

"I have a lot of experience to work from." Colin returned the smile.

"Were you rejuvenated on the winter solstice for this life?"

"Yes. This is my final life."

"Oh. I'll be sad to see you go, Colin, and what happens to Charlotte now that her life cycle has ended naturally? I did put her ashes in the sea."

"Her ashes will return to the Tree of Life. We return to where we came from."

"I see." Tula lowered her head. "I want to hug that tree."

"I know, but Charlotte's soul is everywhere. She can still see and hear you."

Tula raised her head and smiled. "I know, but it's not the same."

"No, and speaking of history, you would be familiar with other Anam Duines."

"Such as?"

"Joan of Arc. Her transgressive role subverted the gender expectations of her day. They executed her for this. The witch-hunt hysteria between the 15th and 18th centuries saw some 50,000 people executed as witches. Not all were Anam Duines, but many were. These executions are mere examples of the power the Kelpie can wield. Joan of Arc and many others' life cycles were not ended naturally. They were murdered, and in more recent years, the Kelpie wore the face of Adolf Hitler and the likes throughout the ages.

The list of Soul Humans who were historical figures throughout the ages is quite extensive. Nostradamus was one of us as well. They say that he died of severe gout towards the end of his life. We know differently. It's like Charlotte and the others, a cause of death will be written in their file. Something will be written. Probably natural causes, even if it's not understood. However, it will reflect the world in which they lived and died. Also, there's Shakespeare. He was Anam Duine."

"If I understand correctly. Those who had their life taken from them, like murdered, and did not complete their full life cycle, died, without ever being able to rejuvenate."

"Yes."

"Nostradamus? Is he still here with us?"

"No. He completed all of his life cycles."

"Shakespeare?"

"Yes. Still with us."

"Go on. Really. Where is he?"

"You saw him in the photo. Graduating class of '92 at The London Academy of Music and Dramatic Arts."

"You need to be a little more specific. I recognized Duncan, and you showed me the photo of your son William."

"That's Shakespeare."

"I don't understand. You said Soul Humans rejuvenate at age the age of 22. Mora gave birth to William."

"I lied. Again. I couldn't tell you this at the time. Mora gave birth to my daughters Iona and Ava. Shakespeare came to live with me for a while when he rejuvenated. He also took my family name, Ridel."

Tula's mind went back to when she was standing at Colin's piano. "That's why I saw only photos of Ava with you and Mora, then with only you. There were no photos of a little boy that would have been William growing up. I only saw photos of you and William together from what looked like his 20s, and the decades that followed."

"That's right."

"Why 22?"

"Because in most of your world societies 22 is an age where a human is more or less self-sufficient. However, in current times, this is questionable." Colin laughed. "But it remains 22 for now."

Tula laughed and closed her little book. "Now I know Charlotte's story. Thank you Colin. Thank you Ròs, Gorm, and Lilac. Also, I understand the visions that were so confusing. Charlotte wanted me to know about all of you, as well as what I didn't know about the world I lived in. I can go back home and know that you are here. She's given me a great parting gift. You must be exhausted. I'm exhausted."

"Yes. We could all do with a good night's sleep. You will stay here tonight."

"Thank you Colin. I did check out of my hotel and was going to check into one in Wick."

"No need. You can stay here for as long as you need."

"Thank you. I'd love to visit the area with you if you have the time. Then, in a couple days, I'll return to Nort."

"My pleasure. However, I don't think you'll be returning to Nort just yet."

"Why's that?"

"We've just scratched the surface of why you came to know this story. Charlotte gave you her ring, and because you have her ring, your story has just begun. Let's get some sleep. We can continue tomorrow."

25

Tula went to bed feeling exhausted, but she was restless and couldn't sleep. *Your story has just begun,* played over and over in her mind. "What else could there be?" she thought. She sat by the open window and watched the Merry Dancers. The unicorns were still outside by the barn.

Earlier that night, when she went for a walk in the field with the unicorns, they told her to look at the Merry Dancers in the sky. "The Merry Dancers are the Northern Lights." they said. "They are the soul of the unicorn. The unicorns are protectors of the human souls and Soul Humans. The unicorn come from the place where you can see the Merry Dancers in the sky. It is their birthplace."

From her bedroom window, she watched the unicorns dance in the light of the Merry Dancers. They danced in the glow of green, pink, red, violet, and silvery-white auras. She could see their eyes glitter even from that distance. She sat by the window and watched the unicorns until they returned to the barn.

She lay on top of the blankets and stared at the ceiling. Then, she realized that she hadn't turned on her phone all day. Once it was turned on, the phone dinged numerous times with text messages, voice messages, and missed calls from Anika. There was nothing she could report back to Anika that would help her wrap up Charlotte's case. As painful as it would be for Anika, Tula had to let her think that she had been defeated.

Shortly after she met Anika, Tula quickly saw that, once she was on a case, she was like a dog with a bone. Furthermore, Sami and Arthur would also be left wondering about the mysterious six dead bodies. These would forever be filed as cold cases.

Tula imagined Anika losing her mind after all available leads had been exhausted, and the case remained opened and unsolved after a period of three years. She would never solve it, even after 5,000 years, even if new technologies or forensic testing could produce any potential leads. It would never happen. "Poor Anika." Tula thought. "She's going to think she lost her touch."

Tula rolled herself under the covers and kissed Charlotte's ring. "Good night my friend." She closed her eyes.

A little while later, she thought she heard someone calling her name. "It can't already be time to get up." she thought.

"Colin." She barely opened her eyes and looked up from her pillow. There was no one there. She closed her eyes and went back to sleep.

"Tula. Wake up."

Tula rolled over.

"Tula. Wake up." A breeze from the open window washed over her face. "Tula. Wake up."

She opened her eyes and sat up in bed. She could see the Merry Dancers from her bed. "Tula." She heard her name as though it was the breeze calling her name. She got out of bed and went to the window, then looked out at the field.

"Charlotte." Tula rubbed her eyes and looked again. She didn't know if she was hallucinating again, like the night she thought she saw Charlotte through her shop window. This time, she didn't drink a bottle and a half of wine nor stuffed herself with chocolate éclairs and then pass out in the chair. She was completely sober. "Maybe it was too much tea, sandwiches and pickles?" she wondered. She looked again.

"Charlotte." Tula poked her head out the window.

In her white gown and glowing in the light of the Merry Dancers, Charlotte waved at Tula to come to her.

Tula slipped on her shirt and pants, and then ran down the stair to the mudroom. She slipped on her gumboots and ran as fast as she could to Charlotte. "Please be there. Please be there Charlotte." Tula repeated over and over again.

When she reached the unicorn barn, she ran even faster to get to the other side and hoped she would find Charlotte in the field.

When she ran around the corner, she heard Charlotte. "You can stop running." Tula stopped running as though she ran into a wall. "Charlotte?"

Charlotte walked towards Tula. A shimmer of glow followed her. Tula could not believe her eyes. "Charlotte!"

Charlotte stopped a few feet in front of Tula. "Tula. It's wonderful to see you."

"Yes, and you!" Tula stepped towards Charlotte to give her a hug.

"You can't Tula. I am light. I am energy. That is what you see and can feel. We can't hug the way we used to."

Tula put out her hand to Charlotte. "Charlotte. I miss you so much."

Charlotte put out her hand to Tula and let it flow over her hand.

"I can feel you Charlotte."

Charlotte took a step forward and put her hands on each side of Tula's face. "Tula. There's so much I need to tell you."

Tula put her hands over Charlotte's. "They told me everything. I understand now."

"There is more. Your story has just begun."

"Yes. I heard this already tonight." Tula smiled.

"Walk with me."

26

In the light of the Merry Dancers Tula walked with Charlotte in the field.

"The Anam Duines need you now more than ever, Tula."

Tula turned to her friend. "Anything for you."

Charlotte smiled. "You never walked away from a challenge. What I'm about to ask of you will be bigger than anything you have ever done."

Tula rolled her shoulders. "I've seen a lot of stuff on this Earth that is beyond comprehension. You and I have seen and been through a great deal together on our voyages around the world. Now I know the influential power of the Kelpie and the human imagination. What do you need from me that the Anam Duines, the serpents, and the unicorns can't handle themselves?"

"Your life."

"My life?" Tula stepped closer to Charlotte. "You always had a flair for the dramatic. You're not related to William are you?" She laughed. "What do you mean by "my life"?"

Charlotte looked down at Tula's hand with the white ring.

Tula raised her hand to her face. "Yes. I know all about this now. By the way, I lost it, in a good way, when I saw the unicorns. I burst into a fit of laughter. I couldn't believe that all of this was happening. Then I sorted myself out and listened to what they had to say. I'm not sure if I would have embarrassed you or made you proud."

Charlotte giggled. "I saw everything. I was in a fit of laughter as well just watching your reaction."

"Well, I'm glad I was a source of entertainment for all of you. So, what's this all about my twilight friend?"

"The Kelpie's power has grown. It is getting stronger and stronger. This is weakening the Anam Duines. When the babies are born from humans, like you, it is more and more difficult for parents to raise their new babies with a knowledge of their imagination's power. Also, the power of the imagination that once proved to be true magic is being eaten away by the Kelpie. There was a time when we were many. Now there is just a handful of us walking the Earth. This exposes human beings to more suffering in ways you cannot imagine. History will not only repeat itself, it will get worse."

Tula went to put her hands on Charlotte's shoulders, but her hand went through her light. Instead, she put her hands out. "Please put your hands over mine, Charlotte."

Charlotte put her hands over Tula's. Her energy was vibrating through Tula stronger than earlier.

"Charlotte, of course I will help you…all of you. However, how can I, one human being, who is not an Anam Duine, help rebuild the power of the triquetra. This seems to be what I'm hearing."

"You are hearing me correctly. The three interlacing arches are slowly unraveling. If this happens, it will weaken the circle at its centre, the human beings. It must be restored."

"How?"

"I didn't come to Nort by accident or for the reason I initially told you about. I did know Nort was the place I was meant to be because of you. You are the reason I was there. It was the reason Duncan and Logan came to me in Nort as well. I am the first Anam Duine, and part of this responsibility is to ensure that I find the human who is as powerful as I was when I lived in your world."

"But I don't understand. I am born of human parents. My parents did not raise me with any knowledge of the power of my imagination. I didn't know anything about the power of the imagination that proved to be true magic. I learned all of that on my own. My life story as an explorer of the world, and most importantly of discovering who I am, took years. I didn't come out of the box this way, and I know you know this. My life was very difficult; it was fraught with unimaginable challenges, and the worst is that I did most of it to myself because I didn't listen to my intuition, nor did I trust or believe in myself. I see that now. I've come a long way from not knowing anything about the true magic of the imagination."

"That's the reason why it is you."

"I don't follow. There are many other humans who were raised just like me, or had it even worse than I ever did. Really, there are people who suffered a great deal. We have seen it for ourselves. What is it about me that you need?"

"Your conviction. Your light shines so bright that we see it from way up there." Charlotte pointed to the sky above the Merry Dancers. "We saw you sitting in your school bench at 5 years old. It was me you were talking to. It's been me you've been talking to this entire time, and yes, you've had others from the spiritual world guide you. They were the ones guiding you to me, and you believe so much in your visions that you allowed them to guide you throughout your life, even when you decided to go against them. You always found your way back to us, and it is this strength that we seek in a human. It is your light, and the only way for me to know was for you to wear my unicorn ring. This could only be done when I died in my human form. The ring, as with the unicorn, is connected to your soul. It sees who you really are. It only remains on your finger because you are worthy of this. It would have disintegrated into ashes the moment you put it on your finger if you were not true to yourself, to your soul, and that's why the dead love you. This is why we gave you the nickname *The Soul Collector*. You have been collecting souls and helping them on their journey back to where they come from. Some humans have a more difficult time with this than others because of the Kelpie's influence on them. Most humans are oblivious to this until they die and meet the Kelpie face to face. This is when your soul reaches out to them and helps them repair who they believed they were to who they truly are, their true soul."

Tula lowered her hand. "I see. I always wondered why I had this gift, but I'm still not sure what it is you need me to do. How does this help rebuild the power of the triquetra?"

"There will be a series of events that, if not resolved, will be catastrophic for human beings. You will be helping humans see the power of the human imagination, and prove it to be the true magic for the wellness of all human beings. Each victory will give birth to more Anam Duines. The birth of each Anam Duine gradually restores the triquetra back to its full powers. This is the life cycle of the imagination. The triquetra needs to be whole in order to help human beings, and human beings need to believe that their imagination is the true magic. They are intertwined. If we lose a battle, the Kelpie gain strength with each victory. We must stop the Kelpie from reigning supreme over all humans and all souls like me, the serpents, the unicorns and the spirits that guide human beings back to their souls. This may cost you your life."

"I see. Do you mind if we sit in the grass?" Tula sat in the grass and patted the grass with her hand for Charlotte to sit with her. "Charlotte you could have prepared me for this a long time ago."

Charlotte sat across from her. "I'm sorry. I could not tell you any this until now."

"And, how do you suppose I'm to stop these events without getting myself killed in the process?"

"The Anam Duines will help you. They will find you. Don't go looking for them. We will guide you as usual. Your visions will tell you where to go and what to do. The serpents and unicorns will be there when you need them the most."

"How will I know about these events?"

"Your visions."

"And when does the first one begin?"

"It's already started. You are here with us, but you will begin tomorrow."

"That's a bit sudden. Not much of a heads-up for what's to come, and what's this first event? It's a bit late for a vision. They usual come a few weeks in advance."

"Sorry. No vision just yet for this first one."

"So, what's the plan?"

"It begins with you going to London and meeting William."

"Shakespeare. Well. This will definitely be interesting." Tula threw herself back on the grass and looked up at the sky. "Well, I did always enjoy a life of adventure and meeting all sorts of people. We can't deny that. This is much more than I anticipated when I came to Scotland to learn more about Charlotte Bourbon." They both laughed.

Charlotte lay on her side next to Tula. Tula turned to her side and faced Charlotte. Charlotte put her hand on Tula's arms. "I'll be with you the entire time."

"I'll expect nothing less." Tula smiled and closed her eyes.

27

The early morning light shined softly on Tula's face. She jumped out of bed and looked out the window for Charlotte. The unicorns looked up at her and smiled. Her room was above the kitchen, and she could hear Colin humming through the open kitchen window.

Tula went downstairs. The stairs creaked with every step she took. She looked down at the steps, and thought: "I didn't hear this last night when I went running for Charlotte."

At the bottom of the steps, she closed her eyes, raised her nose and took a deep breath. "Smells great." She felt a breeze. Colin had opened all the windows in the cottage.

"Good morning." Colin called out. "Hot chocolate is ready!"

Tula walked down the beautiful hallway to the kitchen. "The air and the food smell delicious. I'm not sure which one I want to eat first. Good morning."

Colin poured hot chocolate into her cup. "Pure cocoa, cinnamon and water. Just how you like it."

Tula brought the cup to her nose and inhaled. "How did you know I have this every morning?" Tula lowered the cup. "She told you."

"Of course. How was your visit with Charlotte last night?"

"Delightful." Tula smiled. "Colin. It seems I'll be meeting William Shakespeare fairly soon. What can I expect?"

"He spends a great deal of time in his head. He's honest, open and free-natured. He's creative of course. He likes to explore, especially people. He believes that good eventually triumphs over evil, and that good is rewarded and evil punished. As you know, he is gifted. He can select the right words and arrange them into convincing representations of reality in all of its forms, both material and immaterial. Look out for his verbal dexterity, but he's modified this for current times. Also, if Will can't find a word to fit his meaning, he prefers to invent one, and all this makes him a slightly strange character."

The toast popped out of the toaster. Colin pulled them out and put them on a plate on the table. "The butter is there if you like. The jam's here."

"Thank you. I must admit I'm quite curious about meeting Will, and I'm intrigued with what awaits me, with what awaits all of us. According to Charlotte, we are all in a bit of pickle." Tula reached for a pickle on the plate in the centre of the table, and bit into it."

"She did fill your ear with what's to come if we don't get on with this right away."

"I don't want to make light of this, but do I get a super hero outfit or magic weapon, or anything like that?"

"Just you darling."

"I see, and how will I know when I'm face to face with the Kelpie?"

"Oh, you will know. You will feel it. Trust those instincts of yours. Your gut, and to fill that gut, here you go." Colin tipped the pan of scrambled eggs into her plate. Then he tipped another pan with fried mushrooms and sausages onto her plate.

"Thank you, Colin. Do you think I'm starving or are you filling me up because I won't eat ever again? It smells great!" Tula scooped up a forkful of food and put it in her mouth. "I was wrong. It's divine."

Colin sat across from her with his plate of food. "You can drive to London. Will is expecting you. It's a 12-hour drive or so, non-stop, but do-able in a day with a few stops. I know you've taken longer road trips than that."

"I have. I love road trips. If I leave after breakfast, I should get into London by 11 tonight. I will be making stops along the way."

"Or, one of the unicorns can fly you straight into London. It won't take more than 15 minutes or so, depending on the winds." Colin smiled.

"Is this a trick question Colin? Or... That's funny. I, of course choose the direct flight with Unicorn Airline." They both laughed.

"Ròs will take you."

"Wait. I didn't see any wings on her or the others."

"They have them. They are not visible until they decide to show them."

"I see." Tula continued eating. She buttered a toast and wiped her plate clean with it.

Tula didn't want to eat and run. She washed and dried the dishes with Colin. She tidied up the kitchen and sat with him for another cup of hot chocolate. She knew the world was not going to end that day. In just a short time, she became quite fond of Colin, and she really liked where he lived. It was absolutely beautiful.

Ròs pushed open the mudroom door with her foot and walked in, and then pushed open the kitchen door. "Your flight is ready Madame."

Tula looked up at Ròs and laughed. "How did you manage to get through that door?"

"My head just about touches the top of the door." Tula knew she was not going to get a direct answer.

"Perception."

"That's what I thought." Tula got up from the table and put her empty cup in the sink. She turned to Colin with her arms opened wide and gave him a strong and loving hug. "Thank you for everything."

"You're welcome." Colin's big strong arms hugged her back and raised her feet off the ground.

Tula laughed out loud. "I will miss you."

"I won't be very far. I'm always here. All you have to do is say my name and I'll come to you in a vision. I may just invite myself from time to time when I know you're in a pickle."

"I'll expect nothing less." Tula hugged him tighter. "I'm afraid."

"We know. Let fear be your guide."

Tula looked him in the eyes and smiled. "Time to go I suppose."

"Remember. *All the world's a stage, and all men and women merely players.*"

"Shakespeare's *As You Like It*, Act II, Scene VII." Tula followed Ròs out of the kitchen.

Outside, Ròs stood next to the wooden steps in order to help Tula climb up onto her back. Gorm and Lilac waited on the side to say goodbye. Tula hugged them both. She climbed up the steps with her suitcase and draped her handbag strap over her shoulder and across her chest, as she always carried it.

Ròs fanned her enormously large wings.

"Oh. I didn't see that coming." Tula looked left and right. "Your wings are beautiful."

"I like to think so." The other unicorns and Colin laughed.

Tula leaned forward and stroked the wings. She looked down at Colin. "Tula and Will, Act I, Scene I."

Ròs took flight with Tula. From the air, Tula watched the scene below get smaller and smaller. When she could see Colin, the cottage, and the unicorns no more, she looked ahead. "Ròs. I'm ready."

28

Tula was very comfortable flying so high in the sky. She could see the curvature of the Earth all around her. "I don't know how fast we are flying Ròs, but I can't feel a thing. It's as if we are gliding and everything around us is moving slowly."

"I'm glad you're enjoying yourself. I'll take you on a tour of the surrounding area and into London. Enjoy."

"Wow. Thank you, Ròs."

Tula looked down at the lush green forests, at the farmers' fields, the villages, and towns. The striking panoramic view stretched as far as she could see.

"Just over there, you see, that's Kemble village." Ròs pointed with her hoof. "We'll begin our descent over the Thames Head." Ròs flew low and slow over Kemble village. She flew just low enough for Tula to see the site of a 7th century pagan Anglo-Saxon cemetery.

"From here, we'll follow England's longest river. Look over there, it flows easterly through southern England, including London. However, before I dropped you off in London, I'll take you on a tour.

Ròs glided over the Thames, where it rises north-northwest of Woodstock, in the uplands between Lakes Huron and Erie, and flowed southwest past Woodstock, London, and Chatham to Lake Saint-Clair.

Tula had never seen England from this perspective before, not even from a plane. After they flew over the centre of London, she looked down at the tidal waters of the River Thames, where it meets the North Sea at the Southend-on-Sea, before it opened up into one of the biggest coastal inlets in Great Britain, the Greater Thames Estuary. Tula could not believe her eyes. She didn't want this part of her adventure to end.

Ròs looked back at Tula. "We can land here for a moment if you'd like, then I'll take you to William."

"Yes. Let's take a moment."

Ròs landed in the field. She sat her rear end on the ground and let Tula slide off. They walked around admiring the area.

"Can anyone see us, Ròs?"

"No. Unicorns make themselves visible when they decide that it's safe to do so, and they can't see you either Tula because you are in my energy field. That is how we go undetected."

"I wish I had those kinds of magic powers."

"You have your own. You'll discover them as you go."

"I thought I lived enough of my life to not have to discover myself anymore. Well, not much anyway. I know that's a journey to infinity." She laughed.

"That journey to infinity is one that we are all walking together, but this one right now has a finite moment. Let's go back. I'll fly back the way we came." Ròs lowered her back end and Tula swung her legs over and sat upright on her back.

"We'll be at William's in just a moment."

William looked up from his rooftop garden at Ròs' descent. She glided gracefully over the northern banks of the Thames in London. Tula looked down at William's rooftop gardens and verandas overlooking the water. She could see William watering the flowers. "There he is." she thought.

Ròs landed at the centre of the garden. Tula dismounted the same way as earlier, by sliding down Ròs' back.

"Welcome to my home, Tula." William put out his hand.

Tula giggled. "Thank you." She shook his hand. "He's quite the stallion." Tula thought. She couldn't help but stare at his full head of black and silvery hair, his height, his solid built, his dark eyes, and his beautiful smile. "This is not the Shakespeare I've seen portrayed of him. No hair down to the earlobes or shoulders, with a carefully trimmed moustache and a receding hairline. No moustache or receding hairline on this Shakespeare. This guy has a beautiful head of hair." He rejuvenated extremely well. "I hope he can't read my thoughts."

Ròs cleared her throat. "And we've seen other beautiful things on the way here. Right Tula?"

"Yes. It was a beautiful flight. Thank you!" Tula blushed.

"I'm glad you accepted to join us, Tula." William said as he put the watering can on the ground. "I've prepared a late lunch. Will you stay and join us, Ròs?"

"Thank you. No. I must return to the farm. We have our own work to begin now that Tula has joined us."

"Of course. Thank you again for delivering her to me. I've been looking forward to meeting Tula for a long time. Charlotte couldn't stop talking about you. Ròs, please, send my regards to Colin and to the others. We'll talk again soon." William couldn't take his eyes off Tula either.

"Right. I'm off. You two look after each other." Ròs fanned her wings and was back up in the air before William and Tula had time to look up to see her off. She had already disappeared into the sky when they broke eye contact and looked up.

"Let me take your bag." William carried Tula's suitcase. "I've prepared your room. It's on the top floor." William opened the door. "Please. After you."

Tula stepped through the door and followed William down the spiralling staircase to the top floor. "Over here. This orange door is you room. You'll have everything you need here. There's a full bathroom at the far left corner. Please, make yourself at home. When you're ready, come downstairs for lunch."

"Thank you." Tula closed the bedroom door behind her. She looked out of her window overlooking the Thames. She opened the glass doors and stepped out onto the veranda. "This is where William Shakespeare lives now, and I'm staying in his house as his guest. Thank you Charlotte."

29

After Tula unpacked, washed up and changed her clothes, she went downstairs to find William. The base of the spiralling staircase reached the front foyer. She looked up at the climbing ceiling, all the way up to the top of the staircase, where she first came in from the rooftop.

The architecture throughout the house was exquisite. William retained the unique and fine architectural features of the 15th and 16th hundreds, and decorated with contemporary chandeliers made of colourful blown glass, stained windows, paintings from various medieval, modern and contemporary artists, and very comfortable modern furniture to fill the spaces.

"Over here." William's voice echoed.

Tula followed the echo while looking from floor to ceiling at the bookshelves filled with all manners of books, before arriving at the kitchen. She watched him open a bottle of red wine and pour wine into light yellow glass goblets.

"For you." William put out his hand, holding a goblet of wine.

"Thank you." She took the glass. "You have quite a collection of books."

"Yes. They span the centuries. We will have lunch in the garden."

She followed William outside to the garden.

"Please, have a seat." He pulled the chair out for her and helped her with it.

"Thank you." Tula felt eager to put that goblet of wine down and pinch herself. Instead, she sipped it and composed herself. "This is real. This is all real. This is happening." she thought. "Oh gosh. I sure hope you can't read my thoughts."

William sat opposite her. "In times of uncertainty, being able to rely on friends brings a boost to one's spirit." He raised his glass. "Thy friendship makes us fresh Tula."

Tula raised her glass and smiled. "Thy friendship makes us fresh William."

William served an Italian cold pasta salad, olives, cheeses, and chocolate éclairs, just as Charlotte made them. Tula enjoyed every bite. She could feel that Charlotte ensured William served a meal she would enjoy. "Thank you, Charlotte." Tula said in her head.

William topped up Tula's wine. "After lunch, I was thinking I could take you on a walking tour, if you're not too tired."

"That would be lovely, thank you." She sipped her wine. "William?"

"Yes." He sat back in his chair and gave her his undivided attention.

Tula put her goblet on the table. She looked up at William. "I understand I've come here to…" she paused. She wanted to review everything she knew with William up this moment. She knew that, of course, he already knew everything. She just didn't know what to do or where to start.

"You will know Tula."

"Oh gosh. You can hear my thoughts. Can't you?" She cringed in her chair and took a sip of wine.

"Only when it's necessary. Anam Duines can feel the different energies that allow us to hear thoughts, but we don't hear private thoughts. I will be able to hear every one of your worries and concerns regarding this matter. There are certain things, I, and other Anam Duines, will need to know, especially when you do not wish to say them out loud. This is for your protection. We must be able to act and be at the ready for all eventualities."

"I see. Thank you." Tula smiled. "You're very kind, William."

"That's nice of you to say." William gathered the dishes on the table. "Let's enjoy the rest of the day in London. A long walk will do us both some good."

30

William and Tula spent the afternoon sightseeing around London. Even though Tula had been to London many times, and William had seen its changes over many centuries, they walked around and talked about everything they saw as though it was their first time in London. It was, after all, their first time together in London.

"There's one last place I would like to take you to, Tula." William said.

"Ok. Let's go."

William hailed a black cap. "The British Museum."

"I haven't been there in some time." Tula rolled down the window. "I have great memories of London. I always make time to visit the museum when I'm here. I always seem to find myself spending more time in the rooms with the mummies, coffins and other tomb artefacts. I'm starting to understand why that is." She looked over at William.

"It's one of my favourite places. I spend time in those rooms as well, and I enjoy reading the Rosetta Stone on display in the Egyptian sculpture gallery."

Tula leaned in closer to William. "The galleries also show the use of modern technology for investigating mummies, with x-ray and CAT-scan images of some of the exhibits. Technology has proven to be useful for many, but I fear that it has caused nothing but angst for our Chief Investigator Anika Patel." She leaned back towards the open window and watched the pedestrians cross the road at the red light.

"I enjoy people watching as well." William smiled.

Tula curled her hair around her ear with her finger. "What I also enjoy about the British Museum is that it's a collage of human history, art, and culture, documenting the story of human culture from its beginning to the present. However, now I know it's missing a few things." She smiled.

A few minutes later they were standing in front of the museum's white columns.

"We don't have much time. It closes in thirty minutes. What would you like to see?" Tula said.

"I must confess. I didn't bring you here to tour the museum galleries today." William put his hand on her shoulder.

Tula's heart sank. "It's begun."

"Yes, and I'll be with you the entire time."

"What do we have to do?"

"The ashes of the six other Anam Duines were transferred to the museum. They are kept here for further study and storage. The officials have denied access to the ashes and burial as per the request of the deceased to the next of kin. We must ensure the same for them as you did for Charlotte, otherwise, their souls will be trapped here. The entrapment is the Kelpie's doing, and this weakens the Anam Duines, and the triquetra even more. We need their souls to be released in order to allow for the birth of other Anam Duines, Soul Humans. They are needed more than ever." William offered his arm to Tula.

She wrapped her arm around his. "How do we do this?"

They walked around the gardens. "We have to be familiar with the surroundings of the museum, the inside, and the laboratory where they are being held."

"You mean that we have to break in and steal them?" Tula stopped walking.

"Stealing is not the word I would use."

"What word would you use to fit this story?" She grinned.

"Let's say that we are *Hamletting*."

"Come again? The ghost of the King of Denmark tells his son Hamlet to avenge his murder by killing the new king, Hamlet's uncle. We are not killing anyone." Tula stepped back from William.

"Of course not." William offered her his arm again.

"Hamlet feigned madness, contemplated life and death, and sought revenge. His uncle, fearing for his own life, devised a plot to kill Hamlet.

Charlotte did say this could cost me my life, but I didn't think it would be so soon."

William laughed. "Yes. The King of Denmark did ask his son to avenge his murder and so on and so forth. When we meet the officials who are preventing the release of the ashes, they will appear to us as mad, and they won't be pretending, they will hold true to their beliefs as though it's a matter of life and death, and they will seek revenge when suffering a loss of any form. Just as with Hamlet's uncle, they will behave as though fearing for their life, and devise a plot to kill us. Maybe figuratively. Maybe literally. We don't know yet." William nudged his arm for Tula to take it.

"Oh gosh. The ego. Theirs *and* ours. The mirror reflects back to us three faces."

"Well stated." William smiled. "That's part of the human makeup. It makes for great people watching."

"Hmm. Hmm. You mean you enjoy the messy human. The Id, where the individual's aggression and desires come from. The Ego. Part of the psyche that wants to protect the individual, and the Superego. The part of the psyche that wants to protect society."

"It's never boring." William laughed. "Nothing is easier for the Kelpie than to negatively influence one's sense of self-esteem or self-importance. The ego is essential to the human makeup. It defines who you are and how humans connect with others. The ego becomes an issue when it becomes overpowering. That's the Kelpie's influence. Every human has an ego, whether big or small. It's one of the many aspects of humans that I enjoy observing." He took a step towards Tula. "We must have our wits about us. We must have a clear mind and remain calm when dealing with the Kelpie and the ego. There is nothing more dangerous than a fragile ego."

"In that case, we might as well give up now." Tula wrapped her arm around William's arm. "What a mess."

31

By day three of Tula's and William's scoping out the museum for the locations of the security cameras, the security guards' routine, staff offices, the location of laboratories, and anything else they could think of as amateur thieves, in the event that this was how they would retrieve the ashes, Tula recognized a man walking in the corridor that was for staff access only. He was wearing a white coat with an identification badge and access card around this neck.

Tula pulled William to the side. "That's him. That's the Arthur I told you about."

After Tula and William left the British Museum gardens and their *Hamletting* approach to steal the ashes, Tula told William about the call she overheard Anika having with Sami, what they were talking about and about the chocolate mousse ruse to make Anika believe that she didn't hear or see anything. That night, when Tula searched for Arthur Moore on the Internet, she discovered that he also worked at the British Museum.

She pulled up a photo of Arthur Moore on her phone and showed William. "This is the guy I just saw in the corridor."

"That's who we need to talk to, Tula."

"How can we get access to him?"

"Let's call the museum office and ask for our call to be transferred."

Tula put her phone back in her bag. "And say what? What reason do we have to call him?"

"Good point."

"Wait. Let's just be upfront. I'll tell him who I am. I'm Charlotte's friend. I know Anika and Sami because they are actively working on her case. I can also tell him I know about the six bodies, ashes and all. That should get his attention and he should want to see us, well me anyway. I can't very well tell him William Ridel, a world famous actor and playwright, is with me. People already stare at you everywhere we go and ask for your autograph, and he would wonder why you are a part of this."

"Don't mention me on the phone. I'll be with you when he meets with us."

"Yes. That will work. What do we tell him about the reason he should give us the ashes or to the next of kin, and why you are part of this? I'm assuming the next of kin all know about the Anam Duines, or that their affairs are in order in order to ensure their ashes are sprinkled into a river, lake or ocean?"

"Yes. All is in order for these six. Five of the six next of kin are Anam Duines. Stewart Robertson is not Anam Duine. He's human like you and is gifted with vision, and he knows everything about us, the whole story. He's 92 years old and lives in Edinburgh. He's a retired MI6 who investigated suspicious and unexplained deaths.

A few of us have reached our final life cycle within months of each other. He was assigned to investigate a series of deaths that had all been classified as suspicious and unexplained. With his visions, and his ability to open his mind to many possibilities after reviewing these cases, we knew that we could approach him and reveal ourselves.

He's been an ally ever since and has worked on many more of our cases in order to remove any attention being drawn to them, and close the files, instead of keeping them opened as cold cases."

"If a retired MI6 can't get access to those ashes, then there isn't much luck for us, I would say. Doesn't he have any contacts that could be of some help and spare us from this ridiculous attempt at believing that we can convince a guy like Arthur Moore to hand over the ashes?"

"I'm afraid not. He's done such a good job in helping and protecting us from anyone who would discover us. If we are discovered, they would no doubt hold us against our will, study us like lab rats, and who knows what else they would do. We celebrate the humans' sense of curiosity, and their wanting to discover everything and anything they can. Unlike the Kelpie, the Anam Duines nourish the human mind, the human curiosity, and the human spirit in numerous ways. This is the only way that humans will discover their way to us, to all of this, their entire story, the same way the little girl Charlotte discovered that she was an Anam Duine, and humans believed again in the magic of the imagination, without causing harm to anyone."

Tula removed her phone from her bag. "I'll call the museum and ask to speak with Arthur."

"And say what?"

"I'll tell him who I am and what I said earlier."

"Now that I think of it, I doubt that make him want to speak with you. Really, who are you in all of this, other than Charlotte's friend?"

"You have a point."

"I've always made a point of talking with people in person, not by phone. Well, not that that was an option for most centuries, but you know what I mean. I say, let's see him in person and tell him that we represent Stewart Robertson. Let's just call this a little white lie. Stewart is the last surviving member of one of the Scottish man's ashes, and Stewart is too old and frail to travel, and if he could find some compassion for a dying man's last wishes, maybe he will see us as less threatening or intrusive, and he may just be willing to do what he can to give us the ashes."

"That could work. What about the other six?"

"We can say. I don't know. Oh wait. No. We can't say the families of the six all know each other."

"That could raise more questions." Tula walked to the bench and sat down. William followed her and sat next to her.

"Let me just call and see if he takes my call."

"Yes. Let's just call. Tula what will you say?"

"I don't know yet. Let's see what comes to mind when he picks up." Tula dialed the British Museum's main switchboard number. After a few rings, and listening to a few options to redirect her call, she opted to press zero for the reception. A few seconds later, Tula's waiting time had ended with a woman's voice: "Good afternoon. British Museum. How can I help you?"

"Good afternoon. Can you please transfer me to Dr. Arthur Moore please."

"I can transfer you to his secretary's line. Would you like that?"

"Yes please. Thank you."

"Please hold while I transfer your call."

Tula heard a click as the transfer was made. A minute later, a woman's voice came on the line. "Good afternoon. Department of Forensic Anthropology, how can I help you?"

"Good afternoon. May I speak with Dr. Arthur Moore?"

"I'm sorry but Dr. Moore has left for the day. Is there anyone else you would like to speak with?

"No thank you. Can I leave my name and number?"

"Yes. Of course."

Tula looked up from the floor and across the room. She nudged William on the arm with her elbow. "Thank you. Instead, I'll call back another day. Thank you Madame for your help." Tula hung up.

"Look William. Over there."

William looked in the same direction she was looking at. "What am I looking at?"

"See that beautiful woman over there in the blue dress?"

"Yes. What about her?"

"That's Anika Patel. Chief Investigator Anika Patel." Tula grabbed William by the arm. "Let's get out of here. I don't want her to see me here."

Over the last few days, Tula told William everything she knew about Anika, her two PhDs, choosing to keep her boots on the ground, a clear indication of her dedication, her track record for solving cases, and everything else up until when Tula left Nort to come to Scotland. She showed him all the missed calls, texts, and let him listen to the voice messages.

Anika left voice messages asking Tula to call her back because she had learned more about Charlotte's death from the laboratory results. Anika was so terribly convincing that Tula almost believed her. However, after everything she learned in the last week, she knew that there would be no other evidence Anika could use to help solve Charlotte's case.

Tula was curious to hear what Anika really wanted to talk about, but she resisted the temptation to reply to any of her texts or message until she felt it was the right time to speak with her. She relied entirely on her instinct for this key moment. She didn't want anything to interfere with her new reason for being in Scotland. Charlotte had sent her on a mission to England with Shakespeare, which she was committed to fulfilling.

Anika was an eloquent speaker. She made you feel comfortable and at ease, and William could see how this brilliant woman could get anyone to talk, and he could see why she was so good at her job.

William and Tula walked out of the gallery into the next gallery. This gallery led them towards the museum's gift shop, and from there, they exited the museum. When they walked to William's car, they saw Arthur get into a car.

Tula put her hand on William's arm. "Let's wait here. Let's see where he goes. Maybe we can find out where he lives. Anything. That's how we can find the right opportunity to speak to him in person, like you said."

"Good idea." William removed the key from the ignition. He rolled down his window. It was an unusually warm spring day for London.

"Summer is just around the corner." Tula rolled down her window as well. "Oh, look!"

William looked in the same direction. "That's Anika walking towards his car."

They watched Anika get into the passenger seat of Arthur's car. They rolled down the windows and talked for a few minutes. Anika rolled her hair up into a bun on top of her head. She fanned her face with a piece of paper, then, Arthur drove away with his arm hanging out the window, and Anika leaned over a bit towards the window to catch the cool breeze.

32

William followed Arthur to the distinguished borough of Kensington, in West London, renowned for its prestige and wealth. Tula was very familiar with the exclusive and sophisticated district, with its world-class museums, Kensington gardens and Hyde Park, and the iconic Royal Albert Hall, and garden squares. She visited various friends of friends in this area, especially some of Charlotte's friends who had attended her celebration of life.

William drove slowly along Logan Place, a small residential road. Tula looked over at Garden Lodge Mansion, once the home of the late Queen's lead singer Freddie Mercury.

"Charlotte and I listened to their music all the time. Especially Freddie's solo albums."

"He was one of the greats. We were friends. I was sad to see him go."

"Was Freddie Anam Duine?"

"No. He was not Anam Duine. He was, however, a great soul on Earth."

"Yes, indeed he was." Tula looked over at William. "I would have loved to know him in person. He's come to me in my visions. For a while, he was with me all the time. He had a great influence on one of the books I wrote, and he helped guide me with critical decisions in my life."

"That was our Freddie."

Tula looked around at the other houses and gardens. "And why have you not purchased a home in this affluent buyers' market, William?"

"I like where I am. If I could, I would have bought my original home. It is now a museum on Henley Street in Stratford-upon-Avon. I can't very well claim it back as William Shakespeare." He laughed.

Arthur parked in front of a blue house with a white gate and small garden for a front yard. A woman opened the front door and waved at Anika and Arthur. Anika closed the car door and waved back. William clicked the lock button on the key chain. Tula and William were parked just far enough to not be seen, and close enough to hear the car alarm beep.

Arthur opened the gate and let Anika walk through. A woman walked down the stairs and greeted Anika with a handshake, and she kissed her husband on the cheek.

"I would not have guessed that the salary of a scientist at the British Museum or the Royal Anthropological Institute could afford a place in Kensington." William leaned over to have a better look at the house.

"He comes from money. I read his family profile online, and his late grandfather and his late father were both MI6."

"He has the scientific background, money and MI6 on his side to dig into this further, if it's what he decides to do."

"With Anika at his side, she will encourage him to pursue this and to utilise all of his resources at their disposal. She's not one to give up so easily."

Arthur, his wife and Anika walked into the house. Tula and William stepped out of the car and walked on the sidewalk, across the street from the house. From where they stood, they could see Arthur and Anika through the window. Arthur was reaching for books on the bookshelf, and Anika was scrolling on her phone.

Arthur put the books on the desk and opened them. They leaned over to look at the pages Arthur pointed with his hand. Then, Arthur answered his mobile phone. He walked around the room while brushing his fingers through his hair. Anika watched him walk around the room. Then, Arthur hung up and put the phone on the desk.

When he turned to Anika, he was moving his hands in the air when talking to her. She used her hands when talking as well, and she kept pointing at photos on her phone.

A door opened and Arthur's wife came in the room, carrying a tray of drinks.

Tula looked up from her phone. "Florence. That's Arthur's wife name." She showed her phone to William.

Anika and Arthur took the drinks from the tray. Florence walked out of the room and closed the door behind her.

William's phone dinged with a text. "It's Stewart. Yes. He does know

Arthur's grandfather and father. You mentioned that Anika was like a dog with a bone. Well, they were too, and Stewart advises us to expect nothing less of Arthur."

Tula looked up at William. "Great."

"Now what?"

"I don't know. I know you've been around a long time William, but we are serious amateurs when it comes to any of this." Tula leaned against the wall.

"I say we go to the pub for a beer and supper. Then we can figure out our next move."

"Sounds good to me."

Just as Tula and William got back to the car, Anika and Arthur walked out of the house and got into Arthur's car.

"Let's follow them." Tula pointed.

They followed them for about 10 minutes to a quaint bed and breakfast, surrounded with a beautiful garden. Anika stepped out of the car. She leaned into the passenger window to speak with William. She waved him goodbye and walked up the steps through the bright red door.

"Now we know where she's staying." From the passenger seat in the car, Tula looked up at the building. "Very nice."

"I'll take you to the *Ye Olde Mitre* in Holborn. They say Elizabeth was rumoured to have danced around the cherry tree that once stood outside this pub."

"So it seems. I've been there, and it is said that the Queen valued and supported the theatre and invited you on numerous occasions to perform for her court."

"She was a great supporter. I valued her contribution to my success back then."

"And is she here with us today walking the Earth as an Anam Duine?" Tula leaned over to look into his eyes.

"I'm afraid not. She was just like you." He smiled.

"Too bad. I would have loved to talk to her."

William parked the car. "The pub is just over there."

33

For the next few days, Tula and William followed Anika and Arthur from morning until night. Their routine was the same. Arthur picked-up Anika at her bed and breakfast, they went to the museum, they had dinner at Arthur's, then drinks in his office, where they looked at books, photos, and talked on the phone. On the 3rd day, Anika and Arthur changed their routine at lunchtime. Instead of eating lunch at the museum, they went to a pub near the museum.

Tula and William didn't want to be seen by Anika and Arthur. From across the street, they watched Anika and Arthur sit at a table for four, next to the window. They figured that with a table for four, at least one other person, maybe two, would be joining them for lunch.

Tula and William wanted to remain incognito. They sat at the pub's patio across the street, and watched people going into the pub. From where they sat, they had a clear view of Anika and Arthur, and they could see who else would join them at their table.

By the time Tula and William were on their second Guinness beer, Anika and Arthur were checking their watches. They finished their lunch and asked for the bill. When Anika took her purse which was hanging on the back of her chair, and Arthur had paid the waitress, two men dress in stylish suits showed up at their table.

Tula and William sat up in their chairs. William removed his phone from his shirt pocket, made it appear like he was doing something else, but was he getting ready to take photos of Anika, Arthur and the two men. He zoomed in and clicked the button several times.

"I think you have enough photos." Tula leaned in.

"It looks like a heated discussion. Nobody likes to be left waiting around."

"They're sitting back down. Put down your phone."

"I'm sending the photos to Stewart to see if he knows these two men."

Tula looked down at Arthur's phone when she heard the ding of the send a text and some photos. "They look to be in their 40s. Stewart was way before their time, if they are MI6."

By the time the phone text was sent, Anika, Arthur and the two men were standing up and walking out of the pub.

Tula and William paid the waiter and walked on to the other side of the road and followed their subjects back to the museum.

At the entrance, Tula and William flashed their museum membership card. They had unlimited entries any time of the year. Inside the museum rooms, they followed their usual path to the room closest to Arthur's office where they could see him come and go.

"It's a good thing you suggested we get these cards, William. I'm sure they recognize our faces by now, especially yours. The famous William Ridel."

"I told them I would be here frequently. I was doing research for my next play."

"That's a good way to avoid suspicion, especially the way we are walking around here. We are the least inconspicuous two in here by the way we walk, look at everything and everything else we do that makes us look like amateur thieves. I'm surprised Arthur and Anika haven't found us out yet, or they may have and are playing us for fools."

William took out a notepad from his jacket pocket. "Let's stand here next to this mummy. It will look like we are actually doing something."

Tula stood next to William and the mummy. "Now what?

William's phone dinged. Stewart replied to William's text. "It seems we have a bigger problem than we thought." William stared at his phone.

"Well, what did he say? What's the problem?"

"It's more serious than you know, Tula."

"The suspense is killing me. William, are you preparing to tell me a tragedy of some sort?" Tula smiled.

"Possibly."

Tula's smile vanished. "Ok. Now you have me worried. What is it?"

"These two men are MI6, but they are part of a secret agency of the sorts, within MI6, of which Stewart was a member. These two men have been trained by the best, and they are also relentless when it comes to their job. Right now, their job is to make sure that absolutely no one gets the remaining six's ashes."

"Why would this be a tragedy more so than what we are already facing with William? We already know it's impossible to get even close to these ashes."

"Because it's what they discovered."

"What do you mean, discovered?"

"It's what Stewart managed to keep secret from MI6 and the rest of the world until now." William looked down at the mummy.

"You have my undivided attention, William."

"I must take you back in time before I can tell you about the present."

Tula looked up at the hallway leading up to Arthur's office. "The two men are leaving without Anika and Arthur. Let's follow them."

"No. Let's go back to the garden before Arthur and Anika come out. We can't be seen here anymore." William took Tula by the arm, and they walked out to the gardens. "We can talk here."

34

Tula sat very close to William on the bench. Her leg rubbed against his. "Ok. What is it, Shakespeare?"

"About 4,500 years ago, when it is said that Stonehenge was constructed, seven Soul Humans, the Anam Duines, ended their life cycle. They were not returned to the water to complete their cycle back to the Tree of Life, as you did with Charlotte. Instead, the ashes were kept in stone jars."

"Why?"

What I'm about to tell you has always been considered a myth, a legend, and not one well-researched or of interest to archaeologists, until Arthur."

"Why did Arthur take an interest in this?"

"When the seven Anam Duines, the Soul Humans, died, they were living amongst the most powerful family of Druids at the time. Arthur is a direct descendant of this most powerful Druid family of today's time."

"And what does this have to do with Charlotte and the others?"

"The Druids believed in a supreme God, whom they called Be'al, meaning the source of all beings. The symbol for their supreme being was fire, and it is still fire. They also believed that the human soul was immortal, and that upon death, it passes into the body of a newborn child. Is it because of this Druid belief that when the seven Anam Duines died and the family witnessed their unusual disintegration from flesh to ashes, just like Charlotte and the others, the family ignored the wishes of the seven and did not put their ashes in water?"

"And does this makes the Kelpie even stronger?" Tula looked into William's eyes.

"Yes, and because the Druid's supreme being is fire, they sprinkled the ashes of the seven Anam Duines onto a sacred stone at the centre of Stonehenge.

Before I go on with this story, Tula, you must know that the Druids had never met a Soul Human before these seven. They had only heard stories of the birth of the first Anam Duine, the Boobrie, the triquetra and so on, from generations before. Back then, the Druids considered all of this as a myth, a legend, until the seven were found dead and rapidly turned to ashes right before their very eyes.

Instead of putting the ashes in the water so they could return to the Tree of Life, the family believed that this was a gift from their God. They put the ashes into seven stone jars, put broken twigs from their sacred Oak tree into the jars, and lit the inside of the jar on fire. The family danced in the light of the fire, believing that the smoke and the fire light from these ashes that held the power of protection from the serpent and the magic of the unicorns would, in turn, make their own magic even more powerful. Druids could influence the course of events and control nature. They could also summon magical fog and storms to destroy or disperse their enemies.

Druids were the masters of spellcasting, and had considerable power and versatility. They gained their power through being at one with nature or through a connection to a powerful deity or nature spirit. They were the guardians of the wilderness, and they saw themselves less as masters of the natural order and more as an extension of its will.

They danced all night until the fire burned itself out, and once the fire was out, the stone jars were still fire red and scorching hot. No one could touch them with their bare hands.

"What did they do with the ashes?"

"They buried the seven jars in the ground at the centre of Stonehenge." William looked at Stewart's text again. "Arthur is leading all of this, and Anika doesn't know the truth about Arthur. Arthur is more powerful than you know. He's not MI6, but he's running this secret underground MI6 group for this specific assignment."

"So, Arthur must have known about Charlotte when he called Sami."

"Absolutely. He manipulated her into her telling him about Charlotte and what was happening with her ashes, but because of your gift, your visions, and the fact that you were persistent and consistent with following through with respecting her request, he couldn't convince Sami to hold on to the ashes. He's doing a great job of keeping all of this from Anika. He's probably told her this has only to do with archaeology, and nothing more."

"And what is it exactly that he's keeping from Anika? What is his reason for keeping the ashes? It has to be more than just for the sake of archaeology."

"Yes. As a consequence of not putting the ashes in the water, the family inadvertently put a curse on themselves and all Druids."

"What does the curse do?

"The Kelpie tricked the family into believing that burning the ashes as they did would make their magic even more powerful. Instead, it weakened the Druids ability to influence the course of events and control nature. However, the Kelpie did allow them to keep some of their power to summon magical fog and storms in order to destroy or to disperse their enemies. After all, the Kelpie needed the Druids to do their dirty deeds for it, and it wasn't going to leave them completely helpless. The Kelpie did however leave them with some struggles to summon magical fog and storms to destroy or disperse their enemies, just so the Druids wouldn't use their magical powers against them.

They were no longer master spellcasters of considerable power and versatility. Instead, they were weak and could not adapt. They slowly veered away from gaining their power through being at one with nature or through a connection to a powerful deity or nature spirit. They were no longer the guardians of the wilderness, and they saw themselves more as masters of the natural order and less as an extension of its will. This curse trickled its way throughout their generations and other humans.

The Kelpie had succeeded in weakening the power of the Druids by making other humans see Druids as practicing all sorts of weird and evil rituals. The Kelpie are masters of lies, deceit, and conspiracies.

When the family realized what they had done, and saw their people suffering because of this curse, they performed another ceremony begging the Kelpie to reverse the curse. The Kelpie would grant their request only when the family exchanged the ashes of the seven in the stone jars for the ashes of another seven Anam Duines. It is only when the family has the ashes of the new seven that the Kelpie will cool the stone jars enough to allow the family to remove the ashes from the jars, and replenish the stone jars with the ashes of the new seven Anam Duines. Once they complete this task, they can put the ashes in the water, but not before. If they do not comply with the Kelpie, the curse will get stronger, but the Kelpie would never allow the family to put the ashes in the water. The longer the family has the ashes, the weaker they get, and so do their people, from generation to generation."

"But Arthur has ashes from six Anam Duines. He could have these for a long time. For eternity."

"He chose this profession because it was the best way to ever get this close to the ashes. He has a plan. You ruined that plan when you put Charlotte's ashes in the water. Now he needs one more."

"Just how do you think he will get it? Does he even know how to find an Anam Duine walking on the Earth today, or does he even know which one of you is living his or her last life? This search can also be one that he probably won't complete before his own death. He is a mortal human with a clear death for his end."

"Arthur did not lose all of his magical powers. Over the course of his generations, the Druids learned how to identify who is Soul Human and who is not, and when they suspect a human to be a Soul Human, they take measures to search for the triquetra birthmark. When this is confirmed, they entrap them and keep them prisoners for as long as they can, until they finish their life cycle. The family has performed this horror ever since they agreed to the Kelpie's exchange of ashes, but the Soul Human always escaped before reaching death during their final life cycle. The Kelpie were explicit with their instructions. The Soul Human must not be murdered on the final life cycle."

"Why not? It would seem that this would be the easiest and fastest way of getting the seven's ashes."

"The magic of the unicorn in the ashes would be too weak, and it would weaken the Kelpie."

"That's quite the story. Now, Arthur is not only keeping the ashes where it is impossible to even access them, he is looking for another Anam Duine to imprison until the death of their final life." Tula stood up and faced William. "How do we find out who he's going after to make seven?"

"I already know who Arthur is going to hunt down for his seventh."

"Who?"

"My son."

35

Tula sat back down next to William. "I don't understand. Your son? Who is your son?"

William's eyes filled with tears. "Colin. Colin is my son."

Tula put her hand on William's hand. "Colin Ridel. 72 year old Colin is your son?

William stood up. "We must get to him right away." He walked away from Tula.

Tula hurried up next to him and held his hand. "William, you must explain all of this to me so that I can help you. That's what I'm here for."

William held her hand tightly and walked to the car. He opened the passenger door for Tula and, just as she was about to get in, he put his hand on her shoulders and turned her around to face him. "It's more serious than you know. Stewart said that those two men who are with Arthur and Anika have been specifically tasked with finding someone. These two men know the real reason why they are looking for someone with the specifications that Arthur gave them. Anika believes it has to do with archaeology, mysterious and unsolved deaths. Arthur has not and will not tell her about his family history and the curse, of course not."

"William. What else is there to know so that I can better understand?" She put her hands on his arm and held him.

"I'll tell you in the car. Get in." William closed the passenger door behind her.

It was an unusually warm morning in London, and Tula could see from the perspiration on William's forehead that he felt like it was a heatwave. She sensed that his stress level had surpassed his usual calm and collected

William Shakespeare self which she had come to know and had begun to care for. He was her friend, and now she was really worried about him.

She flicked open the lid of her pink water bottle. "William, have a drink of water."

William drank half the bottle. "Thank you." William drove out of the museum gates and looked over at Tula. "Colin is my son from a life a long time ago.

"I see. Colin mentioned that Soul Humans have children and that the children and parents recognize each other even after their rejuvenation."

"I returned to him when I rejuvenated, knowing this was his last life cycle.

"So this is the most precious life that you are both living together."

"Yes, and if Arthur gets a hold of him, he will not potentially imprison my son and deny him the completion of his life cycle and not return him to the Tree of Life, but this will also kill the three unicorns."

"I don't understand. How? Why?"

"Some of the Soul Humans have special gifts. One of these gifts is what connects them to the magic of the unicorn and vice versa."

"How do you know that they have a special gift, and what gift that is?"

"They are born not only with the triquetra birthmark on their right hip, but with the Tree of Life birthmark that slightly overlaps it as well."

"I remember seeing this on Colin when I helped him with the lamb, and when his pants got stuck on the truck."

"Yes. He told me about that day and when you saw it."

"He didn't tell me about this gift."

"No. Everything has to happen at the right moment. When the Anam Duines, the Soul Humans, are born, the unicorn's soul merges with some of us. This is part of the soul connection between us. It's what allows the magic to work for all of us, and my son Colin is one of those whose soul is connected with the unicorns. If Colin cannot complete his life cycle and return to the Tree of Life, it destroys the unicorn's soul forever, thereby weakening the magic of all the unicorns, and this weakens the Soul Humans, and you. It weakens the human imagination even more, and the Kelpie get a hundred times stronger every time they destroy this link between Soul Humans and unicorns. The stronger the Kelpie get from the loss of the Anam Duines, the more the human imagination gradually gets erased bit by bit. The power of the Kelpie can completely eradicate the human imagination that has created so much good and beauty in this world. It will leave humans without imaginative thoughts. Consequently, they will respond only to fear. For the Kelpie to achieve this, they will manipulate Arthur in believing that their actions aimed at imprisoning him are justified because he will be convinced that 72 year old Colin is old, a burden to society, that he's done with his life, and that he has nothing left to offer the world."

"Well, we can't have that! There is nothing true about any of that for anyone, at any age." Tula drank the rest of the water in the bottle. She looked up and they were already in front of William's house. By the time she gathered her things, William had already opened the passenger door to let her out.

"Thank you, William."

"Let's get our things. Gorm is waiting for us on the roof."

Tula looked up at William with questioning eyes. "How…"

"We can communicate with the unicorns with just our thoughts, and you will be able to do so as well, eventually."

"I see." Tula's previous excitement of flying around on a unicorn was not the same this time. She was terrified for Colin, William, for all Anam Duines and all humans.

Fifteen minutes after taking what she needed from William's house and getting on Gorm's back with William sitting behind her, they were back on the farm with Colin.

36

Arthur was hot on Colin's trail. The day Tula and William left for Wick, Arthur learned who the 7th was, and he was eager to get to him. He knew everything there was to know about Colin's life cycle and where he lived. By lunchtime, he was on a plane to Wick.

Arthur retained the knowledge of every story on how to find a Soul Human living its last life cycle, and every Soul Human imprisoned from generation to generation. The Druids infiltrated every community to find Soul Humans. They followed the cycles of the winter solstice and who suddenly appeared as a 72 year old in their communities. More often than not, the rejuvenated Soul Human remained undetected by the Druids, but from the MI6 records of Arthur's father and grandfather, as well as a result of the other Druids' astute inquiries, Arthur discovered that Colin Ridel was living his final life. Druids were living in Wick, and they reported back to Arthur. Their findings confirmed what the two MI6 men had discovered in the archives and what the Druids of Wick had reported back to Arthur.

The day that Tula and William watched Arthur and Anika from across the street, where they saw them talking, reviewing books and reports, talking on the phone, and where Arthur seemed agitated with his hands and arms up in the air, Arthur was actually putting on a show for Anika. Arthur made it seem as though he wasn't getting what he needed from MI6 who asked him to help them solve these mysterious deaths. All the while, he was being fed information from the two MI6 men who were also Druid and working for the MI6's secret agency, and taking calls from other Druids living in Wick. However, he had been able to dig deeper in the MI6 archives, and he sent the Druids in Wick on a clearer and better path, given the information which he had carefully chosen to share with Anika.

Anika was made to believe that everything Arthur shared with her had to do with only the mysterious deaths of Charlotte and the six others under his responsibility, in order to solve the case with MI6. Where all the while, he was using her for her keen ability to solve crimes. She could dissect every bit of information, ask the right questions, and interpret findings in a way he had not seen in anyone before. When she had served her purpose and he had no more use of her, he was quick to get her out of the way, out of England and back on the plane back home.

Before the morning coffee break, Arthur convinced Anika that her unique abilities added value to archaeology and to the mysterious seven, but like all things, her contribution had reached an end, and Arthur would shelf these files until further data justified reopening these cases. This was the report he co-authored with Anika, to which she agreed, and signed. That afternoon, Anika was on a plane, heading back home.

37

The next day Anika had lunch with Sami. She told her all about her meetings with Arthur and their findings. She wasn't buying any of it, but she had no choice but to sign the report. They really didn't have anything else to go on, but as a keen investigator, she was not fooled by Arthur's charming compliments, and she suspected that he knew more than he was telling her. She had no reason to justify her expenses and get authorization to stay any longer in England. She had to return to the office.

Even though Anika did not solve the case or come any closer to understanding anything more about the mysterious seven than she already knew, she left with a greater understanding of the link between the myths and legends, and the archaeological reports and artefacts that Arthur had shared with her about various beliefs tied with the triquetra.

The information she gathered during this investigation in England was limited, but she sensed it was valuable to solving the case. She just didn't know how yet, but she was going to find out, and this is where Sami's vast knowledge and experience could help her.

Sami was keen to embark on this mysterious adventure with Anika. They had not done anything truly fun and adventurous together since they both got caught up in their grown up life of marriage, family and careers.

Anika returned to Nort to spend time at Tula's bookstore. She figured this would be a good place to start since she remembered the unusual and eclectic book collection of myths and legends that Charlotte recommended for Tula to invest in for her store. After making a list of key subjects she had discussed with Arthur, Anika showed her list of interest to Antonio, the bookstore clerk looking after Tula's shop during her absence.

Antonio examined the list carefully. He invited Anika to come back in an hour, after he'd had a chance to gather books on the topics she was searching for. Some of the books were on display on the shelves in the shop, others were in another room that was only available to staff.

While Anika was at *Le Gâteau* having lunch, Antonio gathered the books available for purchase and put them on the front counter. The other books which were stored away in the other room were carefully examined, until he found the page with the topic Anika had on her list. He photocopied these pages. After 30 minutes, he had photocopied everything from these books and locked the door behind him as he left.

Anika was back in the shop an hour later on the dot, and not one minute later. She examined the collection of books and photocopies that Antonio had prepared for her. Before she could enquire about the photocopies, Antonio was quick to inform her that these came from a special collection of books that were not for purchase, and not to be handled or touched by anyone but him and Tula. He assured her that he had made a copy of the relevant pages of the books.

Anika was grateful for the work he had put into the collection of books and photocopies. The mystery around the untouchable books only raised her curiosity, and she wanted to see the entire book. However, she knew that he could not be swayed to let her see the books. She would have to find another way to see these books. She had a photocopy of the front and back cover, the first few pages about the printing date, publisher, and so on and so forth, and the pages with the topics of interest.

Anika paid for her books and thanked Antonio. She opened the shop door, and turned and asked Antonio when he last spoke with Tula and when she was returning to Nort.

Antonio smiled and repeated the same thing that he had told her before. He remained steady to his script of not knowing anything, and that he was asked to watch over the shop until her return. He also added that he had no idea where she was and when she would return.

Anika returned the smile. She had received the same response from Titi when she was at *Le Gâteau* having lunch, and the same response when she went to Tula's house that morning to see if Tula was there. She ran into Frank Walsh, the pet sitter, and he too kept to the script. The entire village kept to the script. She could not get any information from anyone about Tula's whereabouts and when she was expected to return to Nort.

All she knew was that it wasn't unusual for Tula and Charlotte to go off on adventures for weeks and sometimes months on ends without anyone knowing where they were going and when they were returning. Their adventures were only revealed when they returned to Nort in the form of stories which Tula wrote in her novels and plays, which were performed at the local theatre.

She closed the shop doors and asked Antonio if Tula sold her own novels and copies of her plays at the bookstore. Antonio was please to show her to the shelf that was lined with Tula's body of work. Anika purchased a copy of everything Tula had ever written.

With everything that she had documented during her time with Arthur, he was none the wiser that she was fully aware of his scheme of using her for her astute investigative skills. After reading Tula's stories to learn more about Tula's and Charlotte's lives, she was confident that she was unravelling and would solve the greatest mystery of her career.

38

Just as Gorm's feet touched the ground at the farm, Tula jumped off and ran in the cottage to find Colin. She followed her nose to the kitchen. The house smelled great. She wanted to eat everything. "Whatever you're making, it smells great Colin." She threw her arms around him and held him tight. Colin reciprocated and held her even tighter.

William was right behind her. William noticed how tiny she looked in his son's arms. He always admired his son for all that he had brought to the world in every lifetime. However, nothing compared to his genuine love and care towards all life. He could see that just in the few days that Colin and Tula had become good friends. Also, he loved that everyone loved his son. Colin was not only a great soul, he was a great person with a big heart, and he was damned if he was going to let anyone hurt him.

Ròs, Lilac, and Gorm poked their heads through the opened kitchen window, and greeted everyone.

"It's nice to all be together. I've already poured everyone a whiskey." Colin said. "We will be eating in about a half hour for our very late lunch."

Tula kissed Colin on the cheek and released him. William approached him and he hugged his son and wouldn't let him go.

"Papa. I'm safe. I'm ok."

William was not letting go. He held his son even tighter.

Tula's eyes filled with tears. Now that she knew they were father and son, she could see the resemblance. They were two very handsome men, tall, strong, and impressive in stature. They were gentle, kind and beautiful. To hear a 72 year old man call a 55 year old man "Papa" was strange to her ears. The scene that was being played before her was unusual and beautiful.

William turned to Tula and opened his arm for her to join in the hug. She slipped under their strong arms and disappeared in the family hug.

Lilac cleared her throat and got their attention. They looked over at the unicorns and smiled. "They are on their way." Lilac said.

"We know." Colin said. "Let's sit down and have our drink. Then, we can eat. Papa, I made your favourite."

"Oh. What's your favourite William?" Tula asked.

"Food." Gorm said. They all laughed.

"Sounds like my favourite as well!" Tula added as she smiled.

"But good, healthy food." William insisted. "One can't create with a tired and weak mind and body."

"I agree. I feel the same way. I was an OK cook before Charlotte came into my life. Then, I learned how to really cook, and to be creative with my meals."

"That's our Charlotte. She shared her culinary gift with all of us. Thank goodness, otherwise I think we would have starved or been extremely bored with our basic meals. We are always grateful for our food, but it's much more interesting when you make really good and interesting meals." Colin added. "Let's sit in the living room until lunch is ready."

Tula and William followed Colin. The unicorns walked around the house and poked their heads into the living room window.

William sat next to his son on the sofa and put an arm around him. Tula sat on the sofa across from them. She could see that William was not going to let his son out of his sight.

"Son, do we know who are the Druids living incognito in Wick and the surrounding village?"

"Yes. We've identified them. They are also in Orkney Island, disguised as tourists only when I give my tours."

Tula reached in her bag for her little book. She flipped through the pages with the triquetra and the Tree of Life on the same page. She pointed at the page. "Colin. William explained to me what this means." She turned to the next page. "This illustration is not uplifting. This shows exactly what we don't want to have happen. I didn't know what this meant, but now I do." She put the little book on the table. "And the illustrations that follow go on with the doom and gloom story."

Colin leaned forward as a gesture to soothe Tula. "We are going to do everything necessary to ensure our safety and the safety of humans, even if they fight against us. Indeed, we have already begun. We have put all of our trust in you, Tula."

Tula's eyes grew big. "In me? You put all your trust in me?" She finished her aperitif. "That is putting all of your eggs in one basket." She looked over at the unicorns staring at her from the windows. "And you three, what do you have to say about all of this?" She leaned her head back on the sofa. "You better serve those delicious pickles Colin, because we are in a pickle." She smiled.

"After lunch, we can go to the pub. I promised you a tour of Wick, and a beer at the pub the last time you were here." The timer dinger rang. Colin looked towards the kitchen. "Lunch is ready. Let's eat."

William kept his arm around Colin. "Son. They are coming. Do you think the pub is the wisest move for now?"

"Of course. Let's eat." Colin kissed his father on the cheek and stood from the sofa and put out his hand to Tula. "Come. Let's eat."

Tula took his hand and walked with him to the kitchen. William walked right behind his son. The unicorns were at the kitchen window, ready to join them. There was more to talk about at dinner that needed their guidance.

39

All the unicorns and all the serpents around the world were at the ready to confront the Kelpie. All hands were on deck to keep Colin safe and out of harm's way from Arthur and his cronies, and all of the Anam Duines were on alert. The Merry Dancers were buzzing with energy. No human was immune to the Kelpie, and that was the ultimate power of the Kelpie.

After lunch, Colin drove William and Tula to the Wick pub at the centre of town. The town straddled the River Wick and extended along both sides of Wick Bay. In these waters, plenty of serpents united from various regions to guard and protect Colin. It would present a difficult and challenging barrier for the Kelpie to destroy and get in. However, the Druids were already in Wick and plotting their evil little deeds to capture Colin.

When Colin, William and Tula walked into the pub, Arthur and two young men were sitting at a table in the far corner of the pub. The bartender called out Colin and William's name, and asked them who was the Bonnie with them.

William whispered to Tula that Bonnie was a quintessential Scottish name and word for beautiful, pretty, stunning and attractive. Tula smiled but was utterly distracted by the presence of Arthur and the two young men in the corner. She was perplexed that Colin had no reaction when he spotted them, and William just followed his son's temperament when he walked to bar.

Colin called out three Guinness and he walked to a table at the other side of the pub. They sat around a table. Tula felt as though she was in a western movie. They could see directly across at Arthur's table. Everyone just stared at each other. She was waiting for someone to draw their gun from some mysterious gun sling, and start shooting across the pub. She giggled.

Her giggle was enough to snap Colin and William out of their staring contest with Arthur and the two young men. Arthur and the two men were also distracted by her giggle. She looked up at the bartender when he put the three Guinness on the bar. William got up from his chair and went to the bar, picked-up the beers and brought them to his table. He looked over at Arthur, took a sip of his beer, put his beer back down on the table, and walked over to Arthur's table.

When Tula realized where he was going, she went to stand up from her chair, but Colin put his hand on her hand to stop her. She couldn't believe what she was seeing. She was terrified for William and Colin. She realized at that moment that she had grown so fond of both of them that she would easily give her life for them; for all of them and for everything she had learned about why she was here with them.

She sipped her beer and didn't take her eyes off William, who pulled a chair from another table and sat next to Arthur. She couldn't hear what they were talking about, but she could see they were not smiling. William's face wasn't like anything she had ever seen before. It was stern and fierce, but composed and elegant. No one would ever know they were talking about life and death, and the killing of his son.

It took every bit of strength she had to stay in her chair and not go sit next to William, but she also knew not to leave Colin alone for one minute. Even though he was a strong and sturdy 72 year old man, with all the magic of the unicorn and the power of the serpents to protect him, he was still a vulnerable Anam Duine in human form. If other Soul Humans had been kidnapped and imprisoned in the past by Arthur's family, it could still easily happen to Colin. The others escaped with the help of other Anam Duines. It was just as risky for them. They could have been murdered, but they were willing to give their entire life cycles to save one of them.

She looked at Colin and smiled. She understood when Charlotte said she was asking for her life. Tula was ready to do what was necessary.

There was nothing else to do in this moment but to sit with Colin and watch William at the table. She raised her glass to Colin. They cheered.

40

Tula and Colin looked down at empty glasses. The bartender put three new Guinness on the bar. William looked over at the bartender and then at Tula. Tula didn't know if she should get up and leave Colin to get the beer. She was terrified to take three steps away from him. William smiled at her. She got up from her chair and went to the bar. She turned her head to keep an eye on Colin. Without looking at the glasses, she picked up two glasses and brought them back to her table. William smiled at her again. She reached over with one long leap and picked-up his beer from the bar. She stood there for a moment, holding William's beer. She looked at Colin, and then at William. Colin signalled that it was ok for her to bring William his beer.

She looked around the pub. People were laughing and chitchatting. It was a usual Scottish pub, with the public camaraderie and witty and funny remarks being thrown around. This made it even more difficult to scope out who were the baddies and who were the goodies.

William looked at her and raised his empty glass. She wasn't sure why he was encouraging her to leave Colin to come bring him his beer, but she figured he must have a very good reason to insist, as she could see he was doing.

The bartender called out that he was taking a break for a few minutes. He poured himself a cup of coffee, walked around the bar, came to her table and sat next to Colin. He looked up at Tula and smiled. "Visiting with an old friend."

"Tula. Meet George. George. This is our new friend Tula." George stood up and shook her hand. "Pleasure." He sat back down next to Colin.

Tula was still standing there with one pint of beer in one hand and her other hand still out with a finished handshake.

She swallowed the dryness in her mouth. She reached down for her beer on the table and took a sip. Colin smiled at her and signalled that he would be ok. She nodded at Colin and walked over to William, grabbing two pints of beers.

William took another empty chair and wedged it between him and one of the two men. He wasn't asking him to move over. Tula felt the tension before she could even sit down. William pried the pints from her hands and offered her to sit down.

Tula's body was stiff with tension. She didn't know if she could bend into a sitting position. She smiled to release her anxiety, and giggled a little. She couldn't believe what was happening. William had come to know Tula's different types of laughter and giggles. To ease her tension, he put his hand on her shoulder and kissed her on the cheek. "Darling. Have a seat."

Tula loved the feel of his lips on her cheek. It was totally unexpected. She was overwhelmed with a moment of passion. Then, she quickly snapped herself out of it. When she sat down, William introduced her to Arthur, Tom and Nick. They put out their hand and Tula kept her hand to herself.

"Gentlemen. Let's not be foolish." William said. William was not about to let Tula feel like she would have to do anything that went against her conscience. He knew that she would do anything for Colin, but he would also protect her in every way possible.

Tula could not conceal her concerns, her fear, worry and her curiosity. She rubbed her leg with her hand beneath the table. William held her hand under the table. She sipped her beer, but she really felt like chugging the entire pint, followed by a shot of whiskey.

"What the hell are we doing here?" she wondered. She smiled at William and the others. "Do they know who I am, and why I'm in the picture?"

Behind Arthur, the three unicorns were looking at them through the window. Tula looked around at the table and smiled. The only ones who could see them were her, William and Colin. From where she sat, she could see everyone else in the pub. She scanned the room with her eyes to see if anyone else could see them. What expression on their face would change when they saw the unicorns standing outside the pub by the windows? She sipped her beer to hide her face. She didn't want to make it that obvious that she was people watching.

Arthur and the two young men couldn't see the unicorns. This she could clearly tell. The unicorns were making faces in the window in clear sight of Arthur, Tom and Nick.

"Stop it." Tula thought. "You're going to make me laugh out loud. It will look like I'm laughing for nothing."

"Ok. We'll stop. We've seen you in hysterics. It's quite funny to watch."

"Wait. You can hear my thoughts? I didn't know I could communicate this way with you."

"We said it would happen. Now you know you can."

"Fantastic. So, what the hell is going on here right now in this pub with these…rrr…Arthur and his cronies?"

"They are Druids helping Arthur. They know only what Arthur told them and what his family has been telling all Druids from generation to generation. That's why they are keen to help him. They know you're here to help William, but they don't really know who you truly are."

"I see." She continued looking around the pub for anyone smiling at the funny faces the unicorns were making in the window. Then, she spotted a little girl sitting at the table with her mother. The little girl was giggling when she looked in the direction of the unicorns. From what Tula could see, there was nothing else the little girl could giggle at in the pub from where she sat with four men, other than the unicorns' making faces in the window. The little girl's mother looked at her daughter and looked up to see why she was giggling. The mother didn't giggle.

"The little girl is an Anam Duine?"

"Yes." Lilac said.

"Her mother?"

"No."

"And when her mother sees the triquetra birthmark, she will wonder about this, surely?"

"It became visible on the little girl this morning. She hails from the Skara Brae clan of Orkney Island. Her mother is aware. Not all Skara Brae descendants are born Soul Humans. The little girl's grandmother was a Soul Human. We are showing the little girl who she is. Now she understands the reason for her new birthmark. The children learn through play and laughter, and this has put her mind at ease."

"I see. So Soul Humans are here to protect Colin?"

"Yes."

"Even this little girl?"

"Yes. The presence of Soul Humans is very powerful, especially when they are united in one place. It makes it very difficult for the Kelpie to creep through this veil of energy that surrounds us now."

"That's why I couldn't identify who could see you and who couldn't. Everyone in the pub is laughing at their own jokes and silly conversations, and this little girl wasn't engaged in any adult conversation. She was people watching while eating her food.

William squeezed Tula's hand. She smiled at William. From the look in his eyes and the feel of his hand, she knew he had been listening to her entire conversation with the unicorns. When she looked over at Colin, she could tell from his smile that he had been listening as well. George raised his cup of coffee in acknowledgement.

41

Arthur leaned forward to speak, but Tula was distracted when she saw George get up from the table and return behind the bar. She wasn't going to leave Colin alone. She excused herself and returned to Colin. When she sat down, she realized that she had left her half glass of beer at the other table. William stood from his chair and picked up Tula's glass. He said something to Arthur and walked away to join Tula and Colin.

The little girl followed William with her eyes until he sat down. Tula and Colin noticed that she was staring at them as well. They smiled at her. She said something to her mother, and her mother nodded "yes". The little girl got up from her chair and walked around the table. Her mother said something to her and she nodded "yes".

They watched the little girl walk over to Arthur's table. Arthur and two young men smiled at the little girl. She asked if she could take a seat. Arthur leaned over and pulled the chair out for her to sit.

When she sat down, an orange glow emanated from her. William told Tula that the little girl's energy was extremely strong, and that she was like Colin. That's why the unicorns were present for her to see. It was like her graduation to knowing who she is. She was 9 years old with knowledge and wisdom beyond the many lives that she would live.

When she spoke Arthur, two men stopped smiling. They were no longer humouring a little girl with silly gestures and language fit for any other 9 year old. Instead, they sat upright, and at one point, Arthur grabbed Tom's harm to stop him from grabbing the little girl by the arm.

William assured Tula that the little girl was not in any kind of danger. She could take care of herself. She had the entire situation under control.

Arthur's facial expression was something Tula could not ignore. He was furious with whatever the little girl was saying.

Then, Tula watched George walk over to the little girl and serve her a bowl of chocolate ice cream. George smiled at the men and asked if they wanted another beer. They didn't respond, but George brought them another beer anyway.

With each spoonful of chocolate in her mouth, the orange glow around the little girl glowed brighter and brighter, until she finished the entire bowl. When she was done, Tula thought that Arthur's head was going to explode. He had tolerated the little girl for as long as he could. He slammed his glass of beer on the table, causing it to splash out of the glass.

George walked over with a cloth and wiped away the spilled beer from the table. He spoke some words, and the men sat back in their chairs and drank their beers as proper gentlemen.

The little girl's mother got up from the table and walked over to her daughter. She smiled at the men and told her daughter it was time to go. She put her hand out, and the little girl took her mother's hand.

The little girl looked over at Colin and smiled. She waved at everyone in the pub and walked out with her mother. Everyone knew little Fiona. For a 9 year old, Fiona had already made her mark in Wick as a kind, witty, and brilliant little girl, and when she walked, a veil of orange glow flowed behind her.

Tula was seeing the making of an Anam Duine that she had only seen in her little book. It was more spectacular than she could have ever imagined. She looked at William and Colin, and wondered what their first day of knowing who they truly were was like.

At the other end of the bar, Arthur, Tom and Nick were not in the same joyous spirit. They were still twisting and turning in their chairs at whatever little Fiona had said to them. Somehow, she had managed to anger them more than what William had said to them.

Colin signalled to George for three whiskeys instead of beer this time. George poured three whiskeys and placed them on the bar. William stood up and leaned over to grab them. When he sat down, they cheered and shot back their drinks.

Tula let out a long breath. "Now will anyone tell me what I saw and experienced here today?" She looked over at Arthur's table. "They don't look very pleased with you William, or little Fiona. What did you talk about other than the obvious here?"

Colin signalled to George for another.

"Please. No more Colin." Tula said.

"One last one." Colin flagged George to go ahead. "Let's start with little Fiona."

"Ok. That's a good start." Tula sipped the last of her Guinness.

"As you know, she is like me. We both have the triquetra and Tree of Life birthmarks, and because we are the same that way, we know the day a gifted Anam Duine will know when they learn who they truly are. Today, little Fiona learned who she is, and that is the reason for us being here today. It's sort of a birthday party."

"Ok. That's nice, and what else was going on today?"

William looked over at Arthur. "He's pissed off at us because his plan to kidnap my son today failed."

"Explain." Tula leaned forward with her elbows on the table.

"Before Arthur left London today, he dispatched his so-called army of Druid soldiers to kidnap my son, but the unicorns and serpents and the other Soul Humans were able to fight them off until we got here. The Druid soldiers retreated because their powers had weakened.

The reason we came here was, yes, for Fiona's so-called birthday but, because it's her first life as an Anam Duine in human form, she also needed to see Colin and she needed to see and experience the power of her true nature. Protecting Colin was a great way for her to get to know herself, and being surrounded by other Anam Duines, as we explained before, unites the energy which makes the shield around Colin and all of us even more difficult for the Kelpie to fracture and do its evil little deeds."

Tula put her arm around Colin. She was terribly worried for him, even if he was at this very moment well protected. "And, what else? Why is Arthur and his cronies so angry?"

"Because we set a trap for Arthur's other cronies at the farm. The serpents have entrapped them in an underwater chamber for now, and under the guidance of the unicorns, little Fiona was leading our so-called army of good souls to protect Colin. It was quite a day for her, and when she shared with Arthur the additional barriers placed around his new armies, he would be faced with a great power."

144

"For now?" Tula looked over at Arthur. "And then what?"

"For now, because we cannot cause any harm to any human. That is not who we are. They will tire in this chamber. This weakens their minds and they will submit to whatever the serpent commands before they are released. When they submit to the serpents' commands to behave and conduct themselves in manners that defy the Kelpie, Arthur's army will be forever depleted, and so will the Kelpie's."

"That's great." Tula squeezed Colin with her arm around his shoulder. "But we are not out of the woods yet, are we?"

"No. This will only stop when Arthur stops. When he behaves and conducts himself in a manner that defies the Kelpie. The Kelpie lied to them. It told them that they had to exchange the seven ashes with new ashes for the Druids to regain their magic and the powers that they once had. The Druids believed the Kelpie's lies so much that they are influenced by a lack of belief in themselves. Until Arthur and all other Druids realize this, that they never lost their true magic nor their powers, that it is still with them, within them, and will always be a part of them, they will forever be at the Kelpie's mercy."

"That's very sad. Is there anything we can say to Arthur and the others to get them out of this mindset? This horrible trap the Kelpie has set for them?"

"It's been said and tried for many generations. Fiona has such a great and compassionate heart, that she tried as well today when she was sitting with them. As you can see it just angered them even more. It's really up to them now, and it's up to us now as well to do everything in our power to stop this next horror from happening."

"So, what do we do now? Is it safe to return to the cottage? It will only be us three; no other Anam Duine but you two at the cottage...and I'm just me. No magic powers, remember?"

"Yes. We can return for tonight. I feel like we have a few days before Arthur gathers his army. He will have plenty at the ready for any eventuality. He's angry right now, but don't let that fool you. He won't be so easily defeated."

42

For the next few days, Colin encouraged Tula to rest at the farm and to study the books in his library. She only had a couple of days to become familiar with all the battles that had been fought between the Anam Duines and the Druids. She needed to understand their tactical strategies and how they captured other Anam Duines, and most importantly she had to learn how they also escaped. Her knowledge of the Anam Duines' strengths and weaknesses was as critical as learning the Druids' strengths and weaknesses.

Throughout the day, William and Colin received intelligence from the Anam Duines on the activities of Arthur and his cronies. They were kept informed moment-by-moment. They were leaving nothing to chance.

The serpents patrolled the sea, the rivers and the lakes. The unicorns patrolled the area by air. All communication came directly to William's and Colin's mind. Everyone was on high alert and ready for anything.

By the third day, Tula had read just about every book that Colin had placed in front of her. She studied everything. From day to night, she asked all manner of questions to Colin, William, the unicorns and the serpents.

At a theoretical level she felt strong. She knew she could pass any test placed in front of her, as long as it was an oral exam or on paper. Being in battle for real, she knew was a very different experience. She was knowledgeable and skilled in so many other ways, but as for this, she knew with all her heart that she was not the candidate she would choose to save her own life, let alone someone else's.

That night after dinner Colin gathered everyone outside the unicorn barn. Some serpents had come onto land. They grew legs the moment they were summoned to walk on land. This was also due to the powerful magic of the unicorns. Even Charlotte, Duncan and Logan were present in the light of the Merry Dancers.

Colin announced that their time of hiding had come to an end. They had done and prepared as much as possible, and could not stay removed from day-to-day life. They had to return to society and confront their worst fears.

Tomorrow was the opening of the Highland Games in Wick. The town will come to life like no other day to celebrate the Scottish and Celtic culture. The town will hum of bagpipes, be decorated with flowing kilts, and the cheers from the competitions in piping and drumming, dancing, and heavy events, like the tug-o-war, the hammer throw and tossing the caber, will echo throughout the town. In addition, music, art, theatrical entertainment and all manners of food will flood all the senses. It wasn't a day to be missed, and Colin insisted that they partake in this great festival.

He assured them all that everything that was needed to be to prepared for their encounter with Arthur and his army had been taken care of. There was nothing left to do but to get out there and live life. Being cooped up at the farm for days on end had reached its end.

Everyone, with the exception of Tula, agreed with Colin. She had a list of reasons as to why they should stay where they were, and not throw themselves directly into Arthur's hands. Her reluctance was written all over her face, and when she asked to voice her concerns, they let her go as far as stating that she had concerns. Then, they reassured her that she was ready, and most of all, that Colin was equally ready. He had absolute trust and faith in everyone who was helping him, and that's all she needed to know to lean into the next day.

Tula wasn't that easily swayed into believing that all was good and well. She had come to know all of them all too well by now. It was a definite absolute that they were about to embark on a day of serious adventure with Arthur and his cronies, but she just had no idea of how that would play out. She had read all the books, studied her own little book over and over again, and nothing told her that everything was going to end well...not the way she wanted it to go anyway.

She had her own idea on keeping Colin safe and out of Arthur's grip. She wanted to kidnap him herself, and keep him prisoner in the cottage for as long as possible. Everyone else started laughing at that very thought. She wasn't the least bit amused that they had infiltrated this very thought and made fun of her as well, but she did finish with a bit of a giggle.

All of this was too strange and silly to ever be explained to Anika or anyone else with a stern mind like hers, and she wondered what, if anything, could she ever tell Anika about any of this. It was much too fantastic to keep to herself. Her creative mind was leaping everywhere with ideas for a story, but it would, no doubt, be categorized as fiction and fantasy…nothing else. She imagined, *True Story That You Will Never Believe*, authored by Tula Rose.

William put his arm around her shoulders. "If you survive this Tula, I will help you write it myself."

She looked into his eye. "I am not amused by this intrusion." She smiled and put her arm around his waist.

They all stayed together in the light of the Merry Dancers, until it was time to go to bed.

43

The next morning after breakfast, Colin drove them into town for the opening of the games. Tula yawned the whole way. She had barely slept. Her night was filled with anticipation of the day to come. She looked over at Colin and William who appeared to be well rested. They were chipper at breakfast and chitchatted about this and that, as though they were starting a day like any other day.

Colin and William couldn't have been any chipper when they started singing…

> *Of all the money that here I spent, I spent it in good company,*
> *And of all the harm that here I've done, alas was done to none*
> *but me,*
> *And all I've done for want of wit, to memory now I can't recall,*
> *So fill to me the parting glass.*
> *Goodnight and joy be with you all.*

The Parting Glass, a traditional Scottish song typically played during gathering of friends and family, but she had heard Charlotte sing it as well as a popular funeral song that focused on the meaning of friendship. Charlotte loved the meaning of this song, and loved to play it for friends that held a special place in her heart.

Then, Tula couldn't roll her eyes any longer and she gave in. She sang along with them until they reached town.

Oh, if I had money enough to spend and leisure time to sit awhile.
There's a fair young man in this town that sorely has my heart beguiled.
His rosy cheeks and lovely lips, alone he has my heart in thrall.
So fill to me the parting glass.
Goodnight and joy be with you all.

Of all the comrades that here I've had, they're sorry for my going away,
And of all the sweethearts that here I had, they wish me one more day to stay.
But since it falls unto my lot that I should rise and you should not.
I will gently rise and softly call,
Goodnight and joy be with you all.

It wasn't even 9 a.m. and the town was already buzzing with people, walking and singing everywhere. The smell of beer and whiskey was already in the air. Tula was staying away from beer and whiskey that day. She was much too tired and stressed to add alcohol into her system. She had to stay focused and strong for Colin.

Colin parked around the back of the pub where he had taken Tula a few days before. George was out back sorting stacks of crates filled with beer and liquor.

Tula was seated between Colin and William. She put one hand on Colin and one hand on William, and insisted that they were not starting in the pub. They smiled at her gesture to keep them on the straight and narrow on one of the most celebrated days of the year. When they stepped out of the truck, they each closed their door and left her sitting alone in the truck. They looked back at her, as they smiled and waved.

George laughed out loud and waved at Tula to come and join them. The only thing that came to her mind was, *Charlotte, give me strength.* She could hear Charlotte's great laugh. She watched William and Colin vanish into the pub.

"Well, if you can't beat them, join them." Tula was talking to herself.

"We're supposed to be on a serious mission here, and these guys just want to get drunk." She stepped out of the truck.

George was still outside. He sorted the last crate and opened the door for Tula. "Good morning, and welcome! It's going to be a great day, and you look great by the way."

Tula rubbed her tired eyes and smiled. "I suppose it will be George. Thank you." She looked down at the blue tartan skirt that flowed perfectly around her body, just below her knees. That morning, Colin and William wanted Tula to share in the tradition. Colin unwrapped his wife's blue tartan skirt. Tula wore it with honour, with a white blouse and her white running shoes.

She walked into the pub and found William and Colin standing at the bar waiting for her. They had three Guinness in front of them. "Oh dear."

"It's a great start to this day, Tula." Colin wrapped his big arm around her. Her tired body felt the full strength of his body.

"Yes sir. I believe it is." She smiled and hugged him back. She knew that there was no way she was getting out of this one. She had studied everything she could in preparation for this day and what was to come. She also truly believed and trusted in Colin, William, the unicorns, the serpents and all of the other Anam Duines on this mission with her, and that made her trust in whatever they had planned for that day or any other day that she had no knowledge of, for whatever reason that was. She raised her pint of Guinness, and they cheered.

44

Tula looked into her empty pint. She had managed to finish one Guinness. She waited with anticipation for the guys to order another and possibly a whiskey, but they were kind to her, and said it was just a start. There was an entire day ahead of them, and they needed to pace themselves. Tula knew she was a rookie in the group, and they could have easily gulped down a few more beers.

When they stepped outside, she looked up at the sky. It was a fine day. It was sunny, blue skies, and there wasn't a single cloud anywhere to be seen. The guys called out to her to follow them. She watched Colin and William walking in their kilts. She admired their entire dress from head to toe. Comfortable white t-shirts, age old kilts from their earlier days of many lives before, long socks and running shoes. In one way, she felt she was watching the past come to life. She would have loved to see them in their many other lives.

People filled the streets. The pubs were full. The venues glittered. Everyone gathered to watch the parade kick off the amazing weekend of Scottish entertainment, music, and dancing in Wick.

The Highland Games' atmosphere reached far and wide. The ships, sailboats, fishing boats, and every other water vessel rang their bells, and people blew their whistles in celebration of the games.

Tula couldn't help but to get excited. She loved everything about it. Her hips moved to the music, and she danced hand in hand with William and Colin. They twirled her round and round until she was too dizzy to stand on her own.

She hadn't laughed this much in quite some time. The last time she had laughed so hard was with her dear friend, Charlotte. It was just the two of them, sitting outside *Le Gâteau*. It was a beautiful evening. It was two nights before Charlotte died. They ate a new dish that Charlotte had made with artichokes; drank great wine, and dove into a new chocolate desert. They chatted all night about their adventures together, and remembered all the funny moments that made them cry with laughter.

She could tell by the way William was looking at her that he saw her memories. This time she didn't mind. It was the only way she could share anything about Charlotte right now without bursting into tears. He wrapped his arms around her and held her tight. Then he spun her around one last time before stopping to watch the start of the parade.

Soon after the parade started, Tula felt someone touching her hand. She looked over and recognized Fiona's mother from the day at the pub. The mother smiled and looked down. Tula followed with her eyes. Fiona was standing between them. Fiona smiled and held Tula's hand.

Tula admired Fiona's face painting. Unicorns danced on her cheeks when she smiled. She stretched her arms to show off the orange glitter on her hands and up along her arms. In one hand, she proudly held a yummy fudge tablet. She offered Tula a bite. Tula gracefully accepted and broke off a tiny piece from the corner, and put it in her mouth. Her eyes smiled with delight, as did Fiona's.

Fiona held Tula's hand with the unicorn ring during the whole parade, without speaking. Tula didn't want to be the one to break the silence between them. She was also enjoying the time just as it was. Once the parade was over, Fiona squeezed Tula's hand and let released her. Fiona's mother smiled at Tula and the men, and then walked away. They watched Fiona wave goodbye until she vanished in the crowd.

Tula looked ahead at the dwindling end of the parade. Across the way in the crowd, Arthur and the two young men whom she had seen in the pub earlier were staring her way. She tapped Colin on the shoulder.

"We've been watching them the entire time." William put his arm out for Tula to take. "Let the games begin."

45

Tula's heart began to beat faster. Her eyes got wider and her breathing was shallow. She felt the crowd was squeezing in on them. William nudged her gently. "Steady Tula."

Tula snapped out of the frenzy where her mind was taking her. She could not let fear take control right now. "Why did you have me come with you and Arthur and his cronies at the pub the other day?"

"It was important for you to know your strength in this situation, Tula. You will be face to face with him and his cronies more often than you like, and you will have to be steady on your feet, have a sound mind, and be quick."

"And be quick?"

"For whatever is required in that specific moment."

Colin stood in front of them with his back to Arthur. "Arthur's guards are everywhere. They are at every point of entry into Wick, at every access to various venues, and mingling around in the crowd."

"Yes. I spotted them as well." William scanned up along the road with his eyes.

"How can you tell who are the goodies and who are the baddies?" Tula didn't know how else to say this.

William put his hand on her shoulder. "Steady your mind and look around. The energy field, the Merry Dancers can be seen emanating from an Anam Duine. We are the only ones who can see this. The unicorns and serpents see this as well."

"And the baddies?"

"Those that are under the Kelpie's influence only in this matter we can call the baddies, such as Arthur and his cronies on this quest for the ashes. They emanate a different energy field. Their aura is drained of colour. Instead, they emanate a misty grey, like a fog around them. Those who possess this grey foggy aura are not evil or bad people in most cases. Often, like in this case, they just need time to move on and recover from these negative feelings that are causing this grey foggy aura to appear. The Kelpie is the cause for this aura, but it is also the person's unwillingness to forgive themselves and others. This aura is never locked to specific wrongs. Instead, it emanates from a person when the person's focus and energies become imbalanced in favour of despair and raw negativity, like Arthur, his ancestors and others who have been fooled by the Kelpie."

Tula looked around at the crowd in search of this grey foggy aura. "I'm not seeing it." Her body tightened with frustration.

"It will come since you can now communicate telepathically with the unicorns. Soon, this will come as well when you least expect it. All you need to know is that your gifts and talents are limitless. You are not wearing Charlotte's ring for nothing. You've been chosen for this, and we know you well." William put his arm around her.

Colin stroked Tula's cheek with his hand. "My papa speaks the truth, Tula. We know that you will surprise yourself, and we love you, even if you did decide to return to Nort and not be a part of this. You have free will in all of this. No matter what you do, our love for you is unconditional."

A tear rolled down her cheek. Colin gently wiped it dry with his finger.

William kissed Colin on the forehead. "My son."

"I'm just scared." She smiled.

"We know." Colin said, as he hugged her.

"Not of Arthur and the others, but of my own uncertainty in all of this."

"Yes. That's normal. You will experience all manners of emotions in the coming days that you didn't even know you could have." William kissed her as well on the forehead.

"Look." Tula straightened up. "He's coming over here with Tom and Nick."

Colin turned to face them. His broad stature eclipsed Tula. She couldn't see anything in front of her. William stood next to his son, and with the two of them standing in front of Tula, she felt no bigger than an ant next to an elephant.

Instead of staying small in their shadow, she gracefully stepped in between them to be a part of this trio, as opposed to being protected by them. William and Colin looked down at her and smiled. She knew that they would protect her at all cost, but that everything she did would always be left up to her. It was her life. These were her choices. Always.

Arthur stood in front of Colin. William reached over with his hand and placed it on Arthur's shoulder, and in a gentle motion he had Arthur step away from Colin. When he was standing in front of William, William let Arthur push his hand away. He looked down at Arthur and said in a tone that Tula had never heard before, and enough to scare her as well. "You will not approach my son."

Tom and Nick puffed up, ready to fight, and they stepped up behind Arthur. Arthur ordered them to stand down. "That is not how we will do this."

"No, it is not." William smiled.

"Our army is greater than the one you faced the other day." Arthur rubbed his aching shoulder. "While you've been enjoying your beer and the parade, we dispatched a battalion at the farm. It's all burned down to the ground, including the barns. All of it. There's nothing left there for you to return to Colin."

"I see." Colin said.

Tula's heart sank deep into her stomach. She wanted so much to put her hand on Colin and to hold him. Everything he and his wife had built, their beautiful home, was all gone. All those memories. If Arthur was trying to entice Colin into a fit of anger so that he would fight him and his cronies, she figured this was a good way of doing it.

She held herself steady and sharp next to William and Colin, who were extremely composed. "It's not true." Tula looked up at William. She didn't hear him speak but she heard him in her mind. In this stressful moment where she was also feeling gleeful that she could communicate telepathically with William. She responded. "It's not true?"

"No. None of it. It's impossible with the unicorns and serpents at the farm. They would have told us."

"Sly bugger. He will say and do anything to upset Colin."

"Yes. The moment Colin gives into the Kelpie's 'bad' conduct, to manipulate him into lashing out in revenge, Colin will have stepped into the trap. Once he's in this trap, it will be difficult to release him. All it takes is one moment for the Kelpie to get its hook into anyone."

Colin rubbed his arm against Tula. "Welcome to this new level of communication."

She kept her eyes forward on Arthur and the others. "Thank you."

Arthur looked around at the crowd. "We are many today. There is no way you can escape us today." He looked over at Colin.

William cleared his throat to redirect his attention to him and not his son. "Don't make me repeat myself. I was kind the first time."

Arthur had not doubt that William was a force to be dealt with. He could not show his fear, but he feared that it was apparent nonetheless. He adjusted his posture and widened his shoulders. "They are moving in. Your son will be my special guest for lunch. Sorry. You both are not invited."

Tula's eyes got big. She was staring at a mass of grey fog slowly rolling in around them. The grey fog crept in between every space and washed over the glow of the Anam Duines in the crowd. "We are outnumbered." she thought.

46

The fog rolled around their feet. Tula couldn't move her feet. She looked up at William and, with her mind only, she asked: "What's going on?"

"It's their aura's energy field. They are many. A certain amount of their energy will paralyze us."

Arthur stepped in front of Colin and looked at William in defiance. "He's coming with me." Arthur put his hand on Colin's arm and, with his energy field, he made Colin walk next to him.

William and Tula watched Colin walk away as though he were in a trance. He did not struggle or try anything to push Arthur away. The fog rolled all around Colin.

By the time the fog dwindled away from around William and Tula's feet, Colin was gone. They could not see him through the crowd. Tula grabbed William arms. "We must run after him. I'm sure we can find him."

William held Tula's hand and stopped her from leaving. "What are you doing? We must go now."

"I know where they are taking him, and we must get there before they do."

"Where?"

"Castle of Old Wick.

Tula looked at William surprised. "Old Wick. Ruins." She pointed with her finger in the direction of the castle. "It stands on a spine of rock projecting into the North Sea, between two deep and narrow gullies. All that's left is its four story tower and parts of its seaward side, which has long since collapsed, William. All we can see is the earthworks and a deep rock-cut ditch that used to be the drawbridge. Where, in this dilapidated castle, can they keep someone in prison? There's practically nothing left of it."

William brought Tula closer to him. "Let's get the truck and make our way to the castle." He held her by the hand and walked through the crowd of people so fast that Tula's feet barely touched the ground. When they arrived at the truck, George was waiting for them outside.

"We know." George said. "They are on their way."

George opened the passenger truck door for Tula to get in. "You must go now. Hurry."

Tula was quick to get into the truck without asking any questions. William was backing up and driving off by the time she clipped in her seatbelt.

The festival was in full bloom. It slowed William down, but he manoeuvred the obstacles with great care and caution. "There are subterranean tunnels at Castle of Old Wick."

"What?"

"No one knows about them but us and the Druids. The secret access has never been discovered by them."

"Is that where they will imprison Colin?"

"Yes, and if they get him in there, we will not be able to get him out."

"Why not?"

"The death fairies. The Banshee. It's a common tale of solitary fairies affiliated with death. You can hear the banshee wail, clap her hands, and her eyes are gaunt from mourning. There's also the Dullahan. This one is dark, silent, and headless."

"What about these fairies?"

"They guard the subterranean tunnels. The death fairies are the Kelpie's creation. The Banshee's and the Dullahan's energy is so strong that once an Anam Duine enters its force field, no one ever comes out alive. No one, and we can't even enter it without all of our powers being diminished. All is lost."

"That energy drain only happens to the Anam Duines?"

"Yes."

"Then I'll be the one going in to get him out."

"No. That's too risky. We must find another way, and as I said, he may not come out of this alive. It will be murder. It is not a natural ending of his life cycle. This is what we must protect, first and foremost."

When they drove past the town edge, William stepped on the gas along the narrow road to the castle. Once at the castle, they hurried out of the truck. Tula ran behind William across the field, until they had reached the far corner of the castle.

William bent over and searched the castle wall with his finger.

"What are you looking for?" Tula bent over to look where he was looking.

"I'm following this line of white-speckled stones etched into the larger stone. They are barely visible to the naked eye. Those who know how to look for this secret map know that it leads them directly to the subterranean entrance, and we are the only ones to see the encrypted chart." William lowered himself and slowed down his pace as he walked along the wall. "Here." He pointed.

"What do mean "here"?" Tula looked down at the ground. "I don't see an entrance."

"Yes. It's right here."

William stood up tall. They could hear voices.

"Over there." Tula looked around the corner from where they stood. "It's them. They've seen the truck. They know we're here."

William nudged Tula against the wall. Tula flattened herself against the wall as much as she could. There wasn't much wall for her to hide behind, and there wasn't much castle left to hide into or around it.

"They know we can't enter the tunnels because of the fairies."

Tula looked at him straight on. "No. They know you can't enter the tunnels because of those evil little fairies." Being fully aware of the seriousness of the matter, she couldn't help but hold back a giggle with her hand over her mouth when she said evil little fairies.

William and Tula stayed as low as possible against the ground along the wall of stone. The grey fog began to swirl around the castle. The baddies were approaching, and they had nowhere else to hide.

"They're coming our way. They'll see us." Tula pushed William with her foot. "Are you listening to me?"

"Wait. Let them get closer. We need to interrupt them before they fog us in again and we can't do anything. If we startle them, it interferes with their energy field. It gives us at least a little bit of a chance."

"Really? That's all it takes? Good to know." Without hesitation, Tula jumped out from behind the wall and scared the living daylights out of

Arthur and his cronies. However, it wasn't enough to remove the foggy energy field around Colin and set him free, thereby weakening the baddies.

William jumped up from behind her. They both stood there staring at the same group of baddies who were not amused with any of this.

Arthur pushed Colin forward with his hand, and told him to walk to where William saw the entrance to the tunnels. William stepped back and walked towards the tunnel entrance. "He's not going in there alone."

Tula turned to William. "What? What are you doing? He will kill both of you."

Arthur smiled. "The more the better." Arthur walked behind Colin and told him to stop in front of the tunnel entrance. By this time, more than a hundred baddies surrounded the castle and stood along the road close to the castle.

A sea of fog surrounded them. Tula wondered where were all the Anam Duines. She couldn't see their light through the thick wall of fog.

Arthur stepped in front of Colin. He knelt down and pressed his hand against the stone and called to the Banshee and Dullahan fairies to grant them access into the tunnels. "I have a gift for you." Arthur looked up at his prisoners and smiled.

The fog around the stone dissipated, and a murky film melted the stone away and revealed the opening. Tula arched her head forward to see what they were looking at. She saw a dark opening with just enough light to follow stone steps down into the abyss. At that very moment, without any hesitation, she leapt forward and knocked Arthur to the ground. She fell to the ground on top of him but quickly got up and threw herself around Colin. She called out to him to help her, and to come back to her and William.

Arthur was quick on his feet, and William was quicker to stop him from attacking Tula and Colin. He held Arthur in a firm brace. In the rush, all of the other cronies closed in on them.

The fog thickened. Soon, William and Tula felt paralyzed again. She fought with all her might to set herself free. She looked down at the tunnel entrance. It was darker and wider. Arthur pushed Colin forward, and ordered him to step through the entrance.

47

Panic set in. Tula screamed as loud as she could. "Charlotte!" She felt the unicorn ring vibrate on her finger. She looked down at her hand and she then thought: "The magic of the unicorn. It's here. With me." She didn't know why, but she raised her hand and pointed the ring at Colin. The ring glowed bright whitish orange around Colin. The grey fog shot like arrows around him, and eventually he fell to the ground.

Arthur called out to the others to keep their energies on Colin. "Do not release him."

Tula was not letting go. It took all the energy she had to keep Colin free from the baddies' energy field. She looked over at the spine of rock projecting into the North Sea and from between the two deep narrow gullies she watched the serpents emerged. The unicorns descended from the sky, and the Anam Duines emerged through the thick grey fog.

Within moments, Arthur and a few cronies cowardly ran away to their trucks and left the other cronies alone and defeated. The serpents herded the baddies into underwater chambers, where they would remain until they submitted to whatever the serpent commanded before being released. When they submitted to the serpents' commands to behave and conduct themselves in manners that defy the Kelpie, Arthur's army was again depleted, and so was the Kelpie's.

"This is not the end." William looked at his son and Tula. "Arthur surely has a back-up plan. He is prepared for all eventualities, but we achieved what we had planned to accomplish for today."

Colin hugged Tula. "Thank you. I'm forever grateful at the courage you have shown today."

"Yes. You were very brave, Tula, and you did take some chances. You scared me." William wrapped his arm around her.

"What do you mean by "we achieved what we had planned to accomplish for today"? I didn't know we had a plan." Tula removed William's arm from around her shoulder.

Colin, the unicorns and the serpents gathered around her. William reached for Tula and put his hand on her shoulder. "I'm sorry. There are things we must do to keep you safe at the same time as well. It was us who set a trap for as many Druids under the influence of the Kelpie. We know it is risky for us. It is risky for all Anam Duines in fact, but it's to help the Druids; and now that we were able to safely get some of them with the serpents in the underwater chambers, they are safe and sound. They will emerge with their senses intact. This is how we deplete Arthur's army until we can help him and other Druids get free from the Kelpie's influence."

Tula looked around at everyone. "I see, and what about the ring?" She looked down at her hand.

"We don't know the full extent of the ring's power." William took her hand with the ring into his. "That's the magic of the ring."

Ròs stepped forward. "Arthur's army may be getting smaller and maybe weaker, but he is determined, and this is just the beginning. He won't stop there. This in fact makes him even more dangerous." Everyone agreed with Ròs.

Tula stepped away from the group and walked towards the cliff. She sat down and watched the serpents in the water.

The waves crashed against the rocks. Swirling white water rose and rose until it reached eye level with Tula. Faces appeared to her in the water. They told her that there were the seven Anam Duines whose ashes were kept in stone jars and buried in the centre of Stonehenge.

"We are here to show you the way to us." They showed her how the scorching hot jars with their ashes could be cooled to remove the lids and free their ashes. There would be no exchange of ashes for their freedom and a return to the Tree of Life. This would also restore the magic and power of the Druids. She would be helping them as well, even if she had to battle Arthur and his cronies to do so. They reiterated that these encounters could take her life.

"Tula." William put his hand on her shoulder. "You were far away."

She looked up at him. "Please sit next to me."

William sat close to her. "What is it?"

"I want to show you something." She looked into his eyes and she let him see her vision of the seven faces at Stonehenge.

The others watched while William visited a world that only Tula could let anyone else see. They waited with bated breath to hear what was shown. Tula looked over at them, and allowed them into her vision.

When they returned to the here and now on the cliff with Tula, they were breathless. They knew of her gift, but to share it with her was something they had never seen or experienced before.

She was a seer with impressive abilities who could save the seven in the jars, and they knew she could be giving up her life for the seven in the jars. For all.

Tula stood back up on her feet. William followed and hugged her. "We must continue from here."

"Yes. We must go now." Tula looked at everyone.

Colin hugged them both. The others have gathered around in support.

Tula looked over at the road. "The baddies took your truck Colin."

48

The serpents returned to the sea. Tula, Colin and William mounted a unicorn and headed back to the cottage. On the way, they spotted Colin's truck, abandoned on the road.

Back in the truck, they returned to the cottage.

The next morning, Colin did a final check of the truck before driving to Stonehenge.

Tula followed Colin outside. "Why don't we go by unicorn?"

"We will need a vehicle once we are there, and don't worry, Arthur doesn't know what we know."

William called out that breakfast was ready. Tula wasn't feeling very hungry. She was eager to get going. She felt time was of the essence, but they assured her that it was better to eat before they hit the road.

As they drove away, Tula looked back at the cottage, the land and the sky. "It's so beautiful here."

William put his arm around her. "Yes, I've always been fond of this place."

Colin tapped her on the leg with his hand. "It's my little piece of paradise on this Earth."

As they neared Wick, Colin veered into town. "We need to stop at the pub for just a moment."

Tula rolled her eyes. "No. It's much too early. It's not even 7 a.m. The entire town is just waking up from the night of festivities, and they are preparing for the last day of all-day and all-night partying."

Colin smiled. "No, we are not stopping in for a beer." He pulled up behind the pub. George was sitting on a crate, drinking coffee.

When they stepped out of the truck, they watched Fiona and mother walk around the corner.

"Good morning." George said.

"Good morning." Tula replied. She looked over at Fiona and her mother. "And a good morning to you." Fiona smiled and bit into her toast with jam.

George stood from the crate. "Let me introduce everyone."

Fiona's mother's put out her hand to Tula. "Morag."

"Tula. Nice to meet you."

"And I see you've met my daughter."

"Yes, but we were never properly introduced."

"Fiona."

"Nice to meet you, Fiona."

"Nice to meet you, Tula." Fiona took a last bite of her toast.

Tula was waiting with anticipated breath to hear the reason for this early morning gathering behind the pub. She looked at everyone who were all looking at Fiona and waiting for her to finish eating.

"Your mint tea. Just as you ordered, Fiona." George reached over for the prettiest little cup painted with flowers on the crate behind him. The cup looked like a doll-sized teacup in his big hands.

"Thank you, George." Fiona sipped her tea. "It's delicious!"

"Are you ready darling?" William said.

"Yes."

"May I?"

Morag handed William the small bag back with Fiona's belongings. "This is everything she will need for the next few days."

"We will look after her." Colin said.

Tula was shocked and surprised. She had no idea that Fiona was coming with them, and her vision did not show her Fiona being with them.

The others sensed her surprise. They smiled and Colin said. "We will need two of us to help you Tula. Together, our magic is much more powerful."

"But we also risk that they will take her as well." Tula said. She stepped towards Morag. "She is too young. She is just a child. She is not 22, so I know this is her first life cycle. This is too much to risk."

Fiona took Tula by the hand. "Yes. You are correct. Can we go now?"

Tula was astonished that Morag, a human just like her, was so sure of her decision to let her child go with them on a mission that could cost them both their lives. "Morag, I will do everything to protect her. She will come back home to you."

Morag smiled and kissed Tula on the cheek. "You must go now."

William lifted Fiona into the truck's back seat. Colin sat next to her.

"I haven't driven this old truck in a long time." William smiled at Tula who was seated next to him. "But it drives as I remembered. Smooth."

They waved goodbye at George and Morag.

Fiona waved. "Goodbye mommy and daddy!"

Tula looked back with a look of surprise on her face and thought. "George is your father." They all smiled back at her.

Tula was doing her best to not be such an open book with her feelings, but she also gave up on the idea that there could also be no more surprises of any sort on this mission. She giggled and they all laughed with her.

49

They drove south through the mountainous region and national park in North West England. The Lake District's glacial ribbon of lakes and rugged mountain fells were a wonder for Fiona. She looked everywhere. It was her first trip away from home, and her first time to see the England that she had only ever read about in books.

"Did you know that the Lake District is England's largest national park and a UNESCO World Heritage Site, and home to more than 200 mountains and hills known as fells?" Fiona leaned towards Colin and looked over at William and Fiona anxiously, waiting for a response.

"You don't say! That's why you are here." Colin said. Colin and William had been here many times before in past lives, including this one. Tula enjoyed her memories of the week when she visited the Lake District with her friend Paul. They were all smiling at their memories, and they enjoyed watching Fiona's first experience of seeing the narrow, radiating glaciated valleys, steep fells and slender lakes that exhibited such beauty in her young eyes.

"Did you know that the Lake District also has the deepest lake in England. Wastwater Lake. Seventy-four meters deep, and England's largest lake is Windermere Lake. Fourteen point eight square kilometers." Fiona waited again for a response.

"Your father did say you were prepared for this trip, Fiona." William looked over his shoulder at her. "We are very pleased to have you with us."

They drove past a beautiful cottage, resting on the edge of the lake. "We've arrived." William said. He parked the truck behind the cottage. "It's a 12th century house restored into an inn. Colin and I have stayed here many times before."

"I would think so. It used to be one of our homes once." Colin smiled. "But this area is where I was born. Right over there. Papa built our small house over there, just before the oak trees. I played by those oak trees, and when we rejuvenated, we came back to this place for three life cycles. Then, with the changes in the area, we went to other parts of England and I went to Scotland. We lived in both places from time to time throughout our lives."

Tula and Fiona were both excited with this news. Fiona jumped out of the truck. She didn't even wait for anyone to help her down. Tula followed her. She didn't want to take her eyes off her for a minute. "Wait for me, Fiona." She followed Fiona around the back of the truck and to the gardens. All manner of beautiful and well organized shrubs and flowers covered the grounds. It was as though every nook and turn told a story. It was a magical place.

Fiona ran to the oak trees, looking for any trace of Colin playing here when he was a child. Then, after examining her fourth tree, she found etches of animals in the tree bark.

"Over here." She points at the tree.

Tula came to the tree and looked at where Fiona was pointing, and when they looked around them, they saw those same birds in the trees, red squirrels jumping from tree to tree, a red deer further ahead eating grass, a red fox walking through the garden, and an otter swimming in the lake.

Colin and William carried the bags inside and called out to Fiona and Tula to come check-in. The girls came running in behind them, and when they stepped into the front foyer of the inn, they were in awe of its beauty.

Colin looked around. "It's just as we left it."

Fiona looked up at Colin. "Can I have your room, Colin?"

The check-in clerk smiled at Colin. "Have you been here to visit us before?"

"Yes, a long time ago."

After they checked in, Colin led them up the stairs to their rooms.

"Ladies. You will share this room. This is my old room."

Fiona ran into the room and looked around and out the window. "It's beautiful! We each have our own bed, Tula, and look! There's a basket with treats in it!"

William dropped their bags on the bed. "They serve dinner in one hour.

Let's meet downstairs after you've unpacked and changed. We can show you the rest of the house."

Tula and Fiona were left on their own to explore the room. They wanted to see everything and anything where Colin had once lived.

Tula was glad to have a moment alone with Fiona. She was curious about this young girl who possessed such magic. Tula thought of Fiona as someone who was created of magic. She was in awe of this little girl's confidence, wisdom and courage.

Fiona sat on the bed, looking through her bag. "I would like to wear this for dinner." She pulled out a beautiful yellow dress.

"That's lovely, Fiona. It will shine brilliantly against your ginger hair."

"Thank you! Would you comb my hair for me please?" She handed Tula her hairbrush.

"Of course!" Tula sat behind Fiona on the bed. With one hand, she twirled Fiona's long ringlet and brushed it with the other. "You have beautiful hair, Fiona."

"Thank you! Mommy told me that the unicorns gave me this hair colour."

"Did she say why?"

It is the highest colour of illumination. Orange is optimistic and uplifting as well; rejuvenating our spirit." She looked over her shoulder at Tula.

"And, I would add that orange is a burst of youthfulness, energy, and happiness, and that, my dear Fiona, is all of you!" She turned Fiona's head forward with her hand and continued brushing her hair. While Fiona was getting her hair brushed, she talked with Tula about Tula's gifts. She asked her all manner of questions. When she remembered having her first vision. What she saw. What she understands from her visions, and how she found her way with her here today.

Tula felt no reason to hide anything from this brilliant child who would eventually come to know everything there was to know about her and her gift. She also shared with her stories of her friendship with Charlotte and their adventures together.

"I want to have a friend like that as well to share my adventures with." Fiona looked in the mirror that Tula held in front of her.

"You will darling." She took the mirror away. "Let's go downstairs."

"You look lovely in your silver dress. I like the flowers at the bottom and on the sleeves." Fiona touched Tula's dress.

"Thank you, Fiona." She put her hand out for Fiona to take. They left the room hand in hand and looked around as they made their way down the hall and down the stairs, where the men were waiting for them.

After Colin and William gave them the grand tour of the house and the gardens, they made their way back to the dining room. In the glow of the moonlight shining through the window, Colin and William answered all of Fiona's and Tula's questions about their life at this cottage, and the men shared stories that made everyone laugh.

They learned that William had always been a storyteller, a writer and an actor. Colin was always an animal charmer. He cared for everyone's animals before veterinary medicine was even a thought in anyone's mind. Colin also had two sisters who grew up at this cottage, but they were not born to be Soul Humans. Colin's mother was also human like Mora, Colin's wife.

Fiona had many questions about her own life. She knew her mother and father were not Anam Duines. She was the only child in the family to be an Anam Duine. Her two older sisters and one older brother were human like Tula.

Even though it was Fiona's first life cycle, Colin told Fiona her entire life story, starting all the way from her descendants of Skara Brae and what it meant to bear the birthmarks of the triquetra and the Tree of Life. Colin and William knew that Fiona had been following her instincts, the magic instilled in her from the moment of her conception. She had some knowledge of her existence and what it meant, but this was her first mission, and it was already a great deal for a grown-up to adjust to, let alone a child.

Fiona behaved like a 9 year old girl, and everyone who knew who she really was would have to still allowed her to grow into the woman she would become in her own time. For this reason, Colin and William resisted asking her questions about the mission. They trusted that whatever she needed to say or do would come from her when it was the right time for her to do so, and this was very much like Tula's visions. They knew that Fiona and Tula would guide them through inspiration. They couldn't push them into anything, no matter the urgency of the matter, and as much as Tula and Fiona felt that it was Colin and William who were leading the way, Colin and William knew it was the other way around.

50

After a good night's sleep, Tula and Fiona were up bright and early. They explored the gardens before anyone else was up, and went for a walk along the path around the small lake. Then, they went to the dining room for breakfast. After drinking a hot chocolate, William joined them at the breakfast table. He looked around room. "Did Colin already come down for breakfast?"

"No, not yet." Tula replied. She poured him a cup of hot chocolate. "Here you go."

"Thank you." He took a sip. "Delicious. I'll go see if he's awake."

By the time Fiona's toast arrived, William came rushing back into the dining room. "He's not in his room. I'll see if he's in the garden." He hurried out the dining room and out the front door. Tula and Fiona followed him. They would not let him search for Colin alone, and Tula would not let Fiona out of her sight.

They searched the entire garden and afield along the lake edges and all around and calling for Colin. He was nowhere to be found.

William ran to the front desk and rang the bell for the clerk. The clerk came out from the back office with a coffee in his hand.

"Sir. Have you seen Colin Ridel, the older gentleman that checked-in with us yesterday? William pulled up a photo of his son on his phone and showed it to the clerk. "This man?"

The man leaned in to take a closer look at the photo. "The last time I saw him was when you all went up to your rooms after dinner."

Tula and Fiona were standing behind William. Tula looked around the hallways and back at the entrance. She pulled up some photos from her phone. "Sir. Did you see this man here anytime yesterday or this morning?"

William looked at the photo she was showing the clerk. It was a photo of Arthur.

"Yes. This man was here maybe 30 minutes before you and the young lady came in from your walk, when breakfast was being served."

"Everything is still in his room. His bed looks slept in. So they can't be too far." William looked at the clock on the wall. Eight thirty-eight. "What time did you come down for breakfast?"

Tula looked at the clock. "We went for a walk in the gardens around 7 a.m., and we got back around one hour later."

"So Arthur was here around 7:30 a.m. They've been gone an hour. That gives him enough time to be far enough that we may not get to them before they reach Stonehenge." William pulled his wallet from his jacket's pocket. "Sir. We will pay and check out immediately. Can you please prepare a take-away breakfast for four?"

"Yes Sir. Immediately."

While William was sorting the bill, Tula and Fiona ran upstairs to their room to pack up their things. Then, they went to Colin's room and packed up his things and did the same for William.

Moments later, they were back downstairs at the front desk. William had pulled up with the truck at the front. They hurried to the truck and jumped in. William drove fast but safely through the small narrow roads of the Lake District. Fiona was buckled in the backseat, eating her bagged breakfast, and Tula was watching the majestic scenery wiz by her in the early morning light.

Once they reached a more opened road, it was easier for William to drive and eat at the same time. "Can you hand me my egg sandwich, please. I'm starving."

Tula placed a napkin on his lap and handed him his toasted sandwich. "Smells delicious!"

She looked again in the large bag. The clerk had filled the bag with scones, jams, chocolate brownies, and other treats enough to feed an army. Then, she saw the thermos beneath the bag. She opened it. It was filled with hot chocolate. She poured Fiona a bit of chocolate in her blue bottle, which she found in the backpack her mother had prepared for her. The bottle was for both hot and cold drinks. Her mother had thought of everything.

When the others were settled with their food and drink, she ate her breakfast and drank her hot chocolate, and when she saw a vehicle, she arched her neck to see the driver and if Colin was in the car.

"We don't know what Arthur is driving or which roads he's taking to get to Stonehenge." Tula said. "It's impossible to find them until we actually get there, and where else can he keep Colin a prisoner until his death? Also, how did they find us?" And…"

William put his hand on her shoulder. "We will find him, and we will get answers to all of your questions."

Tula sipped her chocolate. "I'm scared, William."

"I know." They both turned and looked over their shoulder at Fiona.

She smiled at them while eating her breakfast quietly. Once she had swallowed, she said. "Take the next left."

William looked back at her. "Where are we going?"

"We are going to Furness Abbey." Fiona took a bite of her toast.

Tula searched Furness Abbey on her phone. "Interesting. The Abbey is set in a woodland valley near Barrow-in-Furness. It's one of the grandest ruins of its type in the North West. According to English Heritage, the Abbey was founded almost 900 years ago by Stephen, who later became Kind of England, and was the second richest Cistercian abbey in England."

William looked at her as though he had heard this for the first time. "There's more history to this place than what you'll read on the Internet."

Tula kept reading. "It also reads here that when Robert the Bruce invaded England, during The Great Raid of 1322, the abbot paid to lodge and support him, rather than risk losing the wealth and power of the Abbey. The Abbey was disestablished and destroyed in 1537 during the English Reformation, under the orders of Henry VIII. I can read on about the monks who lived there, but I want to know from you two, why this place?" Tula looked over at Fiona and William.

51

William took the next left at the sign pointing to Furness Abbey, 20 miles. He followed the narrow winding road between the fields.

"The fairies at the Castle of Old Wick were one problem, but what we are about to face here is much more serious. The Druids have used Furness Abbey to imprison Anam Duines for centuries. Even though we were able to help them escape, it wasn't without its challenges, and lives were lost." William glanced over at Tula.

Tula looked back at Fiona. Even though Fiona was with them for who she was and her powers to help them, Tula couldn't help but worry for her, especially when talking about Anam Duines dying. She was still a child after all.

"What are we dealing with?" Tula topped her hot chocolate.

William swallowed the last bit of his toast. "You will also read about the folklore and supernatural activity of Furness Abbey."

"And are we just talking folklore or is this what we are up against?"

"They say Furness Abbey is haunted. That's one thing. The ghosts of monks and those who stayed at the Abbey are said to have been seen numerous times at the Abbey. One of these ghosts is the headless monk on horseback. This ghost rides underneath the sandstone arch near the Abbey Tavern, and the death of this monk is linked to an invasion by the Scots in 1316."

"And is any of this real?"

"Yes! The monks, including the headless monk who was killed during the invasion by the Scots was the Kelpie's doing. Some of these monks were Soul Humans. All the monks at this Abbey knew about the Anam Duines, they knew the entire story all the way back to the little girl, Charlotte, at Skara Brae, and when the Druids from Scotland, Arthur's ancestors, were on the hunt for one of us living our last life cycle, they found a monk living at Furness Abbey, but the reason for the invasion was disguised."

"How so?"

"A tunnel runs underneath the Abbey to both Piel Castle and Dalton Castle. This allowed the monks to receive supplies and keep watch on the local settlement, and it is also rumoured that back then and still, it is where the Holy Grail and King John's missing jewels are hidden, somewhere inside the ley tunnel. The Druids disguised themselves as anything but Druids, but instead as Scottish invaders who wanted both the Holy Grail and King John's missing jewels. Where, in fact, they came to kidnap two monks who were Soul Humans, who were living their last life cycle. Peter Thomas and his brother Jacob Thomas."

Tula looked back at Fiona. Fiona was entertaining herself by watching everything in the field as they drove past. She made it look like she was ignoring the adult conversation in the front seat, but Tula smiled at her, knowing that she was paying attention to every word, and she figured that Fiona already knew this story. She turned her attention back to William. "And what happened to Peter and Jacob?"

"They killed Peter in the invasion, and they also killed other monks who were trying to protect the brothers. It was a tragedy of Furness Abbey, and a total failure of the Druids. Some Druids were killed as well in this invasion."

"It was catastrophic on both sides, and I thought you said Soul Humans do not kill or harm humans."

"We don't. The other monks had to fight for their lives and, in doing so, some were killed on both sides, and this is the tragedy. The ghost of Druid Brian who cut off Peter's head continues to search for Peter at the Abbey. Brian wants to take his ashes to Stonehenge. Peter did not complete his life cycle naturally. The other monks hid his headless body and his head until it decomposed to ashes, and then put his ashes in the water."

"If the monks would have left the Druids to take Peter's body and head, they would have brought the ashes of a murdered Anam Duine to Stonehenge. From what I understand now…wait… Let me explain this point-by-point so that I can understand this better myself, first. The Druids murdered an Anam Duine. Peter. Second. Also, because Peter was murdered, the magic of the unicorn in the ashes lost some of its potency. It weakened the magic of the unicorn in the ashes. Third. If they put these ashes in the stone jars in exchange for the other ashes, this would also weaken the Kelpie."

"That's correct."

"Why did they not let the Druids put Peter's ashes in one of the jars to weaken the Kelpie?"

"There was still a chance to save Peter and get him back to the Tree of Life. That's why they took his ashes and put them in the water."

"Why would there still be a chance if he was murdered?"

"Peter sacrificed his life to save the life of his brother Jacob. That's how he got his head cut off."

"More detail please. How did this happen?"

"Brian, the Druid, was chasing Jacob, the monk, and when Jacob was defending himself, he fell to the ground. As Brian was about to bring his sword down onto Jacob's neck, Peter ran to his brother and protected Jacob with his own body. Instead of Brian's sword coming down on Jacob's neck, the sword came down on Peter's neck."

"Oh my. That's tragic. What happened to Jacob?"

"Jacob was in shock. His brother's headless body lay on top of him while his head rolled away. When he turned his head to look away, he saw the sword of a fallen Druid in the mud. By this point, Jacob was hysterical. His brother's blood was draining all over him, and Brian was standing over him wielding his sword again to come down on Jacob's neck. Jacob reached for the sword in the mud and swung it in the air to protect himself from Brian. Jacob swung so hard that his sword pierced right through Brian's heart and killed him. This was the first and last time an Anam Duine has ever killed a human."

"That's so tragic." Tula could not think of any other word to describe this entire story. She just kept thinking: "Tragic. Tragic. Tragic." She put her hand on William's shoulder. She knew she did not understand the gravity of the situation for an Anam Duine to have killed a human.

"And what happened to Jacob?"

"The day after the invasion, Jacob went into seclusion. He isolated himself from everyone. He couldn't find it in himself to forgive himself for killing a human, even under those circumstances, and that his brother gave his life to save his. Then, one day, when he was a very old man, he was 95, which was very old and practically unheard of in the 1300s, Jacob met a young woman named Charlotte."

52

Tula dropped her arm away from William and turned her body towards him. He had her undivided attention. Not that he didn't have it before, but Tula was intrigued as to Charlotte's impact on Jacob's life. Charlotte had a way of leaving her mark for the better on everyone who crossed her path. "Charlotte? What great wonders did she leave us in the 1300s?"

"The monks and Jacob would see Brian's ghost chasing a headless monk, Peter, around the Abbey. Peter was returned to the Tree of Life, but Brian believed that he saw the headless monk. So, whatever Brian's ghost saw and was chasing with his sword is what everyone else saw when they saw the ghosts. Even Jacob saw these ghost."

"And what about Charlotte?"

"These ghosts terrified Jacob. He could not bear to see his brother's headless body around the Abbey, even when he knew that Peter had returned to the Tree of Life. It was his nightmare playing over and over again every night. It didn't matter that he had isolated himself from everyone at the Abbey and how deep he hid away in the Abbey, he saw the ghost every night. It was torture for him, and his friends could not bring him any comfort, no matter what they said or tried. They stayed close by and always made sure that he always had fresh food, water and clean clothes, and left him clean bedding every night. From the Abbey window, the monks watched Jacob stroll in the garden just before sunrise, and retreat back to his room until the next day, where he would emerge a half hour before sunrise. He did this every day until Charlotte came to the Abbey."

Tula looked back at Fiona. Fiona was still looking out the window at the beautiful field and forest. "Jacob carried all this in his heart for so long."

"Yes, and the day after Charlotte arrived at the Abbey, she was in the garden waiting for Jacob. His initial instinct was to retreat back to his room, but you know Charlotte. She had a way about her. She didn't speak. She was there with his favourite berry cake which she had just taken out of the oven. The entire Abbey smelled of berry cake, and she had also picked fresh leaves to make tea. She was sitting on the bench when he walked around the hedges. There she was, sitting quietly, all serene, doing her best work. For the first time since that horrific day, Jacob smiled. He sat next to her and ate cake and drank tea, and never said a word. Every morning after that, Charlotte met Jacob on the same bench with a different cake and tea. Then they walked in the garden and spent their days looking at flowers and planting vegetables and other flowers, in quiet. They never spoke. They did this for several months until one morning, Jacob laid down in the garden where him and Charlotte had prepared his decomposing site. He smiled and closed his eyes forever. That evening, they put his ashes in the water. He returned to the Tree of Life."

Tula heard Fiona move in the back seat. When she turned her head to see what Fiona was doing, Fiona had leaned forward close to the back of the front seat and put herself in between William and Tula.

"We will be there soon." Fiona looked at William. "You need to hurry to tell her why Arthur is taking Colin there, and the problem we are about to face."

William looked at Fiona. "Back in your seat, Fiona." He smiled.

Fiona returned to her seat with her seat belt securely fastened. "We will be there soon."

Tula smiled at William. "And what are we dealing with here? Do they still see the ghost of Brian chasing poor headless Peter?"

"Yes, and Brian's ghost is very strong. The Kelpie is keeping it alive and strong, and Brian can see an Anam Duine who is living his or her last life cycle. The ghost can only come out at night, shortly after sunset. Arthur will keep Colin hidden and contained within the grey fog until the ghost of Brian appears. Then, Arthur will bring Colin to Brian. Once Brian sees Colin, Brian's energy field will entrap Colin, and no one will be able to release Colin from this energy field. No one." He looked at Tula.

"I suppose Colin will stay there in this field until he dies? Then he's released?"

"Yes. They will hide him in the tunnel until that day."

179

Tula looked ahead, and through the trees, she could see the stones of the picturesque remains of ruins. As they approached, her eyes followed the chapter house, the east and west towers of the church, and a cluster of buildings. "I don't see any vehicles." She looked around as they neared the Abbey.

"They are here." Fiona replied.

Tula tidied up the truck. She put all the food away and closed the lid on the thermos of hot chocolate. She always tidied up when she was thinking. "We haven't talked about the other six bags of ashes in Arthur's possession. I can't imagine he left them in London."

"No. He has them with him." Fiona said.

Tula looked back at her. She wanted to say. *"Are you certain?"* But instead, she kept that thought to herself, knowing full well that Fiona was certain.

Fiona leaned forward and put her hand on Tula's shoulder. "Of course I'm certain." She sat back and smiled.

Tula kept looking forward at the ruins through the trees. "Cheeky girl." They all laughed.

53

William drove around the bend and came to the front of the Abbey. They looked up and read "Furness Abbey". The fields were green. The light shined through what would have been windows, and the birds chirped in the forest surrounding the grounds. It was historic, quiet and majestic for a place that held such a tragic past.

William parked the truck behind the shrubs. It was covered just enough by the trees to be out of sight to anyone who drove in on the same road, the only road to the Abbey.

It was still very early in the day. They would have to wait all night to see the ghost of Brian, but they needed to get Colin out of there, so they figured that they had plenty of time before nightfall.

Tula asked Fiona to hold her hand while they walked around. Fiona took her hand, knowing that she would not be left alone for a single moment. She did so more for Tula's sake than her own. Fiona loved the feel of the unicorn ring. She rubbed it with her finger while hand-in-hand with Tula. Tula wasn't bothered by the constant rubbing of the ring. She found it cute of Fiona to do so. Touching was very much a child-like thing to do when they are drawn to something, and she liked seeing the child in Fiona.

William led the way through the Abbey. It was obvious to Tula that he had been here before. He looked around like he knew what he was doing, and where he was going. It was like visiting a house you had previously lived in. William pointed to this and that, and talked about this and that, as though the walls were still up and the rooms were still intact.

When they turned a corner, they heard a sound coming from ahead. The sound was coming from a chamber across from the main centre of the Abbey. A small stone bridge, like a walkway, separated the two. There wasn't much to hide what was ahead, so they couldn't figure out what was making the noise. The wall was low enough to see Colin towering over it if he were there with Arthur.

They followed the noise to the chamber wall. A small wooden door was slightly ajar inward. William pulled it open, and Tula and Fiona were practically on his heels. William and Tula hunched over to walk through the door, and Fiona looked up.

Fiona stopped walking. She tugged on Tula's hands and whispered to William to stop walking. The sound they heard was getting louder. They saw nothing in front of them in the open space with four dilapidated stone walls. At the far end of the room, there was another wooden door. Fiona signalled for them to go ahead to the other door. That door was also ajar, but outwardly.

William pushed open the door very slowly. The door opened up to the forest. They stepped outside and looked around. From straight on, when they first arrived at the Abbey, it didn't seem like the Abbey was a maze, but now, they felt like they were in a mysterious maze. They couldn't figure out how the building they had first entered and the one that had just existed came to this place. It wasn't what they saw when they read the visitors map at the entrance. They should have been in the west wing of the Abbey, and it wasn't what William remembered when he was here many lives ago, before Colin was born.

He had come here to see the Abbey for himself, and to be inspired with a new story to write. He had spent many years in the Lake District and the entire region, just enjoying the beauty and being fascinated with the history of the entire region and country.

Fiona stepped forward and never let go of Tula's hand. She pointed at the small trail through the trees. William looked down and immediately recognized Colin's large footsteps. They followed the footsteps for at least one quarter of a mile through the forest, when they came upon a cave. Footsteps were seen entering the cave, and they then disappeared where the cave floor became stone.

Fiona stopped walking. "This is where we enter the tunnel." She looked up at Tula and William.

They scanned the area with their eyes, searching for an entrance. Fiona squeezed Tula's hand and pressed against the unicorn ring.

Tula looked down at Fiona and smiled. "I see."

Fiona released Tula's hand and walked over to William, and she pointed. "Right here!"

Tula stepped forward and bent over to where Fiona was pointing. "Have you been here before, Fiona?"

"No, but I can feel where Colin is, and he's through there."

Tula raised her hand towards the wall where Fiona pressed her finger. "If we need the ring to get through, how did Arthur get through without the ring?"

William smiled. "The wickedness of the Kelpie. Its powers are so strong that it can melt rock."

Tula didn't bother looking up at him. "Really?"

William leaned forward. "Yes and no. It's because he has the ashes. They are still holding a great deal of unicorn magic, and he uses them for that purpose. It's also one thing for the souls of these ashes to remain close to Colin. The ashes of these six Anam Duines still have a little bit of magic left while they're incarcerated, let's just say, by Arthur. These six are using this magic to protect Colin in their own way. Arthur is fully aware that the six bags of ashes have some power left, and that they would do anything to protect Colin, and that's how they get them to open the door. I can't open the door on my own and neither can Fiona, but with you, the ring and us, we can open this door. You will see over time, Tula, that that we don't always use the same recipe to get through a wall. The ring will work on its own with only you at times, and at other times, it will require us as well."

By the time William was done explaining to her the "yes and no" of the secret passage through the cave, the wall opened up before them, and they were staring down a steep, narrow and twirling set of stone stairs. Tula looked back up at William. "Why this entrance to the tunnels? I'm sure it's not the same entrance that the Druids used during the invasions or anyone else back in the day, to get to the tunnels."

William leaned forward and looked down the stairs. "All the entrances to the tunnel used back then are wide open for tourists, and they don't lead to where Arthur wants to take Colin, and then show him to Brian. He thinks that this is the best way to keep Colin away from us. He doesn't know about the unicorn ring and all that, but the Druid's grey foggy energy field that's controlling Colin right now is strongest below the ground. That's how the Kelpie did it as well. It gives them more power to hide in places I suppose." William took the first steps down the stairs.

Tula asked Fiona to step down between both of them so that she could keep an eye on her. Fiona went down the stairs, holding William's hand. For a staircase going underground, there was sufficient light to see all the way down. Small torches burned from way up high along the wall, and all the way to the bottom of the stairs.

The last step came to a small wooden door in the rock wall. William put his hand on the handle and opened the door outward. The three poked their heads in first and looked around. Much to their surprise, they found Colin sitting in a chair in the corner of the room.

54

Colin looked up from the grey fog and smiled at them. Tula grabbed Fiona by the hand and practically dragged her across the room when she ran to Colin. William followed right behind.

Tula threw her arms around him while still holding on to Fiona's hand. The poor child was being dragged to and fro, and bounced off the chair and Colin's shoulder.

"Colin, are you OK?" Fiona stroked his face with her hands.

"Yes, I'm fine, but make sure the door doesn't shut. There's no handle to open the door from the inside."

William leapt to the door just as it was about to shut behind them. He took off his shoe and wedged it in the door. "There. However, let's get out of here now." He turned to his son. "Son, can you get out from the chair?"

Fiona tugged gently on Tula's hand. "You can let me go now. I'm OK right now."

"Oh, sorry sweetheart, of course." Tula released her grip on Fiona's white hand.

Fiona rubbed her hand and laughed. "A little circulation is needed, and yes, your son can get out of the chair even in this grey fog."

Tula looked at the thick grey fog swirling around their feet. "Why are we not paralyzed by this like we were last time?"

Fiona put up her hand. "Because I'm here with Colin."

"And what great magic are you doing to stop this?" Tula smiled at Fiona and Colin.

William put out his hand to his son. "Come my son. Let's get out of here."

Fiona put her hand on Colin. "You have seen Colin's triquetra and Tree of Life birthmarks. As you know I have the same birthmarks, and when we are together, our powers surpass the paralysis of the grey fog. It's very difficult for the Kelpie to creep in and take control of us, but we must move fast and get out of here because, as William said, their powers are also very powerful down here."

Colin took William's hand and stood to his feet. He had been sitting in the same position, paralyzed, so it took a moment for his legs to regain their strength. Fiona rubbed his legs and, instantly, Colin was as solid and strong as he ever was. He put his arm around William. "Papa. I'm glad to see you." Then he grabbed Fiona by the hand. "Let's get out of here."

When they reached the top of the steps and ran to the cave opening, the Sun was setting. It was too late. The ghost of Brian would be out soon. They had to keep Colin out of sight of Brian, but Tula was puzzled by the sunset. "I can't imagine that it took all day to walk through the Abbey, the forest and down to the room where we found Colin and back."

William put his hand around her. "That's another deception the Kelpie is known for. The walk through the Abbey, the forest, the cave, and to Colin's and back is much longer than you were made to perceive. It's a nasty deception to trick Anam Duines, or anyone who doesn't know about this, to come face to face with the ghost of Brian. Also, the more people Brian scares, the stronger he gets. He has scared thousands of people over the centuries but, in our situation, the Kelpie has tricked us with time today. I wasn't sure if this would happen or not. We had no way of knowing what the Kelpie would do with time today."

"That's a nasty deception, and a frightening one as well." Tula held on to William's arm.

They hurried through the forest in the dark to the Abbey. The wooden door was still open but, instead of taking the same walk out that they took in, William led them around the side of the remnants to a small room with three remaining walls. There, they could see the road through the trees, and just as they were about to step out, they saw Arthur drive up in a car. Two other cars followed behind.

Arthur parked the car in front of the main entrance, and the other two cars parked to the right, blocking any way out by vehicle. When Arthur stepped out of the car, five other passengers got out of his car, and five others in each of the other cars.

"Fifteen of them." Fiona whispered. "That's not so bad."

Tula looked at her. Tula figured one was already too much, but 15, that was still way too much.

They watched Arthur and his cronies walk into the Abbey. One of them was carrying a bag across her shoulders. It looked a little heavy. She held it underneath her arm.

"That's probably the six urns with the ashes." William whispered.

Tula looked around. She couldn't see a way out of there without ramming through the cars, which would make a lot of noise. Just as she finished that thought, the others looked at her.

"It's a good idea." Colin whispered.

Tula rolled her eyes. "Privacy."

They smirked. "We know when not to intrude." Fiona whispered and held her hand.

The trees rustling behind them made them stand to attention. They huddled together and looked behind them. A majestic white deer emerged from the forest.

Fiona stepped forward to greet her. She raised her hand and touched her face. The others did the same. Tula didn't know what to make of this. The doe was brilliant white with big dark eyes. Beautiful was not the word that did her justice. She was exquisite. Then, she vanished into the forest from whence she came.

The others turned to Tula and signalled for her to follow them along the wall.

"But they will see us, and I know you can hear my thoughts." Tula thought.

William encouraged her with his hand to follow.

"Will any of you tell me why she was here?" Tula pointed at the forest.

Fiona spoke to Tula with her thoughts. "Later."

As they walked along the wall, they heard Arthur and the cronies come back outside from the chamber closest to them. When Arthur stepped out into the open, William stepped out in front of him. The others stayed back against the wall.

Arthur looked over and saw them all standing there. The cronies gathered round behind Arthur. The woman holding the bag stepped forward and stood next to Arthur.

William pointed at the bag with his finger. "You won't be leaving here with those tonight, and you won't be leaving here with my son either."

Colin stepped away from the wall and stood next to William. Fiona went to step forward, but Tula grabbed her by the hand and walked ahead of her.

The goodies and the baddies faced each other like in a standoff. "Who is going to make the first move?" Tula thought. Another western movie played in her mind. The other goodies smirked. They couldn't help but watch the movie she was seeing in her mind.

55

Tula turned her thoughts to Arthur and the woman holding the bag. The movie was over. The others returned their attention to the matter before them. Tula turned her head towards the Abbey where the wall was partially destroyed with the arch of what would have been a window. She noticed something that looked like a shadow walking across the room. William turned his head to see what she was looking at, and then everyone turned their heads and looked at the ghost of Brian.

All they could see was Brian walking away from the window. The others waited to see what he was going to do. Brian vanished from where they first saw him, and appeared from behind the wall. They watched him walk along the garden as though he was looking for something or someone.

Arthur and his cronies stepped aside and let Brian walk by them. Arthur was surprised to see that Brian had not seen him nor the others yet. He stepped forward towards the ghost and said his name. "Brian."

Brian continued his search along the garden, then he stopped and looked down. There was the spot where Brian cut off Peter's head and where he died as well. Whatever he saw, he projected into the world he haunted, and it was a scene that both the goodies and the baddies could see.

The others stood silently watching the entire tragedy play out before their eyes.

It was a terrible sight to behold, and a tragedy that should never have happened to any of them, they all thought. However, there was still the matter of the Druids to restore their power and magic, and they weren't about to let this tragic moment get in their way. They desperately wanted Brian to see Colin.

The woman holding the bag of six urns with the ashes walked towards

Brian until she was also in Colin's line of sight. With the magic she did have, she asked Brian to look at her. She told him that she knew where she could find Peter. She told him that she had the other six urns with the ashes, and that they could go to Stonehenge with them.

The ghost of Brian wept over the sight of his dead body, then he turned to the headless monk and placed his hand on Peter's heart. "I'm sorry."

Arthur walked fast towards Brian. "Brian. We have what you want. Look at us." Arthur and the cronies did not understand why Brian was not behaving as the Kelpie told them. William and the others did not understand this either. It's also not what William had seen before either. Many lives ago, he had witnessed the ghost of Brian chasing the headless monk around the Abbey. They all wondered what had changed. They all wanted to know why the ghost of Brian had put his hand on Peter's heart, said he was sorry, and had not looked at Colin.

Tula felt a great sense of urgency to step forward and go to the ghost of Brian. She put Fiona's hand in Colin's hand. With her mind, she said: "Wait for me here."

Tula walked slowly towards Brian. She knew she would have to walk close to Arthur and the woman. This scared her. She knew that anything was possible with them. She didn't know if this was also another trap, and that somehow they were controlling the ghost of Brian to behave differently, but she followed her instinct and walked in front of Arthur and the woman, and then stepped over the flowers and stood next to Brian.

All eyes were on Tula. She bent forward and put her hand on Brian's shoulder. Brian was still weeping over Peter's body. With her mind, Tula told Brian that Peter had been returned to the Tree of Life. She told him everything that happened after Peter died, and she showed him Jacob's life, when Charlotte came along and when Jacob died. She showed him how pain and suffering had been transformed by love and forgiveness for self.

Brian stopped crying. He covered his face with his hands and rose to his feet. Then, Tula kept her hand on his shoulder and showed Brian the ghost of Brian chasing the headless monk around the Abbey so that he couldn't bring Peter's ashes to Stonehenge, and everything else he did to scare others at the Abbey for centuries.

Brian wept. He would not remove his hand from his face. He told Tula that he did not want to show her his eyes. He could not look at anyone.

Whenever anyone looked into his eyes, it gave him and the Kelpie more power, and he didn't want to look into Colin's eyes.

Brian told Tula that he was helpless in this matter. The Kelpie had put a curse on him. The course was set. He could not stop chasing the headless monk, and everything else he was doing to make him and the Kelpie more powerful, nor could he stop or change Colin's fate when they looked into each other's eyes. They were both doomed no matter how much he didn't want to kill Colin. No matter how much he wanted to break free from the Kelpie's curse, he remained a prisoner of Furness Abbey itself.

The moment he took his last breath when the sword pierced his heart, Peter's soul leapt out of Peter's body and embraced Brian's soul, and Peter was not letting go of him. At that moment, Brian saw the error of his ways and understood why and how he had allowed the Kelpie to lead him away from the true heart of a Druid. Ever since, he had been the victim of his own demise and tried and tried to redeem himself and free himself from this curse, but to no avail.

56

Tula reassured Brian that he was not alone. They were here to help him. She asked him to listen to William, Fiona, and Colin. She had allowed William, Colin and Fiona to listen to the entire conversation between them as well. She had let them into her gift of communicating with the dead. Talking with those who have died is the easiest thing she could ever do. Everyone who knew Tula and her gift of speaking with the dead was always in awe of how seamless and effortless of a connection she could make. She always corrected them by saying that she was only a conduit, and that it was always up to the dead to speak with her. She didn't go looking for them. They came to her, and Brian was one of them.

Brian revealed that he had been waiting for her ever since that dreadful day. He shared with Tula that Charlotte had visited with him that morning to tell him that this day was the day he would see Tula. Charlotte had assured him that locking eyes with Tula would not make the Kelpie stronger but weaker. He added that it would also be the end of his imprisonment as the ghost who chased the headless monk.

William, Colin and Fiona kept their poker face. They didn't want Arthur and the others to read any other expression on their faces other than anger towards them for trying to take Colin.

With every passing moment of Colin standing with the goodies, Arthur was getting angrier and angrier. He was anxious to get Colin into Brian's sight. He stepped on the flowers and stood behind Brian. When he was about to grab Tula by the arm, William leapt forward and knocked Arthur to the ground.

The cronies lunged forward to free Arthur from William's grip. It took at least five men to unlock William's arms from around Arthur's body.

"Stop!" Tula cried out. She helped William stand up. When she turned to face Brian covering his face with his hands, Fiona and Colin were standing in front of him.

Everyone smartened up and took their position in their respective groups. William stepped in front of his son and Fiona. Tula stepped in front of him. Arthur pushed his way forward and grabbed the bag from the woman. In his desperation to get Brian to open his eyes, he raised the bag with the six urns with the ashes and let it dangle from his hand in front of Brian.

"Take your hands away from your eyes and look at what we have here. The six urns with the ashes are here. One more and you will be set free Brian."

"That is not true." Tula said. "You know it's not true. It's a trick Arthur. A trick you have fallen for. It will not help you either."

Tula, William, Colin and Fiona knew that Arthur and his cronies could not hear the conversation they had with Brian. They were oblivious to the Kelpie's curse on Brian and to the power of manipulation that they were under.

Tula looked at the bag. They had to save the original seven in the jars. They had to save Colin. They had to save the six urns with the ashes, and they had to help Brian. She looked at Arthur and his cronies. It was an absolute that they had to help them as well, but how?

In a flash, Tula ripped the bag with the six urns with the ashes from Arthur's grip, dangling in front of Brian. She ran away with the bag as fast as she could towards the forest. Everyone was in shock. No one expected that to happen. Arthur shouted at the others to chase her and get the bag back from her.

William ran behind them and knocked a few to the ground on his way.

When Tula reached the forest where they saw the white deer, she ran in the forest and in the same direction where she had seen the deer vanish. She didn't know why, but again, she was following her instincts.

The shout coming from the cronies were getting louder and louder. She turned and could see them through the trees. Her feet began to run faster, as though she had no control over them, and then, she stopped suddenly in front of the white deer.

The white deer stood tall. She lowered her head to Tula. Tula bowed back, but then she realized that the deer wasn't bowing her head as a greeting gesture. Instead, she wanted Tula to loop the bag handle over her head and hang from her neck. Tula quickly did what the deer wanted, and just like that, the deer turned and vanished deeper into the forest with the six urns with the ashes.

Tula was standing there alone. She looked up at the trees and smiled. Then she heard the voices and she turned around from where she had come into the forest. When she crouched behind a fallen tree, she spotted William and told him with her mind where she was. William pretended that he had fallen and hurt his leg. The cronies ran ahead and left him there, and some even stomped on him as they ran past him. Once they were out of sight, William found Tula and they ran back to Fiona and Colin.

By that point, Tula had shared with Fiona, Colin and William that she had given the bag of ashes to the white deer, and they told her that the ashes were now safe. That mission was over, but they still needed to save Colin. Even though Arthur had lost those six urns with the ashes, he would not give up on his own mission. He was frightfully determined, and he would ensure his victory at any cost to the Anam Duines.

57

A few cronies were still huddled around Arthur and Brian. Fiona and Colin remained standing in front of the ghost of Brian who kept his hands over his face.

The cronies that were running after the bag of ashes came running back to Arthur. They were surprise to see Tula standing there. She tricked them and this angered them even more. They wondered how she had run past them without being seen, and they looked at William standing strong without any injuries. They didn't like being made fools of, and it didn't take much to fuel their anger at this point. William knew this, and he watched carefully for any outburst of revenge. Up until now, their plan had been completely destroyed. William felt that Arthur's fury was about to erupt. He had lost everything up until now. All that was left was to get Brian to open his eyes and lock them onto Colin's eyes.

Then, next to the ghost of Brian, a ghostly image appeared before everyone. Without letting go of Colin's hand, Fiona stepped forward and greeted the ghost. He appeared just as Charlotte appeared to Tula beneath the Merry Dancers. "Hello Peter."

Even though Peter had returned to the Tree of Life, he was strong enough to stay next to Brian. He was not going to leave him. Brian raised his head. He did not know that Peter had stayed with him this whole time.

Peter put his hand on Brian's shoulder. "I'm here to take you home."

Brian kept his hands over his face. "The curse. I cannot leave here."

Colin stepped forward. "Brian. We are here to help you. It is your time and our time."

Tula stepped forward. "What do you mean?"

William put his arm around her. "This is the only way."

"For what?" Tula stepped in between them and the ghost of Brian.

Arthur was struggling to understand what was going on. He urged Brian to remove his hands from his face and look at Colin. He even swung his fist to hit Brian in the arm, but his fist swung through the air and through the ghost, and fell forward onto the ground.

The others watched Arthur, who was on the edge of losing control. He jumped back up to his feet and brushed himself off. In his recklessness, he reached for Colin's arms with his hand. William blocked him with his arm. "Not my son."

Fiona looked up at Colin. "It's time." She placed her hand over Brian's body. "We will be with you all the way."

Tula leaned forward and pulled Fiona away from Colin and Brian.

Fiona pulled back. "No. Tula. Please. You must let me do what I came here for."

"And, what is that? I'm to return you to your mother and father safe and sound, Fiona. This is not safe and sound. You must not let Brian see you."

"He has already seen me."

"How do you mean? You've never been here before, and Brian has not removed his hands from his face. He hasn't seen any of us."

"In his dreams, before he became a ghost. Before he was cursed by the Kelpie."

Arthur stepped forward. "That's nonsense. What are you talking about? There's no curse on Brian!"

Colin put out his hand for Friona to take. "We are here to do this, Tula."

"To do what?" Arthur shouted.

William pulled Tula away from the group. "We must stand over here."

Tula tried to release herself from William's grip. "No, William! What are they doing?"

Fiona and Colin put their hands over the ghost of Brian, and the spirit of Peter put his arm around Brian as well.

"We are ready as well." Peter added.

Brian slowly lowered his hands from his face. His eyes were still closed.

"You can open them." Colin said.

Arthur stepped closer. "It's about time. Now we got you Colin, and look at this. Two for the price of one!" He looked down at Fiona.

Fiona smiled at Arthur. "You will not thank me today but you will one day."

Arthur had no idea what she was talking about. He was just eager to see them both get sucked into this trap.

Brian turned his head towards Arthur. He kept his eyes closed, and said: "You will step away, Arthur."

"No. I'm staying right here."

"Then you will die, Arthur."

Arthur smirked. The others weren't laughing. The cronies didn't hesitate. They stepped away from Brian and Peter. Arthur looked around. He felt abandoned by his own cronies who urged him to step away. He let out a grunt and stepped away, and joined the cronies standing at a safe distance from the ghost.

Tula gripped William's hand. "This can't be happening."

He held her hand tight. His eyes filled with tears. Colin looked back at his father. "I love you Papa."

"I love you, my son. I will see you again one day."

Colin turned his head and faced Brian. He squeezed Fiona's hand. "We are ready."

Brian slowly opened his eyes. He looked at Colin and Fiona. A bright orange glow filled the space around them. Brian stretched out his hands towards Fiona and Colin. When they held hands, the orange glow got brighter and brighter.

Arthur shouted: "No! This is not what's supposed to happen!"

The orange glow swirled around Brian, Peter, Fiona and Colin. It was a beautiful sight to behold. The Merry Dancers appeared like long flowing curtains in the sky, and with their long vales, they swept up the orange glow of Brian, Peter, Fiona and Colin. Then, they vanished into the sky as quickly as they had appeared.

Tula and William hugged each other and cried. "What happened, William?"

William wrapped his arm around her shoulder and walked them to Arthur and his cronies. "It's over Arthur. This place will never be a prison to anyone or any Anam Duine." He looked at Tula. "The white deer...she was here to tell us that it was Colin and Fiona's time to return to the Tree of Life. This was how Colin and Fiona knew that they were the ones to help Brian and break the curse. It was the only way. It could only have been done with those who had been born with the triquetra and the Tree of Life birthmarks during their last life cycle."

"But Fiona was just 9 years old. It was her very first life cycle."

"Yes. This was her life. Her mother and father knew this. They know right now what Fiona did. She will visit with them tonight, just as Charlotte did with you." William held her tighter.

Arthur stepped towards them. "This isn't over." Arthur turned quickly on his heels. "Let's get out of here." He hurried to the car. The cronies were quick to follow behind. The woman who was holding the bag with the ashes looked back at William and Tula, and smirked.

The woman sat in the passenger's seat in the car that Arthur was driving. William and Tula watched them having what appeared to be a heated discussion. Then, the woman rolled down her window. She leaned forward and put out her arm. She pointed a slingshot with an arrow-shaped stone at William and Tula. "Next time, I won't hesitate to use it."

The woman pulled her hand with the sling and arrow back in the car. Arthur drove off and waved goodbye at William and Tula.

William dropped to his knees and wept. Tula could not console him. She had to let him cry. All she could do was to sit next to him and watch the night sky. The Merry Dancers were high in the sky. Her eyes followed the waves of colours. She said her own goodbyes to Colin and Fiona. Her heart ached with pain, sorrow and joy. It felt as though she was losing Charlotte all over again. It was as though she was mourning again a great love that had died too young. Mixed emotions from all her memories rushed through her heart.

Exhaustion finally took over her body. She lay in the grass. William lay next to her. Eventually, they fell asleep into each other's arms in the light of the Merry Dancers.

58

The music of songbirds echoed throughout the forest. The squeak and bark-like grunts of the red squirrels resonated throughout the Abbey. It was very early. The Sun was just creeping over the horizon. The grass was wet with dew. William and Tula opened their eyes to a bright blue sky. They looked into each other's swollen eyes.

"I'm sure we look like we've been crying all night." Tula smiled.

"Surely. That is the sight of us right now."

William helped Tula to her feet. After a long yawn and stretch, William looked around. The Abbey felt peaceful for the first time since he first visited it. The curse had been broken and all souls who crossed this way and were haunted, frightened or tormented by the ghost of Brian were also freed.

"The Abbey looks different." Tula said. She walked around looking at the ruins. "Serene." She looked over at William. "That's what I feel now, here. Tragic is not the word I would use to describe this place anymore."

From the main entrance of the Abbey, where the Sun shined through, she saw Brian, Peter, Fiona and Colin appear. William and Tula rushed over. They had to wait for their eyes to adjust to the orange souls glowing in the sunlight before speaking to them.

"My son." William put out his hand.

Colin put out his hand over his father's hand. William felt his energy. He smiled as tears rolled down his face.

Tula put her arm around him. "How is it that you are here?"

Brian stepped forward. "We have come to thank you. Thank you."

"You are most welcome." Tula smiled. She looked at Colin and Fiona. "We already miss you."

"Call to us anytime, and we will be right where you need us." Colin smiled.

Tula looked at Brian. "How is it that you are here with the Anam Duines? You are a Druid who wasn't born an Anam Duine."

"The Merry Dancers will carry me to my home. We have our own Tree of Life. The roots of this tree reach far and wide. We are all connected. I wanted to see you before I went home."

Tula put out her hand to Brian. "It is my pleasure to have met you Brian, and Peter as well."

William could not take his eyes off Colin. "My son."

"Papa."

Fiona was standing in between Brian and Peter, holding their hands. She looked up at Tula. "We have freed the Abbey. It is no longer a prison, but you must still get to Stonehenge and free the other seven. Every day they are there, the Kelpie gets stronger and stronger, and the Druids hold on to the grip of the Kelpie, are more and more of them are in danger of never finding their way back home."

Tula looked around. "We have surpassed what we thought we could achieve. I did not see in my vision how the six urns with the ashes would be returned to the Tree of Life, and the summer is not yet over. We have to wait."

"What you saw in your vision is how you must proceed to free the ashes from the seven jars at Stonehenge." Fiona stepped forward. "It must be done on September 23rd, at 7:49 a.m. Not before and not after. Just as you saw, Tula."

"Yes, on the morning of the autumn equinox. My vision showed me a view of the Earth in a perfect angle, sideways to the Sun, and the day and night were of equal length."

"What else can we do before then?" William asked. "Arthur has his eyes set on other Anam Duines living their final life."

"My vision only showed me what I showed you at the Castle of Old Wick. I can only advise that we follow everything shown to use. As you saw, much of our work will take place close to and on the day of the autumn equinox, but the rest will happen before. This is when we are most at risk of failing at this mission."

"Then, we must return to London immediately." William took Tula by the arm.

The others were all in agreement. Colin put out his hand to his father. The others stepped back, and Tula walked to the truck and gave Colin and William their moment alone to say their goodbyes.

Tula sat in the passenger seat and looked around. Fiona's bag was still on the back seat. Tears rolled down her cheeks.

"Tula."

Tula heard Fiona's voice. She turned around. Fiona was standing outside the truck. Tula went to open the door.

"No." Fiona said. "I wanted to say thank you as well. I saw mommy and daddy last night. They are sad, and they say thank you to you as well. I will visit them often."

"They will like that, Fiona. I'm so please that I was fortunate to meet you my sweet girl. You will always be in my heart, Fiona. I love you so much."

"And I love you, Tula. Now please don't be sad anymore. You have lots of work ahead of you. When it's all done, then you can go back to being sad."

Tula smiled. "You're not making this goodbye easy, my cheeky little friend."

"I must go now. Colin is waiting for me."

Tula put out her hand. Fiona fanned her hand over Tula's hand. They smiled at each other, and Fiona vanished with the breeze, and left behind a stream of orange glow.

59

Anika Patel paced around the stacks of books spread out on her desk in the office. She spent the best part of the summer reading and studying in detail every book she had purchased from Tula's bookstore at least three, four, and sometimes five times.

Her sharp mind began to weave pieces of one story with another, the places, and the mysterious deaths of the protagonists. The world had suddenly become very small in her mind. The many stories were becoming one central account of past and present events of many lives. It was the evolution of a grand mystery, slowly unravelling before her very eyes.

It was 5 a.m. Her family admired her for her curiosity and devotion to her work, especially when it came to Charlotte's case. She could not tell them of the six other mysterious deaths. All she could say to them was that she was working on her most challenging case in the history of her career.

Anika always fought for the victims to whom she proudly gave a voice as well. However, this time, there was no perpetrator to bring to justice. No crime had been committed, and she often wondered why she was so determined to solve this case. Was it because it was a case she had not solved? Was it because she was curious to know who was Charlotte Bourbon? A list of questions lined every layer of her mind.

Her instincts itched incessantly to get back to England. But why? She didn't know what she would be looking for there.

The dawn of a new day shined through her office window. The streets were quiet. Her mobile phone rang.

"Sami. Good morning."

"Are you already in the office, Anika?"

"Yes."

"Getting any closer to solving this case?"

"I can't quite seem to put my finger on it. I'm feeling something, but I'm not sure what it is yet."

"Well. There's another body. Just like Charlotte's."

"Where?"

"Quite a ways south from here. The fishing village of Cambria."

"That's out of my jurisdiction."

"Well. It seems MI6 is involved, and Arthur is on his way to assist with the investigation as well."

"MI6? Arthur? They are coming here? Well! That's all the more reason I need to join him there! I didn't think it would be so soon."

"Neither did I and, of course, you need to be there."

"Sami, when did Arthur call you?"

"He just called. He won't call you himself. He wants me to believe that he's too clever and that I don't know that he's using me as well to tell you what I know. He doesn't know we are on to him. He's going to use you just like he did last time."

"Excellent. We'll let him think that's what happening. What do you know about the body they found?"

"Female. Seventy. Welsh National. Visiting her cousin Rhiannon Cambria."

"Cambria? In Cambria?"

"Yes. It seems her family were the first settlers."

Anika turned to a page in a book and read: "Rhiannon. Really."

"Yes."

"Rhiannon. Like the Welsh mythical goddess of horses, forgiveness, rebirth, the moon, and fertility." She looked at the illustration of a woman dressed in shining gold, and sitting on a horse.

"It turns out her cousin has a horse ranch, and that's where they found her…in the field with the horses."

"Were her clothes gold in colour?"

"Interesting you asked that! Yes."

"Who's the coroner that notified the national medical examiners?"

"Morris Chan."

"Local?"

"Yes."

"I see." Anika took a sip of her coffee.

"Anika, we know that Arthur sent a memo to various national medical examiner offices, inviting them to participate in an archaeological study. We also know that he sent all this before you arrived in England. He also didn't bother telling you this bit of information when you were there. What's he up to?"

"Yes. What's he up to? And in the memo you showed me, he's asking for the same specifications about the data we found with Charlotte. Also, with MI6 letterhead and with some conjured up scientific story, everyone agreed to participate."

"Anika, for some reason, Arthur told me that his research was going great. Over the last few weeks, he received calls from six different medical examiner offices throughout Europe, and one from Cambria. Listen to this: just before calling you, I made a call to these medical examiner offices. Arthur told me who they were. Also, Arthur has already collected the ashes. The last one is of Rhiannon Cambria. In Arthur's memo, he also required that each of the deceased have a will stating that their ashes be sprinkled in a body of water, just like Charlotte. Somehow, the power that be at MI6 and Arthur's involvement for scientific reasons were able to override each of the deceased ones' requests, and take the ashes away from the executor of the will. Without the ashes, the executor of the will cannot carry out the wishes of the deceased people, based on the instructions spelled out in their will or trust documents. From what I've read, each will was well written. The instructions were clear."

"Arthur is a clever and sneaky bugger. Can you text me the details pertaining to that cousin and the farm? I want to get there before they do. I wouldn't put it past Arthur to have called you after he had already landed here. I'd be surprise if he's not already on his way to Morris Chan's office to collect the ashes as we speak. It's 5:15 now. At what time does Morris' office open?"

"It opens at 9:00. I'm sending a text to Morris now to ask him to cause a delay and to not give Arthur the ashes."

"Thank you. I hope it works.

"Anika, remember, this is Cambria. They don't have an official medical office or officer there like we have here. It's all part of their small medical clinic. Morris and his wife are the community doctors. They don't perform official autopsies. He prepares and stores the bodies until they can get it to the coroner. Morris told me that the ranch hand found the body late last night. He heard the horses walking around at night in the field. When he went to see them in the field, he saw Rhiannon Cambria's body. Her cousin called Morris. Morris went to the ranch with the local sheriff. They saw the same thing when Charlotte's body was discovered, as well as the same rapid decomposition to ashes. Since he's the pseudo coroner, the national medical office sent him the memo when it was first received. He didn't make anything of it when he first got it. Then, when he saw the body, the birthmark and rapid decomposition, he remembered the memo, and the rest is history."

"So, the ashes should still be in Cambria. It will take me three hours to drive there. There's no other way to reach Cambria. The village is so remote that the ferry doesn't even go there. Everyone has their own boat, and when you get off the main road to Cambria, I remember that the narrow dirt road takes you into this majestic coastal village, beautifully hidden away from the rest of the world. I haven't been there in years."

"You better get going. Arthur must have flown in or is flying in on some private MI6 flight. Let me know if you need anything when you get there."

"Thanks Sami. I'll let you know when I've arrived." Anika closed all the books on her desk and put them in her big book bag. The night shift was on their way home, and the new shift was slowly rolling in. She waved good morning to everyone. She smiled at her captain. "On my way to Cambria!"

60

Anika called Tula from the car, knowing full well she would not pick up. She left her a message of the highlights of her conversation with Sami, and said that she was on her way to Cambria to retrieve the ashes before Arthur did. She told her that she didn't know why she had such a strong urge to get Rhiannon Cambria's ashes before Arthur, but she had to follow this urge.

Anika had never given up on trying to find Tula. Over the last couple of months, she had left her numerous text and voice messages. Many of the messages were about what she had read in the books, and questions she had for Tula. Bit by bit, she was telling Tula what she was learning, and how she was piecing together the mystery of Charlotte Bourbon. In the hopes of enticing Tula to reach out to her, Anika was very strategic in telling Tula what she was discovering.

Tula and William read and listened to all her messages. They were wise to Anika's attempt to lure Tula out of hiding, but they had no doubt that Anika was a great investigator. It was too soon to tell her anything yet. With each message, they could hear in Anika's voice that she was slowly grasping the mystery of this entire story, all the way back to the little girl in Orkney Island.

Anika's scientific, investigative, and clever mind was beginning to open up a little more into the world of imagination in a way that she had never experienced herself. Even though she was still far from knowing the whole story, she was on the right track. Tula and William were pleased to hear that she was on her way to Cambria to retrieve the ashes before Arthur got there.

A few days after they returned to London from Furness Abbey, William's friend, retired MI6 Stewart Robertson, informed them of the memo that Arthur sent to numerous national medical examiners across the globe. However, by the time Stewart found out, it was too late. Arthur had already retrieved the ashes, except for Rhiannon Cambria's ashes.

Arthur had strong and reliable inside moles that provided him with minute-by-minute updates of a retired MI6 known for snooping around for information. He placed many obstacles in front of Steward Robertson in an attempt to slow him down and prevent him from accessing any information with the goings-on of his mission and the secret agency.

But Stewart was a clever, quiet and gentle man who was wise and powerful, and who had trained many. He didn't acquire the nickname *Master Yoda* from the movie Star Wars for nothing. None of the MI6 agents in the secret agency surpassed Stewart's talents. He had survived many eras of dangerous and deadly missions, and he was proud of what he could still accomplish today.

When Tula and William learned of the six urns with the ashes, they changed their strategy to intercept Arthur. They wanted to be shocked and surprised at how quick Arthur moved and his manoeuvres to get to what he wanted, but they weren't. Arthur was clever, very rich, and had lots of power. He would stop at nothing, and that's what they had to focus on. He was paying a lot of people to get them to do what he needed them to do, and what he wanted. Substantial financing was provided in exchange for the ashes.

Tula saw, in her vision at Castle of Old Wick, that they would be trying to rescue the ashes of seven other Anam Duines, but at the time they couldn't see how Arthur would steal them. Now they knew.

She had hoped that her visions could show her how to stop the stealing of the ashes before it happened. That might make this mission a little easier, but she knew that she couldn't write her own story about any of this until it was over, and if she were to come out of this alive. Tula's visions showed her the games Arthur would be playing. They were getting more and more clever and intricate, and the traps were becoming much more dangerous.

The voices of the ashes in the seven jars at Stonehenge called out to Tula day and night. She could feel their desperation. Tula and William were now just three days away from the autumn equinox, Saturday September 23rd at 7:49 a.m.

61

Thursday, September 21ˢᵗ.

At 8:15 a.m. Anika was driving on the dirt road that opened into Cambria. She drove just over the speed limit, without stopping. She was now running empty on gas. Lucky for her, there was a small gas station at the entrance of Cambria where she could fill up before taking the road at the far end of the village, and up along the coast to the ranch after meeting Dr. Morris Chan.

At the gas pump, she noticed that she couldn't pay with her credit or debit cards. It was an old-fashion pump station from before the days of swiping cards. She filled up and went inside the gas station and paid the attendant.

It was 8:25. She had to wait 35 minutes before Dr. Morris Chan's office would be open. That was too long. It was imperative that she get to him before Arthur did. On her way out the door, she turned to the gas attendant.

"Would you happen to know where Dr. Morris Chan lives?"

"Yes. The clinic is just around the corner."

"Does he live at his clinic?" Anika let the door go and walked towards the attendant. She showed him her badge.

The attendant smiled. "Yes." He pointed with his finger in the direction of the clinic. "The house is behind the clinic. It's the small blue building next to the pharmacy. The house is yellow."

Anika realized that she might have been a little too aggressive. He was telling her what she wanted to hear. "Thank you." She read the nametag. "Thank you, Derrek."

"You're welcome. Enjoy your day in Cambria. It's the fish festival today."

Anika smiled and walked out of the gas station. She looked around and noticed the fishing boats coming in. People were opening their stores, fishermen were unloading their catch of the day, and some were cleaning their boats.

"First light of day is a magical time on the water." A fisherwoman called out from her boat. She was unloading her catch of the day.

She got back in her car and drove around the corner to the little blue medical building. It was still closed. She read on the door. *Dr. Betty Chan, M.D. General Practitioner and Dr. Morris Chan, M.D. General Practitioner.*

She parked the car in the one-car parking lot. People were walking around and looking at her sitting in her car. Someone called out. "The docs are not in today."

She waved and smiled and stepped out of the car. A small path in the grass curved around the building. She followed it to the yellow house. As she was about to climb up the stairs, a man opened the front door.

"Good morning. How may I help you?" Morris Chan asked.

"Good morning. I'm looking for Dr. Morris Chan." Anika showed him her badge. "I'm Chief Investigator Anika Patel."

"I'm Dr. Chan." He walked down the steps and put out his hand. "Pleasure to meet you, Chief Investigator Anika Patel."

Anika shook his hand. "Nice to meet you as well. Do you have a moment to talk?"

"Of course! Let's sit over here." He pointed at the chairs on the porch. "Please, after you. Would you like some coffee?"

Anika would have killed for a coffee, but she wanted to get to the point of her visit. "No thank you." She sat down.

Morris sat next to her. "How can I help you?"

"Dr. Chan."

"Please. Morris."

"Morris, I understand that you have Rhiannon Cambria's ashes. Is that correct?"

"I did have the ashes." Morris leaned forward in his chair.

"You don't have the ashes anymore Dr. Chan, err... Morris?"

"No. You're just a little too late I'm afraid."

"Too late?" Anika removed her phone from her pant pocket. She scrolled her photos until she found a great photo of Arthur. She wanted to be sure it was him who took the ashes. "Is this the man who came by to collect the ashes?"

Morris looked closely at the photo. "This man left here about 15 minutes ago."

"He did? And did you give him the ashes?"

"No. He was very persistent though. He even showed me an official MI6 document, and he was ready to offer me a great deal of money for the ashes of Rhiannon Cambria."

"I see, and why didn't you give him the ashes?"

"Because they were not mind to give. Guinevere was adamant that her cousin's ashes be protected and not be given to anyone by the name of Arthur Moore."

"Guinevere?"

"Yes. Guinevere Cambria. She's Rhiannon Cambria's cousin. She owns the horse ranch two miles around that way along the coast." Morris pointed with his finger. "Her horses roam free in the field and on a long stretch of beach. It's a beautiful place. She also has the most beautiful barns painted white with bright orange shutters and doors. The horses only go in the barns to sleep at night. That's if they want to go into the barn."

"I will make my way over there after my visit with you. Thank you. Did Guinevere say why the ashes were not to be handed over to Arthur Moore?"

"No."

"And how did you get Arthur to accept your answer? How did you get him to leave without the ashes? I know him. He can be very persistent."

"Like I said. First, they were not mine to give. Guinevere was very clear about this. I've known her since she was 22, when she moved here from England. It's also when my wife and I moved to Cambria. It was on her birthday and she invited us to the farm to celebrate with her. I can't believe it was already 26 years ago."

"And why did Arthur leave empty handed?"

"He left empty handed because I didn't have the ashes. I told him I didn't have the ashes." He looked around. "That man was furious with me. I didn't know what he was going to do. I must admit that I was a little terrified of him, not only for me, but for my wife as well. He had two other very large and solid men with him. Even though they were dressed nice and well put together, and very polite, their eyes told a different story."

"I'm sorry they frightened you and your wife." Anika put her phone away to hide the face of the man that scared him.

"And where are the ashes now, Dr. Chan?"

"With the woman Guinevere told me I was to give them to?"

"What woman was that?"

"Guinevere said I was to give the ashes to Tula Rose and only to Tula Rose, and no one else.

62

Thursday, September 21ˢᵗ morning.

Anika looked around and thought. Tula is here. She pulled her phone back out from her pocket and scrolled to a photo of Tula.

"Morris. Is this the woman you gave the ashes to?"

Morris leaned forward and looked at the photo. "Yes. That's her. That's Tula Rose. She's a beautiful woman."

"Yes, she is. When did you give the ashes to Tula?"

"She knocked at my door at 7:30 this morning. She stayed for some hot chocolate, and left shortly before that man Arthur Moore arrived."

> Anika looked around and thought. "She must still be here." Morris pointed at the photo. "She was very kind. I can't remember the last time I felt such a gentle energy from anyone. It's like being around Guinevere, and I felt the same gentle and kind energy from the man that was with her."

"A man?" Anika had no idea who this man could be. "Can you describe this man for me?"

Morris described William to a tee. Anika searched her phone, but there was no one matching the description Morris had just given her.

A woman came out of the front door. "Good morning."

Morris stood up. "This is my wife. She's also Dr. Chan."

Anika stood up. "Good morning, Dr. Chan."

"Please, Betty. Lots of visitors this morning. Breakfast is getting cold. Will you come in for breakfast?" She held the door open.

Morris turned to Anika. "Please come in for breakfast."

Anika was puzzled that Tula was in Cambria. She figured she couldn't be too far, and that she would be able to find her. "I'm afraid I'll have to decline your kind offer."

Betty opened the door a little wider. "Let me give you something to go at least." When she opened the door a little wider, Anika noticed hand drawings encased in beautiful frames.

"Those drawings are beautiful Morris." She pointed with her finger.

"Thank you. I did those myself."

"Really? You drew those? You do great work!"

Betty was back at the door with a toasted tomato sandwich, with a takeaway coffee. "Here you go."

"Thank you. Morris, would you be able to draw me the face of the man you saw with the woman who collected the ashes?"

"Yes, of course. If you come back in 30 minutes, I can get that to you. The clinic is closed today because of the fish festival, but they know where to find me if they need me."

"If you don't mind, I will take my lovely sandwich and coffee, and walk around the village and come back in 30 minutes."

"Please. Enjoy the village and your breakfast, and come back when you're ready."

Anika bit into the delicious sandwich and walked back to her car. She was starving and dying for her coffee. She couldn't eat and drink it fast enough, and she was eager to walk around this small village and run into Tula. She had to still be there. The only way out was on the road she came in, and she would have seen her, and there were no other cars all the way in or out, unless she came in by boat somehow, and then left by boat as well.

For 30 minutes Anika walked everywhere and into every shop, and showed everyone a photo of Tula, asking everyone if they saw this woman. Her efforts were to no avail. No one had seen Tula anywhere. Anika felt frustrated that not one person had seen this beautiful woman walking around this village this morning. How could anyone miss her?

By the time she returned to Dr. Chan's house, she was feeling more frustrated at the dead end she had encountered. She put on a smile on her face and knocked on the front door. She could see Betty walking down the sunlit hallway. "Good morning again Chief Investigator Anika Patel. Come in." Betty opened the door.

Anika walked in. She followed her to the kitchen. Morris was sitting at the table, finishing up the drawing. He raised it at eye level. "It is done. Here you go Mrs. Patel." He handed the drawing to her.

Anika held the drawing straight up in front of her. "This is amazing. Very handsome man."

"Do you know who this is?" Morris said.

"I don't, but now I have a great likeness of him. May I take a photo of it?"

"Of course, but it's for you. Please take it with you."

"Oh. Thank you. That's very kind. I appreciate you taking the time for me today."

Anika said her goodbyes and, unknown to her, she walked away with a specular likeness of William Shakespeare, also known in today's world as William Ridel. When she got back to her car, she looked at the drawing again and wondered. "Who is this man with Tula?"

63

Thursday, September 21ˢᵗ morning.

The village was buzzing with all manner of voices and preparations for the festival. Back at her car, Anika unrolled the drawing on the hood of the car. She put a stone on all four corners of the sketch to keep the breeze from moving it around. She took a photo of the sketch with her phone, rolled up the sketch, and put it on the back seat. When she got back in her car and started to reverse, her phone dinged. It was from Tula. She stopped her car immediately and read the text. *"I'm sorry for not getting back to you. Keep up the great work. I will see you soon."*

Anika read the message a few times and wondered. *What is she up to? What does she need me to do for her, and will I see her soon in Nort or somewhere else?* She reversed the car onto the one and only road through the village. The speed limit was 20 miles. "Any slower and I'll be driving backwards." she said to herself.

At the end of the village, she followed the road up along the coast for 2 miles. She knew that she had arrived when she saw horses running along the beach, and to her right, the barns were painted white with bright orange shutters, and the doors and the pink-coloured house were just as Dr. Chan had described them.

When the horses saw her, they stopped running and watched her drive towards the house. From the front, the house looked like a flower. The window shutters were light green, and the wraparound porch was a beautiful green-brown earth tone. It was a mix of colours that she had never seen put together for a house, but it worked. She couldn't take her eyes off it.

"How delightful!" she thought. When she parked the car, she saw a woman walk out from one of the barns. Anika thought the barns were also quite majestic. "How beautiful! I've never seen anything like it before for a ranch."

The woman waved at her. She was carrying a glove in one hand, and pitch fork with the other. The woman waved for Anika to come towards her. Anika stepped out of the car and did as the woman asked.

It was a beautiful day. The sun was shining and the sky was blue. "A perfect end to summer", she thought. The air was a bit cool. It felt like September. It also began to smell like the end of summer and the start of a new season. The air was a bit sweeter and, being by the ocean, it was also a bit salty. She liked that.

"Good morning." the woman said. "I'm Guinevere Cambria."

"Good morning, and nice to meet you Guinevere. I'm Chief Investigator Anika Patel." She held out her badge and put out her hand.

Guinevere shook hands with Anika. "Welcome to my home…to our home." She pointed at the horses watching from the beach. "How can we help you?"

Anika picked up on the 'we'. "How could the horses help her?" she wondered. "I'm here because I just came back from Dr. Chan's."

"I see, and how are they doing this fine day? It's the fish festival today. They will be part of the celebration. I'll be heading there myself soon. Will you be staying for the festival today?"

"They are well, but I'm afraid I won't be staying for the festival." Anika looked up at the barns and the horses. "It's quite the home for them."

"Of course. The best for the best." Guinevere smiled. "What is the purpose of your visit with me?"

Anika removed her phone from her pocket. "I would like to ask you a few questions."

"Of course."

She showed Guinevere a photo of Arthur. "Have you seen this man?"

"Yes. He was here with two men. They just left by boat. They are gone now."

Anika looked over at the ocean and thought. "Always one step ahead." She noticed the horses staring at her, and then she brought her attention back to Guinevere. "And may I ask what he wanted?"

Guinevere leaned the pitchfork against the barn wall and put her gloves in her back pant pocket. "This man is dangerous Anika. I would not advise you continue to follow him and the two men accompanying him."

"Why not?"

"It will not end well for you."

"I see, and what did they say or do to make you say this?"

"I've known of them my entire life. My cousin warned me about him, and every time he came here, he was always trying to get information from us by throwing loads of money at us. He's been after my family for a long time. We know how powerful he is and what he can get done."

"Yes. I know this about Arthur, and how is it that you and your family have managed up until now to refuse him without bringing any harm to yourselves?"

"With us he is only so strong. We are always prepared to deal with him."

Anika thought that answer was vague and cryptic. She also picked up the same vibe from Guinevere that she did from Tula. They were not about to say anything they didn't want her to hear or know. "Guinevere, why did you ask Morris to give your cousin's ashes to Tula when you could have put them in the water yourself?"

Guinevere looked at Anika straight on.

Anika thought. "Got ya!" She would have to tell her something that would help her crack open this mystery.

"That's what my cousin wanted. When she was dying, she told me that I was to give her ashes to a woman by the name of Tula Rose, and that this woman, Tula Rose, would do what was necessary with the ashes."

"I see." Anika adjusted her body to release some frustration. "Did you ever meet this woman, Tula Rose?"

"In a matter of speaking, yes."

"What do you mean by "in a matter of speaking"?"

"I knew her friend Charlotte."

"Where did you meet Charlotte?"

"Scotland. She also told me you would come here as well."

"I see, and what about Tula Rose and Charlotte?"

"Charlotte told me all about Tula and showed me a photo of Tula. She also told me how she knew my cousin. Before you ask, Rhiannon and Charlotte were lifelong friends from when Charlotte used to visit Rhiannon in Wales and Rhiannon visited Charlotte in France. Sometimes they traveled to Scotland together. They often went to Orkney Island and to the small town of Wick as well."

"When was the last time you saw Rhiannon before this visit?"

"She didn't leave Wales very often to come here. The last time she came to Cambria was on my 22nd birthday, when I moved here."

"Do you, by any chance, have a photo of Rhiannon before I go? It's just so I can put a name and photo to the file." She was telling the truth. There was no photo yet of Rhiannon Cambria on file. Her body was too decomposed by the time Morris sent photos and sent them to the national examiner's office. She had already asked Sami for a photo but she didn't have one either. No one had her passport either. "The passport must still be here at the ranch." Anika thought.

"Yes. I took a few photos of us when she was here." Guinevere took the phone out from her pant back pocket and scrolled with her finger through different photos. "Here. This is my cousin Rhiannon Cambria."

Anika looked closely at the photo. "May I?" She put out her hand to take Guinevere's phone.

"Of course."

Anika took the phone in her hand and looked at it closely. She tapped the photo with her fingers to widen and zoom in to make the photo bigger. It was the same woman that she had seen in a photograph hanging in the one of the shops while she was waiting for the sketch of the man with Tula. She returned the phone to Guinevere. "I've seen this woman before. It was hanging on the main wall of the bakery. This woman was standing with other people in front of the bakery. From the clothes they were wearing, it looks like the photo was taken in the early 1800s." She watched for a reaction from Guinevere's face.

"Of course, you would have seen this face. We all look alike from one generation to the next. The Cambria clan established this village many generations before that photo was taken."

"But she looks exactly the same."

"That's the Cambria Clan. What can I tell you?" Guinevere reached for the pitchfork and removed her glove from her back pocket. "Was there anything else? I must finish my work and then head to the village. They will be waiting for me there. I'm volunteering. I'm cooking the fish."

"No. That's all for now. Thank you for your time. Here's my card. Please send me the photo, and if you have anything else you wish to share with me, or if Arthur returns and you need my help for anything, please don't hesitate to contact me."

"Thank you. I will. Are you sure you don't want to spend a bit of time in Cambria and enjoy the fish festival?"

"Yes. I'm sure. I have a three-hour drive, and I must get back to the office." Anika turned to look at the horses on the beach. The beach was empty. She then turned and looked behind her. A herd of horses was standing behind her. "How could she not have heard or felt so many horses walking behind her?" she thought. She turned to face them. They were all very large, tall and beautiful.

"No need to be afraid, Anika." Guinevere stepped forward. They are here for their treat before I go.

"Anika loved horses. She loved all animals and admired how free they were on this ranch.

"A large bag of carrots and apples is waiting for them inside. Would you like to help me bring them out and feed them?"

"I would. Thank you." Anika followed Guinevere in the barn and, together, they carried out the bags of carrots and apples.

"Over here." Guinevere walked to the long trough at the back of the barn. She poured a bag of apples in the trough. "Pour that bag over in that one."

Anika did as she had been instructed and, by the time the bag was empty, the horses were behind her at the trough. She smiled at them, and she could have sworn she saw them smile back at her.

By the time Anika had helped Guinevere put everything away, she felt a strong urge to spend the day with Guinevere at the festival. She knew that she wasn't going to get anything else out of Guinevere that Guinevere didn't want her to know. However, what was strange for Anika was the strong urge she felt to stay in Cambria and enjoy the festival. She couldn't explain it, but she was feeling what Morris described about Tula and Guinevere. Guinevere's energy was calm and inviting, and Anika did want to learn much more about the beautiful and mysterious village of Cambria.

"How different but how similar it was to Nort." she thought. The people she spoke with were not saying anything she wanted to hear. The answers to her questions were deflected in the most eloquent and polite manner. It felt like they were all in on a secret, except for her, and she was determined to find out what that was.

After an hour of enjoying the festival and talking with the locals, her urge to stay in Cambria left just as fast as it had come up. Common sense and comprehension of what was happening to her was thrown out the window. Her feelings overshot every logical thought rushing through her head. This time, she couldn't leave Cambria fast enough, and her urge was now fixated on getting on the next flight to England.

64

From Cambria, Tula and William flew by unicorn over the rugged and steep rocky inclines of Northern Wales' Carneddau Mountains, in Snowdonia National Park. They glided over the soaring peaks, scrambling ridges, serene lakes and green pastures. When they found the herd of wild ponies, they descended at their feet. The ponies were waiting for them by the lake. Tula and William scattered Rhiannon's ashes in the lake where she spent most of her time with the ponies. They had fulfilled her wishes. The ponies gathered around and thanked them for bringing their friend home. They were please to know that Rhiannon had returned to the Tree of Life.

By late afternoon, Tula and William were back in London at William's house. The many plans they had intended to execute went out the window every time something changed. This time, it was a bigger change than they anticipated, even though they had been warned by Tula's vision that Arthur would get other ashes.

He acquired six, and almost had his seventh. He was now on the hunt for the seventh, and on his way to Stonehenge. However, now, they had no idea who Arthur would be going after. They wondered what trick he had up his sleeve this time.

It was a race against time. The clock was ticking. They looked up at the clock when it struck twelve.

"Today is Thursday. Saturday at 7:49 a.m. is the autumn equinox." William pointed at the calendar on the wall.

Tula's phone dinged. She raised the phone with her hand and turned it around for William to read the text. "It's from Anika. She's flying back to

England on the next flight. Her plane lands at Heathrow Airport tomorrow, Friday at 4 a.m. Then, she's driving to Stonehenge. That's only an hour's drive or so from the airport. By the time she lands, gets her car and leaves the airport, she will be at Stonehenge on Friday morning, around 6 or 7 a.m."

"Clever woman. I doubt she has figured all this out, but what is more worrisome is that Arthur may have also laid down crumbs for her to follow. Why does he want her involved at this point? Surely, she has served her purpose for him by now."

"I agree. We won't be able to stop her from coming here."

"No. That's impossible. I say you reply to her text, but let's not call her just yet."

"I agree." Tula tapped the phone. Her text to Anika read. *We will see you there. Be careful. Arthur is not to be trusted. He's very dangerous. We will see you at Stonehenge.*" She put the phone back in her pocket. "The unicorns are waiting for us on the rooftop in the garden. Let's go."

65

Thursday late afternoon, Stonehenge.

Tula and William flew to Stonehenge by Gorm and Lilac unicorn airline. Before landing, they flew over Amesbury, where they booked three rooms in a bed and breakfast. Amesbury was the nearest town to Stonehenge in the county of Wiltshire, on the Salisbury Plain.

In flight above Amesbury, Tula followed the bank of Durrington with her eyes, then south to Woodhenge, and then to the Avon River, snaking its way across the landscape east of Stonehenge, and West Amesbury Henge on the northern bank of the river, and then over to where Coneybury Hill gradually dropped down into Stonehenge. Stonehenge came into view when the unicorns continued soaring westward.

Many buses and cars were parked in their designated areas. Some tourists were just arriving, some were leaving, and many others were walking around admiring the majestic outer ring of vertical standing stones, each around 13 feet high, 7 feet wide, and weighing around 25 tons, and topped by connecting horizontal lintel stones. However, no one could see the unicorns flying overhead with Tula and William.

A few yards away behind a mound of tufts, like trees and shrubs, the unicorns descended, and Tula and William dismounted. From there, they walked out from behind the mound without attracting any attention to themselves, and joined the tourists at the Stonehenge monument.

It was during normal business hours. Like all other tourists, Tula and William could not walk up to the stones themselves and touch them. The nearest they could get to the stones was about ten yards. A rope wrapped around the monument created a low barrier to prevent people from approaching. However, it was possible to walk up to and among the stones outside of public business hour if you were one of the early morning or late evening tourists who paid for a private access tour.

Tula and William walked along the footpath that runs along one side of the stones, just a few feet from the one that paying visitors were using. From where they stood, they could see and feel that the stone circle was not only special, but also very tight.

They looked up at the mound and saw the unicorns walking around. By the time Tula and William finished walking along the footpath, the unicorns were waiting for them at the end near the roped off section.

Tula giggled when she walked around the unicorns. How could she ever describe to the tourists that, not only were they standing in front of a most unique and prehistoric monument, but they were also amongst unicorns that they could not see, unless the unicorn wanted to be seen.

William watched Tula people watching. He could see and feel her mind busy with stories that she so desperately wanted to write about. He also knew that she would write about all of this one day. Her little book only told part of the story, and all of his books and his son's books also only told part of the story. She would keep this imaginary and fantastic tale alive in her stories as well.

Tula scanned the area with her eyes. "The equinox is at 7:45 a.m. This will be peak time for private tours. We won't be able to get to the seven jars buried in the centre of the stones with people walking around." She put her arm around William's arm.

"And this cannot be done even if we do this with you and no one can see us." Lilac said. She looked at the stones. "The energy from the jars and the fury of the Kelpie will be very strong. It may kill people. It would be like an explosion. All they will see is a flash of bright light, and we also risk the total collapse of the stones. It can completely destroy this monument. They, too, will be turned to ashes, and not one scientist will be able to explain what happened, but if Stonehenge is completely destroyed, it will make the Kelpie even stronger, and will most likely completely rip away whatever magic is left from all the Druids. It will destroy them completely, and they will live on Earth for only a very short time and, for the first time, without any magic, and they will all die. For now, they only believe that they have lost their magic. Without any Druids living on Earth, the Kelpie's power will multiply. To how much, I don't want to find out."

Tula held on to William's arm even tighter. "This is frightening news, Lilac."

William put his hand on her arm. "First, we need to intercept Arthur before the equinox." He looked at his watch. "Thursday. Three o'clock. We need to get those six urns with the ashes before Arthur comes here tomorrow."

"We don't know where he is." Tula said.

Gorm stopped playing around the tourists who were completely oblivious to his presence. "Ròs is looking for him. She'll let us know when he's been found."

"Oh. There she is." Lilac looked up in the sky.

They all looked up. Their eyes followed Ròs gliding over the monument and just above the people's head. It was obvious that she was having fun. Some people felt a breeze over their heads, others in front of them, and some looked behind as though they thought that they were being followed. She was purposely making them feel her. It's what unicorns did sometimes to have fun.

66

Ròs descended next to Lilac. "That was fun." She laughed.

Lilac nudged her with her foot. "What did you find out?" She smiled. Playing was a unicorn's pastime, and lately, they didn't have much time for it.

"Gather round." Ròs let a tourist walk in front of her without playing a trick on him, before telling the others what she had learned. "As you know. Well." She turned to Tula. "Tula. People have lived in Amesbury, or this area, for a very long time. As you say in your world, as far back as 8800 some years before Christ."

"Ok. That's a long time." Tula smiled while looking at William. She had to make it seem like they were the ones talking, as opposed to appearing like they were talking to invisible people in front of them.

"When you flew over, you would have seen the evidence of these prehistoric times." Gorm pointed with his nose towards Amesbury. "The landscape bears the evidence of large-scale prehistoric structures and settlements in the whole area." He pointed west. "Over there, Bluestonehenge, at West Amesbury." He looked around. "With the numerous other monuments around Stonehenge, and let's not forget the Neolithic village in the neighbouring parish of Durrington."

Lilac nudged him with her foot. "Ok. She gets it. People have lived here long enough. Let Ròs finish."

Ròs looked around and said. "As they were saying, people have lived here for a very long time, and these people were the Druids. So, what I'm saying is that they are well established in this area. They are everywhere in Amesbury. You will have a difficult time getting close enough to Arthur. His army consist almost of the entire population of Amesbury and the surrounding area. As I've said, *almost*, so not all of them. Anam Duines live

226

here as well…and here comes one of them now." She looked over the mound from where the unicorns descended with Tula and William.

Tula looked where the others were looking. "Who is the woman walking with the unicorns?"

William smiled. "Guinevere. Known today as Guinevere Cambria."

"Rhiannon's cousin from Cambria." Tula said.

"Oh, more than that." William put his arm around Tula.

"Well, enough with the suspense." She squeezed him with her arm around his waist.

Ròs turned to Tula. "You know all about this story…this legend. Amesbury is part of the legendary King of Britain's story, King Arthur being a central figure in medieval literature."

Tula looked over as Guinevere walking towards them. "King Arthur's wife. The beautiful and noble queen. They say her life took a tragic turn when she fell in love with Lancelot, one of Arthur's bravest and most loyal knights. It is also said that Amesbury is where the convent to which she retired is located, and where she was buried." She looked at William. "Kind Arthur and all that were real?"

"Hmm Hmm."

"Fascinating. She's Anam Duine?"

"Yes."

"King Arthur?"

"No." William looked into Tula's eyes. "She can tell you everything after we are done with all this."

"That will be the first order of business after all of this. That's for certain." She looked and smiled at Guinevere walking along the footpath with her unicorn.

"She's here to help us." Ròs said. "Arthur is in Amesbury with his many cronies and the six urns with the ashes."

"And he needs a seventh." Tula said. "We don't have much time to find out who that is, and get them to safety."

William held her tighter with his arm around her. "We already know who he's coming after."

Ròs took a step closer to Tula. "You must be strong." Ròs looked at William.

Tula looked at William. "No. I don't understand."

"Yes. It's me. This is my last life cycle."

Tula held him tight. "I thought you were…"

"I know. I couldn't tell you until now." William brushed her face with his hand. "Let's greet the queen."

Tula held his hand against her face. "My vision showed me a man in danger, but it didn't show me the face."

William kissed her on the forehead. "Come."

The unicorns opened a path for Guinevere to walk through. She was not as Tula had imagined.

Guinevere brushed her fingers through her dark brown pixie hairstyle. She was no taller than Tula, and about the same size and frame. Dressed in a t-shirt, jeans and boots with her jacket tied around her waist, Guinevere put her arms out and hugged Tula.

Tula embraced her and held her tight. "It's a pleasure to meet you." She didn't know if she should say "Your Highness" or Guinevere.

Guinevere put her hands on her shoulders. "Guinevere is what my friends call me."

"Guinevere it is."

William wrapped his arms around both of them and kissed Guinevere on the cheek. "It's been a while. Sorry I couldn't stop by when we were in Cambria."

"I saw you leave with Gorm and Lilac, and I knew I'd see you here."

Tula looked at William. He could read her thoughts, and she knew that they could all hear her thoughts. They weren't nice ones, so she left it there. "Thanks for keeping me in the loop." They all laughed.

The sound of bus and car engines purred. People climbed in the buses and their cars. One by one, vehicles left their parking spots and drove down the road. Others were driving towards the monument.

Guinevere looked at the monument. "They are here to visit Stonehenge at sunset, and some will come late at night. They have to come with a torch, as there are no street lights here. Each year on the autumn equinox, Druids gather at Stonehenge early in the morning to mark the equinox, and to see the sun rise above the stones."

Tula watched the buses and car leave, and watched the new arrivals' park. "I don't see how we can ever come back without anyone being here if they come any time of the day and night. What will we do when the Druids gather here on the morning of the equinox? What about you?" she looked at William. "What are we to do about you?"

67

They watched the sun's rays rained down on the stones. Shades of yellow-orange streamed across the bluish sky. When the bright bulbous sun came eye-to-eye with the stones, it lingered there for just a moment, as though it knew it was being watched before it said goodnight.

The night tourists cheered the day's end goodbye and welcomed the night. Some turned around and looked at Tula, William and Guinevere, and returned their attention to the stones. There would have been many against three should they have decided to come after William right there and then.

The unicorns scanned the area. They had perfect night vision. Arthur was nowhere to be seen in the night crowd.

Guinevere put her hand on Tula. "We must not let Arthur get William anywhere near or in the convent where I retired many lifetimes ago."

Tula looked over at William. "Why not?" She didn't hide the fact that she was still furious with all of them for not telling her that Arthur would be coming after William.

"When I rejuvenated, I left the convent shortly after. I was in the protection of the nuns back then, until the Druids made a pact with the Kelpie. The nuns were under threat of starvation and dying a violent death if they didn't comply with the new rules of the region, which were to let the Druids know any time an Anam Duine took refuge in the convent. You see, back then, no one, and it didn't matter who you were, could enter the convent without having received the authorization or an invitation from the abbess. The abbess was and still is the spiritual leader of the convent and her authority is absolute. No priest, bishop, or even patriarch could override an abbess within the walls of her own monastery, but the Kelpie's powers were such that it even scared the Druids into submission. They forced their way into the convent and tormented the nuns into such fear that they succumbed to their torture. I managed to escape a few days before this horrific day in the history of our existence, and one of the most shameful of days in the history of the Druids. Even though they know what they did was wrong beyond what they could ever imagine they would and could ever do to another, they have hidden that shame deep inside themselves, and have allowed the Kelpie to rule. Since then, the convent has become a place of entrapment for the Anam Duines. If Arthur gets William in the convent, he will murder him. The convent is the only place where the Kelpie has made it so that, when an Anam Duine is murdered, he or she still keeps his or her powers, and then transfers these over to the Kelpie. The Kelpie made this possible by feeding on the nuns' fears and their anguish from what they suffered, and by the Druids belief that they have lost all of their magic. Because the Druids' self-doubt concerning the loss of their magic was so strong back then, and even stronger today, the Kelpie is getting more powerful than ever. There is one other thing. The Kelpie's power is like a shield all around the convent and its grounds. Not even the unicorns and serpents can break through it to help us if we get trapped there."

"But we were able to break the curse at Furness Abbey. Can we do the same here?" Tula looked at all of them with fear in her eyes. "Surely, something can be done, right?"

"Yes." William kept her close in his arm. "Your vision. What you saw and showed us at the cliff near Castle of Old Wick."

"Yes. It will be dangerous, and even more dangerous now that I know that the man they showed me was you. In this vision, I saw myself dead." Tula stepped towards Guinevere. "You must tell me everything about the convent. I must know every way in and every way out. I will share my vision with you, and with this insight on how we can save William, Guinevere, you will tell me and show me the rest while William stays away from the convent." She didn't wait for a reply from Guinevere. She grabbed her by the hands and let her see her vision.

When it was all over, Guinevere's eyes were wide open with fear. What they were about to undertake was beyond anything she had ever done, but if the nuns survived after suffering such horror, and reclaimed their inner peace in the face of ultimate fear, she could endure what they were about to attempt.

It was too close to the autumn equinox for Arthur to keep the six urns with the ashes anywhere else but with himself. He was also fighting against time and couldn't waste any moment with any interference. An army of Druids was stationed at Stonehenge right in front of them, amidst the tourists. The Druids were proud to show themselves. They made no qualms about being seen. If looks could kill, Tula, William, and Guinevere would be dead, and so would the unicorns, had they been able to see them.

The three and the unicorns walked around the tourists towards the mound where they descended. From there, they mounted the unicorns and flew to Amesbury. A few seconds later, they were standing outside the bed and breakfast. The unicorns went up to the roof for the night to rest and watch over the others. Tula, William, and Guinevere walked to the pub across the way.

68

By the time their dinner arrived, Tula, William, and Guinevere had finished their Guinness. Another was ordered before the bartender had a chance to ask if they wanted another one. They watched and felt the Druids' eyes watching their every move. It turned out that most of the people in the pub were Druids, and wanted them dead. Even amongst the music of the jovial fiddler playing in the corner of the pub, the tension was so high that you could cut the air with a knife

All three sat with their backs against the wall. It was a tight fit, but it was too risky otherwise. The desperation in the Druids' faces didn't leave them with any room to give the Druids the benefit of doubt that they would bring anything but harm their way. Some even knocked their chair with their legs when they purposely walked by the three. Others took a long time in the loo, waiting for one of them to break free from the group and ambush them in the toilet, but they weren't falling for any of their tricks.

The three scanned the room for the glow of the Anam Duines amongst the grey fog creeping around the Druids. Some Anam Duines were sitting quietly in different areas of the pub, some were at the bar and others were walking in.

Tula's imagination brought her back to a scene from a western movie and a standoff in the bar. Guinevere and William started laughing. The Druids turned to see what reason they could have for laughing so much and so loud. It offended them that the three in the corner were enjoying themselves and, at the same time, Tula let all of the other Anam Duines in the pub see what they were laughing about. They too were struck with uncontrollable laughter at the scene playing before them. One of them got up from her seat and pretended to pull out a gun with each hand from her holsters, and said: "Bang bang."

Well that just got them all laughing even more. The Druids were confused and banged their beer glasses on the table in protest.

The bartender told them to settle down. He was an Anam Duine, and he had been kind to everyone who had walked in, but he tolerated no breaking of glasses in his pub.

When the laughter settled, all eyes turned to the front door. Arthur walked in, carrying a bag across his chest with two cronies at his side.

Tula's imaginary standoff just got more interesting. It was the best gunfight ever. Tula and Arthur in a duel to settle the dispute over who walks away with the six urns with the ashes, as well as William, who is alive and well. The showdown in her mind was transmitted to all of the Anam Duines in the pub. They were all infected with a contagious belly laugh. Deep snort hilarity was on display for all to see.

The Druids were trying to read the room, but they were none the wiser for the joviality in the air, which they deemed inappropriate under the current circumstances. That just made the Anam Duines laugh out loud even more, and then they all cheered. Tula was victorious in the best western movie showdown they'd ever seen. When it was over, they all stood to their feet and clapped, and Tula took a bow.

Arthur waved his hand and told everyone to be quiet. His attempts to quiet the disgruntled crowd was to no avail. The more he tried, the more they laughed.

Tula looked over at the bartender whom she thought would ask the crowd to quiet down a bit, but he was nowhere to be seen. She stood up to have a look over the bar where she heard something, and there he was bent over with laughter. He was practically rolling hysterically on the floor.

William took Tula's hand and brought her back to sit down before she went into a fit of laughter herself, yet again. Guinevere was barely sitting on her chair since she was also in a fit of laughter. She pulled Tula by the hand. "I haven't laughed this much and this hard in so long. Thank you."

Tula sat back down, barely keeping herself together as well. "You're welcome. Anytime." She sipped her beer and, while laughing, she said: "We still have this matter to attend to, don't we".

That just made William and Guinevere laugh even more. William pulled them both to his side. "Let's send Arthur a beer." They all giggled, and William waved to the bartender who had finally come up for air. "A Guinness for our friend over there."

The bartender still couldn't speak. He nodded his head in acknowledgement. When the head of foam reached the top of the pint, he raised the glass with his hand and walked over to Arthur. He bent over and put the pint on the table. "Our condolences. From your friends over there." The bartender turned on his heels with a big smirk on this face and walked back to the bar.

Tula, William and Guinevere waited for Arthur to look their way. When he did so, in defiance, they raised their glasses and cheered. Arthur raised his glass and clearly showed them his middle finger on the side of the glass facing them.

"Well. That's just ungrateful." Guinevere laughed.

A little while later, the bartender announced the last call. Tula checked the time on her phone. "If all goes as planned, Anika should be on her way to the airport by now."

Guinevere leaned forward and rested her elbows on the table. "She's quite the investigator. I like her."

Tula nodded. "Me too. She's certainly a force to be reckoned with. I didn't know if she would make it this far. I didn't know if I would make it this far, but I'm glad she's on our side, whether she knows it or not."

William put his arm around Tula. "Me too."

They emptied their glasses and wished the bartender goodnight. When they walked outside and crossed the road to their bed and breakfast, they looked up at the Merry Dancers in the sky. They could see the unicorns dancing on the roof and waving down at them.

Tula held William and Guinevere by the arm. "What if Arthur takes one of us away in the night like he did with Colin?"

William brought her close with his arm. "That may happen. The unicorns will stay in the room with us tonight. The serpents are at the ready, as well in the River Avon. Rest assured that you can close your eyes and sleep tonight, Tula." He kissed her on the cheek.

"Thank you for reserving my room." Guinevere said. "My room is right next to yours, Tula. William will be on the other side."

Together, they walked through the main entrance and upstairs to their rooms.

"Goodnight." Tula said. She opened the door to her room. William and Guinevere waited outside until she closed the door and they heard the click of the lock on the door.

69

The overhead seatbelt sign dinged and the light came on. Anika buckled her seatbelt. Her phone was on silent. She felt it vibrate in her jacket pocket. While reading Tula's text message, *We will see you there. Be careful. Arthur is not to be trusted. He's very dangerous. We will see you at Stonehenge*, the flight attendant asked her to put her phone away. The plane was taking off. Anika put her phone away and put her head back. It was dark out as the plane was speeding along the runway. She looked out the window and wondered: ""We". Who is "we"?".

The day took every ounce of energy she had, and even what she had in reserve. Before the wheels even came up, she had closed her eyes and fallen asleep.

Friday, September 22nd. Heathrow Airport 4 a.m.

"Mrs. Patel." The flight attendant gently stroked Anita's shoulder with her hand. "We've landed."

Anika practically jumped out of her seat. "What?"

"We've landed."

"Oh. I'm sorry." Anika went to stand up and was jerked back by her buckled seatbelt. "Please excuse me." She unbuckled the seatbelt and got up from her seat. Almost everyone was off the plane. Her reflection in the window was not a sight to behold, she thought. She ran her fingers through her hair and straightened her clothes. When she reached for her bag in the overhead compartment, her phone dinged. Instead of reading it and make the flight attendant wait for her, she gathered her belongings and exited the airplane.

On her way to the car rental reception desk, two men intercepted her. She recognized them from when she had spent a few days with Arthur in London. They were always around here and there, but never with them. One of the men stepped in front of her, and the other stood beside her. They made certain that she could see their guns in the holster underneath their jackets. She knew they would never use it as force, especially in an airport. Intimidation was the result they were after, and unfortunately for them, it was not her reaction.

In a clear and demanding tone, the man in front of her asked her to follow him. Anika was not in the mood for Arthur's goons. She had her own plan, and she was determined to see it play out just as she saw it in her mind.

The villagers of Cambria may not have been forthcoming in the secret they kept so close to their heart around the mysterious deaths and the ashes, but they also weren't unfriendly to her. They invited her in to listen very carefully to the stories they shared with each other over a feast of fish and beer. These stories which had been passed on from one generation to the next carried with them many of the accounts of what could be deemed as imaginary mythical people and events told to children and adults for entertainment. However, the stories from the past were all too familiar to the lives she was getting to know a little more with time. Her imagination was expanding beyond what she could have ever believed.

Anika remained polite and excused herself. She turned and walked towards the car rental reception desk. The man behind her grabbed her by the arm with a firm grip. "Anika. Please come with us. This is not a request. Let's do this quietly. Your car rental has been cancelled."

Anika never did tolerate being manhandled by anyone, and he was no exception, even if he were MI6. She tried to pull her arm away without making a scene. They had the upper hand and she knew it, but didn't want them to know she knew she was out of luck. They were not letting her go anywhere.

She looked straight up at the man. "I will come with you if you remove your hand."

The man released her. He carried her handbag and luggage, and signalled with his hand to follow the other man.

"Never put your hands on me again. I won't be so kind next time." She followed the man ahead of her. The other man stayed close to her side.

With achieving her eighth degree Dan black belt in taekwondo, she knew she could defend herself easily with these two, but this was not the moment, and she wanted to know what Arthur was up to.

When the airport doors opened automatically, a black car was waiting for them in front. It was not an official parking spot for arrivals, but the authorities controlling the comings and goings of the vehicles did not look at or approach the black car. They all respected the invisible boundary around it.

A man stood next to the car and held the door open. He signalled with his hand to Anika to sit in the back seat. When she sat, she leaned forward and asked for her shoulder bag. She had put her phone in the bag when she didn't read her text while leaving the airplane. The man ignored her and shut the door. Before she could open the door, the car door locked immediately. She couldn't unlock it. The man walked around the front of the car and sat in the driver's seat. He ignored her request to unlock the door. The man holding her bag put the bag and her luggage in the trunk of the car, and then he opened the other back seat door and sat next to her. The other man sat in the front seat.

Despite her many questions, the men remained quiet. The man sitting next to her handed her a bag. The smell of a salmon sandwich and coffee rushed up her nose when she opened the bag. She didn't want her facial expression to show that it smelled delicious.

"Thank you. Am I allowed to eat it now or is there some instruction you want me to follow before I dig into this?" She wanted a rise out of them, but she knew they wouldn't give her one. They just ignored her. She ate the sandwich and drank the coffee before they were even out of the airport boundaries.

She wasn't accustomed to being controlled by an authoritarian figure like Arthur and his goons, and to show her defiance, when she was done eating, she threw her trash on the car floor. She knew it was childish, but she did it anyway.

70

Friday, September 22nd.

Tula tossed and turned all night, replaying her visions over and over in her mind. At one point she heard Fiona's little voice calling to her to remind her: "What you saw in your vision is how you must proceed to free the seven jars with the ashes. It must be done on September 23rd at 7:49 a.m., not before nor after."

With her head on her pillow, she looked at the dawn of a new day shining through her window. She jumped out of bed and ran to the door, opened it and stepped into the hallway. On one side, she knocked on William's door, and on the other, she knocked on Guinevere's door. She waited in the hallway in anticipation. The two doors opened at the same time. William greeted her good morning, and Guinevere invited them into her room. "I have already ordered breakfast for all three of us."

While they were eating, a piece of paper was slipped under the door. William got up and took the paper from the floor. "It's from the front desk. It's a notification that, due to maintenance on the road and the grounds around Stonehenge, all tours have been cancelled for today and tomorrow. They will reopen on Sunday, September 24th."

"You have to give it to him. Arthur is clever and has the power to do anything." Tula sipped her hot chocolate.

"And I bet the workers will all be Druids." Guinevere bit into her toast. "That's how he's surrounding the stones with his army."

"We haven't underestimated him yet, and we can't in the slightest going forward." William put the paper in the trash bin.

Tula walked over to the window and looked outside. The village was just waking up. "I can see the convent from here. It's just over there. That's where Arthur has taken refuge. The coward. The Druids have taken it over again. I'll have to go in and get the ashes." She looked at William and Guinevere. "There's no other way. I'm the only one who can go in."

They knew that's what her vision had shown her. It was also futile to talk her out of it, and there seemed to be no other option in front of them.

William sat back down and drank his coffee. "Arthur will not leave the safety of the convent. He fears an attack from the Anam Duines. Since yesterday, we are many in Amesbury and surrounding area. We have surpassed the number of Druids in Amesbury and the surrounding area."

"The mass of the Anam Duines crept in quietly while we were in the pub." Guinevere said. "He knows that if he leaves the convent, there will be a full-on attack, and he will lose the ashes. That was not possible yesterday. The Druids were positioned throughout the region in search of Anam Duines. There were small battles here and there between them and the Anam Duines, until the Druid armies were dismantled and captured and handed over to the serpents, and kept in the underwater chambers."

Tula sat down. "He will have to leave the convent eventually to make his way to Stonehenge in time for the autumn equinox. He will do so even when I get the ashes from him. He will do everything in his power to stop us from rescuing the other seven jars with the ashes."

Guinevere poured her another cup of hot chocolate. "Let's go over the convent layout." She reached for her bag and pulled out a folder. They cleared the table and unfolded the sketch of Amesbury and the convent. Guinevere pointed. "Here. This is where you will enter." Her finger followed along a line. "These are corridors." She followed the lines. "This is where you need to go. This is the room where you'll find Arthur."

"How do you know that's where I'll find him?" Tula pointed on the sketch with her finger.

"It's the most secure room in the convent. It's where I've stayed. It's where we've all stayed. It's very difficult to get to this room, and very difficult to access. There are secure passages throughout the route. I will walk you through each one."

Tula turned the sketch to face her. She looked closely at the layout and pointed. "This is the bed and breakfast." She looked out the window. "This line, the corridor, is it underground?"

"Yes. The thicker lines are the underground corridors, and the thinner ones are the above-ground corridors."

"So I'm going underground to get to the convent?"

"Yes. Arthur and the other Druids don't know about the tunnel that goes from here to the convent. It's always been a well-kept secret. It's how I got out. It's how the others like me got out as well. We only used it because we were only a few throughout history to ever have had a need for it. Otherwise, if it was used by the nuns to escape, there would have been too many, too often, and that would have increased the risk of breaking the secret location of this secret passage. The nuns made this decision, and that decision was obeyed. You will be the first one to use the tunnel since I've escaped."

"I see. Where is the entrance to the tunnel?"

"In the kitchen. The big brown wooden door opens into a pantry. From there, behind the cabinet and against the right wall when you walk in, there's a lever at the bottom. Press down with your foot. That lever will unlock another lock. However, that lock is not in the pantry. You will have to leave the pantry, shut the door and walk back out and into the kitchen, to the outside. Next to the house is the large oak tree."

Guinevere got up from her chair. "Come here." Tula and William followed. "See, that tree? That's the one. When you get to that tree, just there below, is a stone in the ground that looks like it's been there forever. The lever that you pressed in the pantry will unlock this stone. Press your foot down on the stone, and that too will unlock another lock. However, this one is just over there." She pointed ahead at the shed. "In the shed, there's a trap door that takes you down to the root cellar. The trap door is hard to find. You have to feel for it with your bare foot. The wood feels a little different from the rest. The spot is in the far right corner of the shed." She looked over at Tula. "I know it's long and convoluted, but it's the only way. Let's sit down."

Guinevere pointed at the underground tunnel. "Here, the trap door will open. You will walk down the steps into a very old root cellar. There's a door on the far wall. Open it. This door opens into the tunnel that will take you all the way to the first tunnel in the convent. Right here." She followed the thick line from the root cellar to the tunnel in the convent with her finger. "It's a very quick walk. You'll be there in two minutes tops."

Tula stood up from her chair and looked out the window. "It seems it would take longer than two minutes."

"That's just how it seems. Walking outside from here to there will be longer than two minutes because you are walking to the front of the convent. The underground tunnel takes you to this side, the closest side to us, and the tunnel reaches out beneath the ground. The convent is like an iceberg. Most of it is beneath the ground, and that's another secret."

William buttered some toast and served them to Guinevere and Tula. "Eat up. Once we leave this room, we may not be eating until tomorrow."

"May I have a slice of cheese please?" Tula held her toast out in her hand. William cut the cheese and put it on her toast. "Thank you, and from here, where do I go?"

"You will follow these three tunnels underground." Guinevere traced the way with her finger. "These will be less difficult, but keep an eye out for traps. The tunnels were built with flooding in mind, should it ever be necessary to do so. They are linked to the River of Avon and to the other rivers in the area. They generally run under a foot all year long, but that's also deceiving underground. At each intersection from one tunnel to the other, you will cross a small bridge. Don't step on the light blue stone. The colour is very faint blue. Step on that one, and the flooding begins. The stone is hard to reach as a precaution of course, just so we don't accidently step on it. However, it can still happen depending if one is being chased or not, but you will be alone, the light is dim, and you will be nervous. The pressure of your foot on the bridge will activate the blue stone, but it is only triggered to release when you put your full weight on it and press down until it lowers into the water below the bridge."

Tula followed the tunnels with her fingers and crossed all three bridges. "This is easy enough, with my finger." She laughed. "Where do I arrive above ground?"

"Right here, after the third tunnel. This is the most dangerous part."

Tula felt a flash of light rush through her head. She dropped her toast in her hand on the floor and fell back in her chair.

71

Tula scanned the entrance before stepping into the convent refectory. The dining hall chandeliers dangled across the tall ceilings. It was silent. When she stepped out of the tunnel and on to the hall floor, the sliding door shut closed behind her and was flush with the wall. The wooden wall panels appeared as though there was never a door.

There were three entrances to the dining hall. The largest and main entrance was to her left, the second largest was to her right, and the smallest narrow entrance was directly in front of her. Every five minutes, the Druids' changing of the guards came through all three entrances. She therefore needed to get across the hall and through the smallest entrance, and pass the guard without getting caught. To make sure no one was getting in or out of the convent without being seen, Arthur had posted guards at every door entrance, in every corridor and at all intersections between every single nook of the convent. It was impossible to go anywhere unnoticed.

Tula didn't know if they were at the beginning, in between or the nearing the end of the 5 minutes. The guards were nowhere to be seen, and when the Druids first took over the convent, they increased their chances of catching intruders by setting a trap in the dining hall, the biggest room in the convent and with three points of access. Everywhere had one or two traps, unless you climbed in from a window or jumped out from a window.

Tula stepped gingerly, searching for the rigged stone floor. Some of the stones were wired to set off a quiet alarm that alerted the guards of an intruder in the hall outside of meal-time. Since she couldn't very well do this mission when everyone was in the dining hall eating, this was the only time she could chance it.

Each stone was 4 feet by 4 feet. They were rough to the touch and grainy around the edges, but the stones were not all the same. The distinction between the rigged stones and the others was the small hairline fracture along the lower southeast corner of the stone. This is where the damage was done to install the wiring.

With each step between the rows of tables and benches, Tula searched for the hairline fracture before taking the next, while at the same time counting up to 30 seconds to reach the other side and hide, before the guards appeared. It was like watching the fast and slow motion images all at once.

She glided her feet across the stones like a pro. Then, she heard a click. Her feet froze where she stood and her arms reached for the table closest to the entrance. With all her might she jumped up onto the table. Furthermore, from a standing position on top of the table, she flung herself through the narrow entrance. When she hit the floor, she slid along the floor and pushed the panel on the wall closest to the floor. It opened just wide enough for her to slide through and disappear from view. Just as the panel shut behind her, she heard the guards' footsteps.

The dim yellow light above her head indicated that she had safely reached the above-ground web of corridors hidden in the convent's walls. Tula followed the row of yellow lights along the ceiling. The corridor followed every room in the convent. There was a hidden panel to access each room. She looked up along the wall. Every two steps, weirdly shaped apparatuses were installed about a foot over her head. This allowed her to hear everything being said from the other side of the wall. However, those on the other side of the wall could not hear anyone talking nor moving in the hidden corridors.

When she reached the junction to either go left or right and up, she went right and up, leading her to the top floor and to Arthur's room. The tricky part was when she got to the secret panel to Arthur's room, and to open it and enter his room without him seeing her come through the secret panel, and thereby revealing the hidden corridor between the walls.

Just as she was taking the last turn to the corridor leading to Arthur's room, she put her hand in her pant pocket and removed a small vial that William and Guinevere prepared for her. The vial contained a mixture of nightshade, thought to have been used by Juliet in the final act of Romeo and Juliet, but with an added ingredient, unicorn dung. This was not meant to kill Arthur. It was mixed just right to place him into a catatonic state and immobilize him long enough for Tula to take the ashes and escape the same way she had entered the convent.

When she reached Arthur's room, she listened for his voice and any other voice in the room. After a few seconds, with her ear close to the apparatus, she knew with certainty that Arthur was alone. In her other pocket, she removed another vial. In this vial was the antidote made with unicorn tears and spit. It would prevent her from falling unconscious when she opened the other vial to knock Arthur out. Tula inhaled the antidote before opening the other vial. After a minute, she opened the other vial and placed the opening of the vial in the hearing apparatus on the wall. The fumes from the vial drifted across the wall and into Arthur's room. A few seconds later, Tula heard a thump like a body falling to the floor. She pulled the vial out from the apparatus and kept it opened in her hand. With her foot, she pushed against the panel in the wall. With her hand, she gave it a gentle nudge until it opened all the way, just wide enough for her to squeeze through.

When she stepped into the room, she saw Arthur face down on the floor. The bag he carried across his shoulder was on the bed. She stepped over his body and took the bag. The bag felt light. She opened the bag and found nothing in it. Then, she remembered how brilliant Arthur was. Of course he wouldn't leave the ashes in the bag in his room. He would hide them in the most obvious of places.

She bent over and put the vial on the floor next to Arthur's nose. He needed to be knocked out for as long as possible. She didn't want to take any chances. Then, she looked around the room. "Where would it be right under my nose?" Everything in the room appeared to be in its place. She looked again, up, down, and all around. Six urns with ashes were a substantial size to hide. That's where she found them, hidden behind the panel of the very wide bedroom doorframe.

The door entrances to the convent were deep and wide, and the frame around the doors was made of decorative wood with wooden tops, carved into flowers. She remembered seeing herself in the vision where she removed the wooden flowers by screwing them off. She also remembered seeing urns with ashes hidden in the frames. The larger outside frames were hollow and just big enough to hide the urns.

She took the vial from the floor and fanned it along the crack, at the base of the door. A second later, the guard standing outside the door fell to the ground, but she had to move quickly before the next changing of the guard. When she entered Arthur's room, she heard them greeting each other and moving along to another station, and replaced by others. She had five minutes. "Plenty of time before the next changing of the guards. "They will sound the alarm once they see the guard that has passed out in front Arthur's room. They will all come running." she thought.

As fast as she could, she ran around fanning the air in the room with the vial and under the door crack to keep it potent in the air. Then, she pulled the chair to the door and climbed up it. With both hands, she screwed off the wooden flower cap and reached into the frame. Right at the top, she felt an urn. She pulled it out. She searched for a second, and then pulled out another. All was going well until she came to the sixth urn. She was too short, and her arm wasn't long enough to reach any further. In a panic, she jumped off the chair and pulled the table to the door. The top of the table was clearly higher than the chair. When she climbed up onto the table, she heard Arthur move. She jumped down from the table and shoved the vial up his nose, and then climbed back up onto the table. When she put her arm into the frame, the tip of her fingers rubbed against the urn. She jiggled her fingers just enough to pull the urn out.

With all six urns, she jumped off the table. "I'll take this." She grabbed Arthur's shoulder bag and put the urns in the bag. When she bent down and pulled the vial from Arthur's nose, there was a loud and powerful bang against the bedroom door.

Panic set in. Tula needed to get out of the room before they broke open the door and Arthur woke up, but the secret latch to open the secret panel was not in an obvious spot, like on the wall, next to the panel, but above the window. She needed to drag the table across the room and place it in front of the window, climb on top of the table, and then press her finger against the painted flower on the wall just below the ceiling. Furthermore, as for the row of painted flowers, she had to pick the right one. It was the third from the left.

As she was about to climb up on top of the table in front of the window, the guards pushed the door open. Tula turned around and faced her attackers. One of the guards raised his sling and arrow, aimed it right at her and pulled. The arrow shot across the room and struck her in the right shoulder.

She screamed so loud that it brought Arthur back to his feet. When he realized what was happening, he grabbed Tula by the throat and pressed his hand down against the arrow.

Tula screamed and passed out.

"Wake up, Tula." William rubbed her cheek with his hand. "Sweetheart. Wake up. You're safe. You're here with Guinevere and me." He held her up in the chair. "Tula."

She opened her eyes. They were filled with tears. "I'm here."

"Yes. You're here with us." Guinevere said. She wiped her face with a cold cloth.

"That feels good." Tula said.

"Here, drink some water." She placed a glass of water against Tula's lips. "That's enough for now. Let's lay her down."

William carried Tula to bed. "Tula. Look at me. You are safe."

Tula looked up at William and Guinevere. "That's what we saw at the cliff at Castle of Old Wick, and up to when the guards broke down the door. Except the ending when Arthur put his hands around my neck and pushed against the arrow in my shoulder." She rubbed her shoulder as though it were there. The pain was all too real. It was something she would never forget.

"Your visions are powerful. They showed you the entire structure of the convent and the hidden corridors. You don't need this map to find your way. You know it already." Guinevere smiled.

William walked to the door. I'll get her things from her room. Let her rest for a few minutes. Then, she must shower and get changed. We will leave here in 30 minutes."

Tula turned her head on the pillow and smiled at William. "Thank you."

72

The men in the car did not speak with Anika until the man sitting next to her said: "Mrs. Patel, you have a call." He leaned forward and pressed the button on the console between them. The console unfolded into a screen. He removed Anika's cellphone from his jacket pocket. "Here's your phone, but you can't use it just now. Please wait." He handed her the phone.

"Thank you. Who is the call from?"

"Please." He pointed at the screen. "The call is coming in."

Anika watched the screen come to life. The face of a very old man appeared. "Mrs. Patel. Please excuse this rude and forceful way of getting you to us safely."

"Who are you, and what do you want from me?" Anika asked as she leaned forward.

"Mrs. Patel. My name is Steward Robertson, and the two men with you, the one next to you is Cole and the other is Martin, and the driver is Mat. We are MI6, and we are working with Tula Rose and William Ridel."

"Tula. Why? And who is William Ridel? I don't understand, and why did you say you are keeping me safe? Also, please stop calling me Mrs. Patel. Call me Anika please."

"Anika. For your safety, we've been following you for quite some time now."

Anika looked at the two men. "These are the men who were following me and Arthur when I was in London."

"That's correct. They were there for your protection."

"Protection from what?"

"We've been following your case of Charlotte Bourbon. As you've been told, Arthur is a very dangerous man. He can't be trusted. We squashed

249

his plan to get you out of the picture. He was going to kill you this morning when you arrived. We intercepted his men and took you out of harm's way before Arthur could strike."

Anika was shocked. "Why would Arthur want to kill me?"

"Arthur is a very unreasonable man these days. He's on a mission that may be difficult for you to understand and believe. He will stop at nothing to get what he's after and why he's doing this. You have served your purpose for him and he doesn't want you investigating this any longer. He wants you out of the picture for good."

"What is it that I won't understand and believe?"

"Before I tell you, please be assured that we are taking you to Tula. She's in Amesbury. We will get you there safely. However, Arthur and his men are there as well."

"What's going on? Can you please tell me sir what it is that I'm up against, and what's with all the mystery around this?"

Stewart narrated the entire tale as though reading a bedtime story to a child. He related the accounts of Orkney Island, the Anam Duines, the triquetra and the Tree of Life birthmark, the unicorns, the serpents, the Kelpie and the Druids, all that's happened since Charlotte's death, with Colin and Fiona, the six jars with the ashes at Stonehenge, the autumn equinox, Guinevere and the truth around the entire King Arthur tale, and Tula's visions up until this very moment. He left no stone unturned.

Now she knew the name of the man in the sketch. Shakespeare. William Ridel. Anika listened quietly. She was attentive to everything being told to her. Of course, there were many moments where she wanted to burst out with laughter and tell this old man to stop feeding her such nonsense, but she refrained and allowed the old man to tell his story.

When he was done, Anika burst out laughing. She couldn't hold it back any longer. "I've never heard such b.s. in my life. Really. You expect me to believe all of this?"

"You will see when you get there. This is the truth, Anika, and you must be very careful when you're face to face with Arthur."

"Sir, we will be there in 3 minutes." Cole said.

"Very well. Anika, I can't stress enough that you must remain extremely vigilant. Today may be the day you die, and he needs William to accomplish his mission; so there are many lives at stake here." The screen went dark.

Anika sat there, feeling as though she had been kicked in the gut. This was all too strange and weird for her. "I'm a bright, educated, and a sound-minded woman." She thought to herself. "This can't be real, and this is certainly not the day I'm going to die...and not at the hands of these nut bags."

"Here we are." Cole said.

"Where is "here"?" Anika asked as she looked out the window. She looked up at the front of the Amesbury bed and breakfast, and when Bruce opened the car door to let her out, Tula, William, and Guinevere walked out of the lodge.

73

Tula was the first one to greet Anika with a hug. "I'm glad you're safe." Anika returned the hug. "Me too. How are you, Tula?"

Tula turned to William and Guinevere. "Please, let me introduce you."

William put out his hand. "It's finally a pleasure to meet you in person, Anika. Tula has told me a lot about you."

Anika shook his hand and she turned to Guinevere. "And we meet again!"

Guinevere stepped towards her and put out her hand. "Yes. It's good to see you again."

Anika wondered. "Who are these people?"

Cole stepped forward with her handbag and luggage. "Anika, I'll bring your bags to your room."

"My hand bag please, and thank you." She took her bag from Cole and draped the strap across her chest.

"Please let's sit in the garden. I'm sure you have lots of questions for us." Tula replied. She walked towards the stone table and bench.

William gestured with his hand that Anika could go ahead. William and Guinevere followed behind.

Anika sat across from all three. At first, she stared at them wondering what nonsense they were going to try and get her to believe, and she wanted to know what her role in all of this was.

Tula smiled at Anika. "First, let me say that I'm sorry that I didn't reply to your message, and I didn't tell you about any of this. I was also none the wiser about any of this until I came to Orkney Island to try to understand Charlotte's death. This is what I learned and how I learned it." She removed her little book from her back pant pocket and placed it on the table. She told her the entire story as she had experienced it.

Anika remained quiet. She didn't want to miss a beat of what was a lie and what was the truth. She was very good at reading people, but up until now, she hadn't seen anything that was said or done in order to deceive her.

When Tula finished narrating the events that led them both here, Anika asked: "And this is all happening today in that convent over there?" She looked in the direction of the convent.

"That's correct. We must get the ashes away from Arthur, just as I described."

Anika looked around at the garden as though she were looking for something. "And what about the unicorns?" She looked up at the sky. "I'm told that they are real and that they fly as well." She smirked. This was the moment of truth, she thought. If they could produce these unicorns just as it was told to her, she would believe the rest of this weird story that no one would ever believe.

"Here they come." Tula said. She pointed behind Anika.

Anika turned around, and right before her very eyes stood four unicorns. One by one, they approached her and introduced themselves.

"I'm Ròs."

"I'm Gorm."

"I'm Lilac."

"I'm Viri."

Viri was the only one she recognized from Guinevere's farm. He was the one who smiled at her, but he also looked different than he did before. His bright green eyes smiled at her, and he had a long twirled horn sticking out of his head. One by one, they fanned their wings and took flight over their heads.

Anika's mouth was wide open. She couldn't believe her eyes. When she turned her attention back to the three sitting across from her, she said. "Well! I suppose we better get to work then! I'm told that this is a matter of urgency. I will want to talk more about all of this after we do what we have to do in order to stop Arthur from doing what he needs to do." She stood up. "Let's go. The clock is ticking. Where's the kitchen?"

"Yes. Of course." Tula jumped up from her seat, and the others did the same. They were witnessing the legendary Chief Investigator Anika Patel in action. They were just as amazed with her as she was amazed to learn that all of this was real.

74

In the kitchen, William put his hand on Tula's shoulder. "This is where we split up. You and Anika go to the shed. I will press all the levers, and when you get there, you can open the last door to get down into the root cellar. In the meantime, Guinevere will make her way to the far end of the convent grounds, where she will be waiting for you."

Tula looked at Guinevere. "Wait! We are not coming back out the same way we're going in, and you two will be separating. That's too dangerous for William."

"I know the grounds very well, and this will be the safest and fastest way to get you out, Tula. You already know your way. You saw it in a vision. You will take the other corridor that is hidden in the walls, starting at Arthur's room. It's behind the bed. You have seen this before, and you have done this in your vision. It will all come back to you before you even get there. Now, when you take that corridor, stick to all the right turns, until you reach the junction with three options, left, straight ahead, or right. Go straight ahead, all the way to the end, where you will come to a staircase that will take you to the far end of the grounds. At the top of the steps, look up. There's a small latch made of stone that you push and turn anti-clockwise. This will open the hatch door that opens out onto the edge of the forest. Dirt and other debris from the forest floor will sprinkle down on you. So, keep your eyes closed until it stops. I'll be there. When you get out, you will close the hatch and it will vanish into the forest floor. It will no longer be visible to the naked eye."

Anika listened intently, and her eyes were big and wide. She couldn't believe what she was hearing. "We got this Tula." She patted her on the back as though she had done this a million times.

Tula giggled. "Well, it's now or never, and just so you know, Anika, I get shot with an arrow flung from a slingshot in Arthur's room…and it hurts like hell!"

"What? What are you talking about?" Anika asked.

"I'll tell you on the way." She checked her pockets. "I have the vials."

"Excellent." William said. "I will make my way to Stonehenge. I must see what they are doing there in preparation of receiving the ashes in the jars. They are up to something, and I must find out what that is before we all gather there."

"That's way too dangerous, William." Tula put her arm around his arm. "It's you they're after and they…"

"I know, but it's the only way right now. We have to stay ahead of them and that's what we're doing." William put his arm around Tula and kissed her on the cheek. "I'll see all three of you at the stones."

"Wait!" Anika said. "How do we know what each other is doing? We don't have radios or anything to stay in communication with one another."

All three smiled at her.

"What? What am I missing?" Anika smiled back at them.

"I'll tell you on the way as well." Tula said. "Time to go!" She walked to the back door. "Follow me, Anika."

Tula completed the same walk through the underground and above ground corridors, all the way to Arthur's room, just as she had done in her vision. Anika couldn't believe how well they had executed this part of the mission without getting caught when the alarm went off in the dining hall.

Even when Tula knew where she shouldn't step, she stepped on another stone that was rigged to set off the alarm. This time, from what Tula had told her, the guards were more aggressive in their search for them.

In the vision, she only saw herself. She didn't see Anika with her. Now, there were two of them to hunt down, and the guards were ferocious in their search. Tula and Anika could hear everything from the hearing apparatuses on the wall.

Anika felt that she was in one of the mythical and fantasy stories that she had read to her children. Tula assured her that it was all too real, and to keep her wits about her. Even though they were in these hidden corridors, it didn't guarantee their safety. Anything was possible at any time. Her visions were a source from which she prepared and planned, with imagination and wisdom, but there were also many unpredictable moments and events that couldn't be foretold. This was the trickiest and most dangerous part of all this.

In the corridor behind Arthur's room, Tula said: "Guinevere is in position. Arthur is at the stones."

Anika was just about to ask her how she knew this, but she refrained from asking the question. Mind-to-mind communication was new to her. In this situation, she was an observer and had to trust Tula. However, she did want to ask her a question. She put her hand on Tula's shoulder.

Tula turned to her and, before she asked her question, replied: "You are here to protect me. Possibly save my life, Anika. Before you ask your next question, yes, at certain moments, when it is critical for me to do so, I can read your thoughts."

Anika removed her hand and smiled. "I hope it doesn't come to that."

"You didn't just happen to get caught up in all of this, Anika. Had you decided to sign off on Charlotte's file and leave it as a cold case, never to be solved, your life would have continued just as it did, but that is not you. Your persistence to solve the case and be a voice for the victims, even if you couldn't prove that Charlotte's death wasn't criminal, you persevered, and you are here today. The moment you delved deeper into Charlotte's case, you set the wheels in motion. The higher power that be in the Anam Duines' world, with their unicorns and serpents, found a purpose for you, and that was to keep me safe to the best of your abilities because I, or we, rather, may well all die today."

"I suppose that we all have to do what we have to do." Anika put her ear up to the apparatus. "It's quiet."

"Wait. He's in there. We just need to make sure if he's alone or if someone else is in the room with him." Tula leaned against the wall. Her casual and calm disposition was the opposite of what Anika was feeling and showing.

"Breathe Anika. It's all about to happen." She removed the antidote vial from her pant pocket and pulled off the lid. "Breathe in slowly and deeply."

Tula opened the other vial and placed it up close into the apparatus. They heard two thumps.

When they stepped into the room, they couldn't believe their eyes. William had passed out on the floor, right next to Arthur.

75

Tula shoved the antidote vial up one of William's nostrils. He woke up instantly. There was no time to ask him why he was in Arthur's room. Tula fanned the vial under the door crack. When they heard the thump, William dragged the table in front of the door, jumped up on the table, unscrewed the wood flower, and pulled out all six urns with the ashes.

Everything was happening all so fast. Anika followed every instruction thrown at her as though she was under a spell. She didn't think; she only acted. By the time William was about to pull the bed away from the wall, and Tula was up on the table in front of the window to press down this time on the fourth flower from the right, the guards knocked down the bedroom door.

It was critical for the guards and Arthur to never discover the secret corridors. So, William stepped away from the bed. It was just as Tula had seen in her vision. The arrow flung across the room and hit her in the shoulder. Arthur was up on his feet and charged towards Tula, but before he could reach her, Anika's taekwondo skills were on full display. Arthur was back on the floor with her foot pressing down on his neck.

Tula was moaning in agony. The guard raised the sling and arrow, and aimed it at Anika. Because of the distance between her and the guard who was pointing his arrow at her, she was defenseless without her gun. Her choices were to release Arthur and charge at the guard who was ready to kill her with an arrow, or to figure something else out without getting killed. However, if he missed her, Tula was in his line of sight as well, and he would for sure hit her in the heart this time.

All the while, William was communicating every moment-by-moment event directly to Guinevere. The danger had escalated too much to stick with their original plan. Before William could show her what was happening, she ran to the convent and stood outside of Arthur's room window. With one Anam Duine in the convent and another just outside its door, she could feel the Kelpie getting stronger and stronger. The guards were more enraged. When they saw Guinevere outside by Arthur's room, they raised their sling and arrows and aimed.

She called out loud in her mind: "William, throw me the bag with the ashes. William removed the bag that was hanging across his chest and flung it hard enough to smash through the window. At that very moment, the guard released the arrow from the sling.

From where she stood, Anika saw how her and Tula could escape the arrow that was heading straight for them. She crouched down to the ground with her foot still on Arthur's neck, and William ran to Tula and pushed her to the ground, just as the bag flew in front of them and was struck by the arrow. The power of the arrow was so strong that it helped to propel the bag through the window with great force.

Guinevere ran for the bag with her arms in the air. The bag landed on the ground in front of her. When she bent down to pick it up, she could feel the arrows brush against her back.

When she got back up on her feet, she saw the nuns looking through the window of the abbess' office. They were pointing up. She looked up and there, in the sky, were the unicorns flying over the Kelpie's powerful invisible shield that blocked them from getting any closer. She then saw a group of other nuns marching from around the corner of the building and armed with slings and arrows. Behind them were more Anam Duines, ready to take on the Druid guards who had held the nuns captive for so many centuries. The nuns told Guinevere to run away with the ashes. This was their fight.

Guinevere could hear the sounds of arrows being shot through the air, as well as the moans and groans of the guards when they were struck. Midway through this battle, she turned around to see who was still standing. Under any circumstances would the nuns and the Anam Duines be capable of aiming and killing any of the guards. They struck them only in a way that they could completely immobilize them.

The same was happening in Arthur's room. Anika had enough of Arthur's wiggling around, trying to escape her grip, that she knocked him out. Now that she was free to leave him on the ground, she and William fought the guards for as long as they could. She even managed to get a sling and some arrows into William's hands so that he could very quickly immobilize any guard that came through the door. However, eventually, he ran out of arrows, and there were more guards than the two of them could fight, whilst remaining alive.

Tula was still on the floor with an arrow in her shoulder. The pain was so bad that she would fall in and out of consciousness. Then, when she opened her eyes, she saw Ròs stick her head through the window.

William and Anika turned towards her and dropped to the ground. The guards didn't know why they had dropped to the ground, and they couldn't see what they were looking at. William looked up at the guards and said: "Prepare yourselves for the fight of your life".

The unicorns and the serpents came in from the window at the speed of light and showed themselves to the guards. The guards fought until they could fight no longer. One by one, the serpents carried them to the underwater chambers.

When Arthur came about, he found himself alone in the room with William, Anika, and two nuns tending to Tula's wound.

76

Arthur ran to the window. All he saw was the Druid army being dismantled and taken away by the serpents. He knew that he was now on his own. The failed mission was not only a personal failure, but also a failure for all Druids. They were doomed to live forever without their magic, and they would soon all die.

The nuns gathered outside and looked up. They raised their slings and arrows at Arthur. They were victorious and regained control of their convent after centuries of oppression by the Druids who were under the influence of the Kelpie. Their will to defend themselves against all the odds that they believed in front of them, and the nuns' courage to stand together and preserve the sanctity of their convent as a haven and a home for the Anam Duines and anyone else who needed them, emanated such an energy field around them that it destroyed the Kelpie's energy field that blocked the unicorns and the serpents from entering the convent.

Tula joined Arthur at the window and put her hand on his shoulder. "This is not the end, Arthur. We need you to help free the seven Anam Duines in the jars at Stonehenge. You are the only one who can do this."

When Tula lay on the ground in agony with an arrow through her shoulder, the vision revealed more details. This is where she saw that all the while, it was Arthur who had been chosen to free the seven jars with the ashes, but with their help. Before Arthur could even approach the seven jars with the ashes, he would have to return to being himself, as the Druid he truly was, with all of his magic.

All of the other Druids who found themselves in the underwater chambers were shown the truth of who they really were, and how the lies of the Kelpie had led them away from their true selves. However, in order for the serpent to release the Druids from the underwater chambers and help Arthur, they would have to believe with all their heart that they had been led to deceive themselves, and have a true and pure knowledge of themselves, that they were Druids with all the magic that was gifted to a Druid. This is the same journey where Arthur had been left to discover and come to terms with before the autumn equinox, but without going to the underwater chambers. He was the chosen one and, for that reason, the serpents could not bring him to the underwater chambers due to the power of his defiance and strong belief in the Kelpie. Arthur's belief in the Kelpie curse on the Druid was so powerful that his energy would poison the Druids' recovery back to their true selves.

While Tula and Anika were making their way through the corridors to Arthur's room, William walked up to the convent's front door and announced his presence to Arthur. The guards led him to Arthur's room. It was there that William told Arthur what he needed to do in order to save himself and all the Druids, while freeing the seven Anam Duines. Consequently, the fate of the Druids, of the Anam Duines, and of human imagination were all in Arthur's hands.

With all the excitement, the day had escaped them. Night was upon them. It was time for dinner at the convent. The bell ringing from up high in the convent steeple announced that it was time for dinner. The ring echoed throughout the abbey.

The two nuns in the room invited Arthur as their guest of honour. He was free to choose to stay or go. Arthur quietly contemplated everything that was said to him about being the chosen one and his strong belief in the Kelpie's curse. Everything he believed, as well as his choices in life, flashed before his eyes. A strong sense of doubt washed over him. He didn't know what to believe anymore. As much as he wanted to hang on to the salvation of all Druids, as well as to what that would mean for the Anam Duines, and the human imagination without any hesitation, it was impossible for him to do so. At the same time, the guilt of the misgivings he had inflicted upon other Druids filled his heart.

The nun opened the bedroom door and put her hand out for him to take. Fear washed over him when he took her hand. She led him to the dining hall, and the others followed behind.

Anika wanted to arrest Arthur for everything he had done, but what would the report read? She did find it humorous. Tula and William smiled at her. Their sentiment was also leaning towards giving Arthur a good thrashing for the trouble he had caused them and to so many, but that was just their edgy side of revenge which they had tucked away in the corner of themselves, and it was never to be set free, of course. Giving Arthur an imaginary thrashing was good enough. The nuns turned to them and smiled as well.

In the dining hall, the nuns stood around the tables, waiting for their guest of honour. When the nun walked in with Arthur, hand-in-hand, they greeted him by saying his name and raising a glass of wine.

Shame washed over Arthur. He could not understand why they were so kind to him and honouring him after everything he had done that was so wrong.

"It smells delicious, doesn't it Arthur?" Tula commented.

He averted her eyes in shame. The nun walked him to the table where Guinevere was sitting. They had set a special place for him. The table was decorated with flowers from their garden, and with an array of dishes for him to choose from.

Arthur sat quietly at the table and, when he couldn't decide what to select, Tula served him a plate. He watched everyone around the table, eating. They were talking and laughing as though they were oblivious to the villain sitting at the table with them.

The passage of time from when all of this evil was set in place, from one generation to the next, up until this very moment flashed before his eyes. He was sitting by himself, alone with his thoughts and his memories, digesting every bit of self-doubt he had swallowed over and over again.

When he took the fork in his hand and put the food that the nuns had prepared for him with such love in his mouth, a thunderous boom and flash pounded the convent's walls. The Kelpie was in full view to claim its most valued Druid. A huge grey foggy hand smashed through the window and wrapped itself around Arthur.

All the nuns rushed around Arthur. They gathered in a circle and held hands. Tula, William, Guinevere, and Anika all joined in. In Scottish Gaelic, they sang the story with its distinct melodies and tempo, about the Druids' spiritual truth that was found in nature, as well as all things that were interconnected. The rhythmic sound of their voices resounded through the convent and the convent grounds.

Arthur began to feel his blood pressure lowering and calmness taking over. While in the Kelpie's grip, he let his body sway in a pleasant and gentle swinging rhythm, rising and falling with the tune of the singing voices.

The more they sang, the more Arthur's mind and body went into deep relaxation, relieved from the anxiety that the Kelpie had squeezed around his body, and he found the seat of his peace in his mind, body, and soul. He imagined a different world for himself, for all Druids, for the Anam Duines, and for all human beings, knowing with all their heart that they have the gift of imagination, and that this gift is what will serve them best in the matrix of their lives. Furthermore, with a sudden burst of energy, Arthur stood from his chair and stared at the Kelpie right in the eyes. "No more!" He removed the grey foggy fingers from around his body and freed himself from the foul grip to which he had clung his entire life.

The Merry Dancers glowed brightly in the sky, and reached down into the convent and wrapped their colourful veils around the grey fog, and carried it away. Arthur looked around at the humans' and the Anam Duines' circle. He put his hands together in the prayer position and thanked them all.

Tula looked out the window. The dawn of a new day was about to reveal itself. She hadn't realized that the singing circle had taken all night to free Arthur. They were moments away from the autumn equinox.

77

The instant Arthur freed himself from the Kelpie, the serpents released the Druids from the underwater chambers. The serpents gathered from every corner of the world and carried the Druids to Stonehenge.

The Merry Dancers delivered a few more unicorns to carry all of the nuns to Stonehenge. Tula, William, and Guinevere were met by their unicorns. Guinevere put her hand out to Anika. "You're coming with me!" Anika jumped up on the unicorn and laughed out loud. "This is something I'll never be able to tell anyone."

Tula put her hand out to Arthur. "And you're with me!"

Ròs led the way, and they were off. A second later, they descended upon Stonehenge, amongst the Druids and the serpents. The Merry Dancers moved rhythmically in the sky, and all the way down and around the stones. The colourful veils swayed graciously around everyone.

Tula walked hand in hand with Arthur to the centre of the stones. William, Guinevere and Anika stood behind them.

The stone over the seven jars with the ashes glowed bright and hot. It was too hot to touch. Tula and Arthur kneeled next to the stone, and gently waved their hand over it. Everyone around them held hands and began singing. With every note, the stone's glow got dimmer and dimmer, and with every musical note, they could feel the Earth's North Pole begin to tilt away from the sun, and the South Pole also began to tilt towards the sun. When the sun began to peep over the horizon, Tula and Arthur lowered their hands onto the stone. Together, they lifted the stone and placed it aside. There, in a hole a foot deep in the ground, were the seven jars of ashes, glowing bright orange.

Arthur reached in with his hand and removed the jars, one by one.

Each time he removed one, he'd say *"I'm sorry"*, and placed it on the ground in front of him. When all seven jars were lined up, the veils of the Merry Dancers carried them up into the sky. With them, in the glow of the orange light, appeared Charlotte, Colin, and Fiona, and all the other Anam Duines who had been rescued and had returned home to the Tree of Life. The Druids at Stonehenge and all of the other Druids throughout the world opened their mouths and released a big exhale. A bright orange light shot down into their mouths. Their magic was restored. Tree leaves shuddered all around, and Mother Nature's water flowed through their veins once again.

Later that day, Guinevere invited Anika to take her back home by unicorn. Anika accepted without any hesitation.

"Anika, I will see you in Nort sometime." Tula said. She gave her a big hug. "Thank you for all your help. We could not have done this without you, and now that you are one of us, you will be called upon from time to time, when needed, should you accept the challenge when called upon."

"You're welcome, and of course, I will help whenever I am called upon. I'll see you when you get back." Anika mounted Viri. Guinevere and Anika waved goodbye and vanished into the sky.

Back at the Amesbury pub, Stewart waited for Tula, William, and Arthur. When his pint of beer was half full, Stewart announced his retirement as head of the secret MI6 agency, and that he was passing the torch on to Arthur. There was no else he could think of to entrust this duty to but to Arthur Moore. William removed a unicorn silvery-white ring made of spiralling bone from his pocket.

"Arthur, you found your way to yourself and back to us. It is this strength that we seek in a Druid, just as we did with a human." He smiled at Tula. "Arthur, it is your light that we see now, and the only way for us to know that your heart is true to the Druids' magic gift, is for you to wear this unicorn ring. The ring, as with the unicorn, is connected to your soul. It sees who you truly are. It will only remain on your finger if you are truly worthy of it. It will disintegrate into ashes the moment you put it on your finger if you are not true to yourself, and to your soul."

Arthur was terrified he would fail them once again. He took the ring from William and slid it onto his finger. The anticipation around the table was palpable. Within seconds, the ring glowed on his finger.

They raised their glass to Arthur's new role.

William and Tula were now free to let the love between them blossom. Tula accepted William's invitation to come and live with him at their new cottage in England with her two cats and two dogs. Also, William accepted her invitation as well to live in Nort. To add to the collection of the Anam Duines' stories, William wrote a play based on Tula's new book, *A True Story That You Will Never Believe*.

Printed in Dunstable, United Kingdom